The Shadow
of Evil

THE BAKER STREET MYSTERIES

The *Shadow* of *Evil*

TIM PIGOTT-SMITH

Illustrated by Chris Mould

Hodder
Children's
Books

A division of Hachette Children's Books

First published in Great Britain in 2009
by Hodder Children's Books

1

A Catalogue record for this book is available from the British Library

ISBN-13: 978 0 340 96006 6

Typeset in Garamond by Avon DataSet Ltd, Bidford on Avon, Warwickshire

Printed and bound in Great Britain by
CPI Bookmarque Ltd, Croydon, Surrey

The paper and board used in this paperback by Hodder Children's Books
are natural recyclable products made from wood grown in
sustainable forests. The manufacturing processes conform to the
environmental regulations of the country of origin.

Hodder Children's Books
a division of Hachette Children's Books
338 Euston Road, London NW1 3BH
An Hachette UK Company
www.hachette.co.uk

To Pam and Tom

My thanks to John Lloyd for help
on Victorian detail.

PROLOGUE

Soon after he ran away from home, Sam Wiggins started having nightmares. He came to dread sleeping, because sleeping meant dreaming.

It always started as the same dream, a nightmare version of the time when he arrived homeless on the streets of London, and did not eat for several days. Alone and hungry, he stole a bag of roasted nuts from a barrow. A beggar spotted him, raised the hue and cry, and Sam had to run for it. He managed to lose all his pursuers, save one – a huge man who chased him relentlessly. Sam ran, as if the Devil were at his heels. He got away in the end, and bumped, literally, into Sherlock Holmes and Dr Watson. In his life this was a turning point, but in his nightmares, there was no relief. Occasionally there was hope, but in the end, it was always dashed. This was one of Sam's dreams . . .

Night. Mist. Sam is running for his life. He fears being caught. He fears being beaten. He fears prison. Most of all, he dreads being banished to a penal colony on the other side of the world. These terrors invade Sam's mind as one last pursuer, a giant of a man, hunts him through the dark streets of his dreams.

Sam nips between two buildings – through a narrow gap that only he knows of. He pauses at the other end to catch his breath, but he can still hear the flat thump of heavy boots coming after him. He sets off again, shooting in through the doorway of a slaughterhouse.

He runs between hanging carcasses of meat, the worn leather of his old shoes slipping on the blood-soaked floor. A beam of light splits the gloom, catching the blade of a meat cleaver, temporarily blinding him. A man, armed with a great meat-saw, blocks his path. Sam stumbles past and plunges out of the slaughterhouse into the passage that runs between the backs of the warehouses. Now, at last, he can hear nothing behind him.

He does not stop running, but heads swiftly up the passage and into the street that will lead him to safety. But his way is blocked – his foe is a move ahead of him. Sam screeches to a standstill. Sometimes, at this point, he can see his pursuer's face – a different face in each dream. On this occasion it is his stepfather – the loathsome man who replaced his dead father, and whose use of the belt finally drove Sam to leave home. The repellent features – thick lips and heavy brows – turn Sam's stomach. With this hated foe close behind him, closer now than ever, Sam sets off as fast as he can in the opposite direction. He turns a corner to find himself trapped in a dead end. He cannot turn back. The unrelenting boots echo behind him in the narrow street.

Sam has no choice – he runs, jumps up and grabs the top of the wall. Before he can scramble over, he feels an enormous hand grasping his calf through his threadbare trousers. He can hear the angry threats that chill his blood and remind him of the unhappy time he lived under his stepfather's thrall. He is losing his grip on the wobbly top brick, but kicks out frantically, shaking the gigantic hand off, hauling himself up and scrabbling over the wall. He drops down into a builder's yard, landing on a mountain of sand.

At last he is free, but now he finds it hard to move. His feet stick like glue in the shifting sand. He struggles down the mud-like slope, sand clogging his shoes. He falls. He crawls laboriously between several piles of bricks, which sway dangerously above him. He stands.

He tries to run again. He trips on some cement sacks, but regains his leaden footing and stumbles heavily out of the yard, as the night-watchman emerges from his hut, brandishing a stick and cursing.

Sam finds he can move faster again on the firm concrete. He sees his friend Titch on the other side of the road. She is waving and calling to him, smiling. Wanting to join her, Sam starts to cross the road but the cobblestones turn to water beneath his feet. He finds himself sinking, swallowing the foul water and fighting for breath. He makes desperate swimming movements, but cannot stop himself being sucked downwards. He sees Titch trying frantically to reach him, but it is too late. He is drowning. His body plunges deeper and deeper, the salty water catching in his throat, choking him as it floods his lungs.

A grey-black cloud appears above him. However quickly Sam sinks, this dark shape moves closer. Sam tries to work out what it is, inky and huge behind him. He turns to see if it is his stepfather who has again caught up with him, but the murky water clouds his view. It is certainly a man, for large hands now close around Sam's throat. He glimpses a bushy moustache, before the hands force his head away so that he cannot see. The man draws close to him. Sam can feel the stiff bristly whiskers on the back of his neck. His stepfather is clean-shaven. Who can *this* be? Is it the law? Sam's lungs are full of water. The pressure of the powerful fingers on his throat makes the blood pound in his temples.

The man's hands are squeezing the remains of life out of him. Sam can feel consciousness draining away as his body goes limp. His dangling feet touch the ocean bed, and to his surprise, he sinks into the sand. Light as a feather, he slips easily through the seabed. Leaving behind the water and sand, and the tight grip of the fingers strangling him, he emerges into a fresh, white, open universe. His lungs are blissfully clear. He can breathe again and he floats free into a cloudless sky.

He feels a momentary elation as if he can fly, but before he can gain control, he is falling through space. Gathering speed, faster and faster he falls. Looking down, he can see the earth rising swiftly towards him. With terrifying force he plummets, fast and hard, into panicky, breathless wakefulness. He sits up suddenly, stifling a scream. His heart is racing. His eyes are open, but through the darkness of the windowless basement where he sleeps he can see nothing – there is nothing to see. The dream is over. His mouth is dry. His brow is wet, and his whole body is clammy with sweat, but cold as ice.

He peers through the dark and can just make out Titch, sleeping. At least Sam didn't disturb her as he sometimes does. He feels for the horseshoe Edie gave him, and clutching it to calm his nerves, he snuggles down under his blanket and tries to gather his thoughts, but fear sours everything. When will this demon of his dreams catch up with him – *really* catch up with him? Will Sam round the corner one day and find himself face to face with this phantom? He tries to sleep but it is useless. He lies there, hoping that Titch might wake, or daylight might come.

But there is nothing. Just the darkness. Just the fear. The dread.

1

ONE EYE OPEN

Before leaving London on a mission of international importance, Sherlock Holmes despatched Sam Wiggins to the Tower of London on what he admitted was a 'somewhat hit and miss affair'. He instructed Sam to watch for Major Sebastian 'Tiger' De Ville. He referred to the Major as 'the second most dangerous man alive'. When Sam asked Holmes the purpose of this operation, the Great Detective replied ominously that he was really interested in De Ville's boss, the villainous Professor Moriarty – the *most* dangerous man alive – so Sam knew from the start how perilous this assignment was.

When he first encountered the Great Detective, Sam had been involved in the rescue of a kidnapped friend, an incident known as the Case of the Dragon Tattoo. Holmes always feared this kidnap was 'the tip of the iceberg – the bit you can see'. He was convinced that it hinted at Professor Moriarty's vaster, more fiendish activities – 'the bit you *can't* see'. He explained to Sam that the true purpose of the 'white slave' operation they had unearthed during the kidnap rescue had been to create a nationwide network of operatives for the evil Professor. 'Wiggins,' Holmes muttered darkly, 'that demon Moriarty sits like an ugly spider at the centre of an international web of crime. Truly, I am afraid.' Sam had not imagined Sherlock Holmes to be capable of fear. 'I feel it in my bones,' Holmes went on. 'Moriarty is preparing something on an apocalyptic scale.'

Sometimes on a gloomy day, a shaft of sunlight will break through the clouds and even the dingiest alley will take on a pleasant aspect. No matter how much the winter sun shone upon the ancient grey-white stones of the Tower of London, for Sam it never lost its ominous atmosphere. He could not look at it without the shadow of its gory past blackening his thoughts. His mate, Potts, had told him loads of gruesome stories: of Sir Walter Raleigh, imprisoned for months before having his head chopped off; of two young princes – one stabbed, the other suffocated under his own pillow; of Anne Boleyn, ill-fated wife of King Henry VIII, executed on Traitor's Green. In those days, when

London was protected by a wall, the severed heads were displayed on spikes above the gates to the city. A grisly warning to anyone entering London!

Sam was outside the Middle Tower – disguised as a shoeshine boy for cover – for four days and three increasingly bitter nights. His friends, Titch and Billy, brought regular supplies, and Potts dropped by whenever he was free. Although it was a busy period for Potts's boss, the betting king Jacky Dyke, Potts always made time for Sam. Sam was glad to see his friends, but he didn't mind being on his own. He could think, and he liked thinking. Alone by the Tower, watching for De Ville, he shone shoes and pondered the changes in his life since he had run away from home.

Sam and his four friends, whom Holmes called the Baker Street Irregulars, now spent a good deal of their time performing tasks like this current one, but Sam was very conscious that it was Dr Watson who had made the real difference to all their lives. He was looking after Edie properly, helping to prolong her fading eyesight. He was supporting Billy in his pursuit of a career in hotels. Potts was already quite independent, earning money as a bookie's runner.

As Sam watched, polished and waited, he

acknowledged to himself that it was he and his best friend, Titch, who owed Watson the greatest debt. He had bought Titch a boat, and she was already making money on the river, as well as running a line in songbirds at the bird market near Brick Lane. The good Doctor made sure Holmes remunerated them all properly for their work. Sam and Titch suspected that Watson topped up their earnings occasionally with secret donations of his own. This helped Sam build his growing savings – guarded in a sock – to help him realise his dream of becoming a doctor. Watson was flattered by Sam's interest in medicine, and encouraged it. Occasionally, he allowed Sam to work at his Paddington surgery.

During Sam's four-day vigil at the Tower, Titch and Billy brought sandwiches, baked potatoes and home-made lemonade, supplied by Mrs Hudson from the kitchen of 22lb Baker Street. The winter sun rose and fell. And then, on the fourth night, when the crush of hansom-cabs that made up the evening rush hour had faded, the moon appeared in a crystal-clear sky, eerily illuminating the cruel battlements of the Tower.

A cab drew up outside the wall by the Bastion Tower. Through the postern gate came the instantly recognisable figure of Tiger De Ville. Just as Holmes had described him, he was a tree of a man with unnaturally long arms and enormous hands. With huge strides, De Ville stalked round the cab, checking the area. He returned to the gate and ushered through it a man with a large bald dome of a forehead. His face was white. He had an aura about him. He moved slowly, deliberately. Sam was mesmerised. He had not the slightest doubt who this was – Holmes had warned him that he might also see Professor Moriarty. De Ville led the evil Professor to the cab and watched as the horse pulled off.

When the cab was safely under way, De Ville whipped round unexpectedly and looked straight at Sam. Stunned by the intense glare in De Ville's savage eyes, Sam flinched. De Ville walked towards him. His brow was deep-lined, and he had a huge, straggly moustache. He moved fast, and as he came closer, Sam realised how he had come by the nickname 'The Tiger' – his grey hair contained two streaks of black, running in a V from the centre of his forehead.

'Don't move, kid. Stay right where you are!' De Ville growled.

Before Sam could gather his things and run for it, De Ville was on him. One mighty hand clawed his shoulder and forced him to the ground. De Ville

stamped his foot on Sam's shoe box. 'If you're here to shine shoes, kid, get shining.' Kneeling, trying to conceal his shaking fingers, Sam applied a great blob of polish to De Ville's massive leather shoes. 'And don't clog the lace holes,' De Ville snarled. Under his intimidating glare, Sam shone the boots in silence. When he was nearly done, De Ville asked, 'What's business like at this hour, kid?'

'Not great, sir,' Sam mumbled, keeping his head down.

'I bet it isn't.'

'But I don't have nowhere to go for home, so I stay here.'

'Rubbish. You don't fool me, kid. You or your mates.'

The hairs on Sam's neck stood on end – De Ville had obviously been observing *him*. He sensed De Ville watching now, as he buffed up the shine.

'That'll do,' said De Ville, whipping his foot away. Sam put his brushes and duster away clumsily, frightened of what De Ville would do next.

'Get up, kid.'

Sam rose nervously. De Ville's feral eyes fixed him. His mouth was wide. At each side, long, tobacco-stained teeth protruded, reinforcing the image of the tiger. Through the tendrils of his overhanging moustache, between his thick, shiny lips, was a glint of gold. De Ville's hand shot out, encircling Sam's throat and pinning him to the wall. His thumb pushed Sam's head to one side. Sam could feel the thick hair on the back of De Ville's hand brushing the underside of his chin. But what really chilled his blood was De Ville's ample moustache. De Ville leaned forward, bringing his lips close to Sam's ear, scratching the side of his neck with his whiskers, reminding him of the black underwater phantom of his dreams, whose bristles he could feel even as it strangled him.

'I am known as Tiger,' breathed De Ville. 'Can you guess why?' Sam shook his head. 'Because I sleep with one eye open, kid. Like a tiger. And I shall always have one eye open for you. Get it?' Sam grunted. De Ville was so close Sam could smell the pungent odour of cigar on his breath and clothes. De Ville's rough tweed suit rubbed against him like a pelt. 'I don't ever want to see you again, kid,' he sneered. Sam felt enveloped by this vile-smelling, hairy creature. De Ville tightened his grip on Sam's throat and forced him up on to his toes. 'Here or anywhere. Get it?' Sam struggled to nod, but couldn't. He tried to speak, but couldn't. Suddenly De Ville loosened his stranglehold. Sam's knees buckled and he clutched his aching throat. 'Scarper.'

Forgetting his shoe box, Sam ran for it. He didn't look round. He didn't need to. He could feel De Ville's eyes burning into his back. He knew the man was after him. He could hear the slap of his boots. Just like his dream.

It is nearly five miles from the Tower of London to Baker Street. Sam ran every yard of it, but it was not until he nipped out of Soho Square and crossed Oxford Street that he felt he could relax. Still cautious, he engineered his way through some of the obscurer crannies around Wimpole Street. By the time he reached Marylebone Road, he sensed he was out of danger, but not for one moment did he slacken his pace, legging it past Madame Tussaud's into that short neck of road between Baker Street Railway Station and the corner of Regent's Park, where Sherlock Holmes and Dr Watson had rooms. There, on the first floor of 22lb, Sam saw a light burning in the study, and finally, he felt safe. Looking back at the street, he raised the heavy brass doorknocker.

Despite the late hour, Sam's friend Billy Chizzell, the page-boy, opened the door. Sam stood panting, unable to speak.

'You all right?' Billy said, welcoming his friend. 'Come down to the kitchen and cool off.' He chattered on. 'Mrs Hudson's gone to bed. We can have the place to ourselves.' Sam fell into the hall, put his hands on his knees and struggled to get his breath back. 'Close the door, Sam. It's real nippy.'

As he pushed the door to, Sam just managed to spit out the words, 'Is Mr Holmes back?'

'No. Sorry.' Putting two and two together was not Billy's forte, but he suddenly realised *why* Sam was in a state. 'Oh crikey! Have you got news?' Sam nodded. 'Wow! Brilliant!' cried Billy, clapping his hands.

'No word from Mr Holmes, though?' Sam gasped.

'No!'

'Then I must speak to Dr Watson.'

'He's got someone with him – some American – Mr J. Wilson Booth blooming Senior. Just barged in – well after hours if you ask me! They're up there now, and between you and me, it doesn't sound as though it's going too well. Listen.'

As they climbed the stairs, Sam became aware of voices raised so loud that, even from the landing outside the study door, he and Billy could hear what was being said.

'I had a contract with Mr Holmes, Doctor...' The voice was deep and resonant, with a rich Texan drawl.

'With respect, sir,' Watson interjected, 'Holmes has never used formal contracts.'

'A Gentleman's Agreement then,' the speaker snarled gruffly. 'Your Mr Holmes undertook to protect my company's ships from sabotage. And what does he do? Disappear. Since he shook my hand he has been hiding from me, Dr Watson, and you know where.'

Watson had a pretty good idea where Holmes was, but he had been sworn to secrecy. All he could do was assure Mr J. Wilson Booth Senior that Holmes was a man of his word. From the landing, the two boys could hear Watson blustering away.

Billy looked at Sam. 'It sounds to me as though the old Doc needs helping out in there!'

'I don't think it would help if we went in now, Billy,' said Sam, who just about had his breath back.

Before either of them could do anything, the study door opened and Mr Booth came storming out. He was a large man. Tall. Broad. He wore a linen suit whose expert tailoring immediately displayed its owner's wealth, and a Texan leather cord tie, held at the neck by a chunky bull-horn clasp. This imposing figure was stopped in his tracks, not by Billy, whom he continued to ignore as he had when he arrived, but by the sight of Sam – a grubby, sweating street urchin, in tattered clothes. He simply stood and gaped.

'Sam here was waiting to see Dr Watson,' said Billy with a grin. 'Have you finished?'

Booth was flabbergasted by Billy's cheek, but it didn't take him long to find his tongue. 'Out of my way, you ragamuffins!' he cried, charging past the two boys, brandishing his Stetson hat. As he descended the stairs, he called out, 'Dr Watson, you will be hearing from my attorney.'

Watson appeared in the study doorway looking somewhat deflated. Holmes was always putting him in situations like this. But, as Sam had observed before, Watson never complained – his loyalty was unquestioning.

Sam looked at the dejected Doctor. 'Where *is* Mr Holmes, Doctor?'

'Don't *you* start, Wiggins!' replied Watson.

As he made his way along the hall, Mr Booth overheard Sam. 'That's a damned perspicacious question, young whippersnapper,' he called out, 'and one to which I too would like an answer! Where *is* Mr Holmes?'

Leaning over the banisters and addressing the fiery American fuming in the hall below, Watson shrugged apologetically. 'At this moment, Mr Booth, I am unable to answer your question.' Watson was quite pleased with this truthful evasion, but it was too much for Mr J. Wilson Booth Senior. Planting his Stetson firmly on his head, and flourishing his cane, he strode to the front door.

'That's a dashed slippery answer, Dr Watson. You are no gentleman, sir, and your Mr Holmes is a charlatan! A charlatan and a phony! Goodnight.' So saying, he slammed the door.

'And goodnight to you too, Mr Booth,' said Billy under his breath.

Sam looked at Watson. 'Was it something I said?'

Watson smiled fondly at his two young friends. 'Come in here. Tell me your news. And I will tell you all about Mr J. Wilson Booth Senior.' Watson ushered them into the study. 'It is quite a story!'

The SS *Arcadia*, one of the ships about which Mr Booth was so concerned, was being battered by the fury of an Atlantic storm. The swirling wind and the mountainous sea hurled the boat around like a cork in a whirlpool. Most of the crew were safe in their quarters, but three gallant sailors were holding a rope over the side, at the end of which dangled a fourth man. Hurled to and fro by the tempestuous waves and wind, this man was either foolhardy or unusually courageous and perhaps both.

The identity of the man risking life and limb to save the SS *Arcadia* and the lives of all on board was known only to the captain of the ship. He was, in fact, the very man Mr J. Wilson Booth had called a charlatan and a phony: Sherlock Holmes himself – the Great Detective! One of the sailors yelled to their brave companion, 'Can you hear me, sir?' His cry was drowned by the roaring of the wind and the crashing of the waves.

Holmes was attempting to remove a limpet bomb which was clamped to the SS *Arcadia* just above the water line. In spite of the violence of the storm, Holmes could hear an ominous ticking. If this bomb exploded, Holmes would be blown to pieces, and the ship would sink – in weather like this, she would go down in minutes. The water flung Holmes one way. The wind picked him up and threw him another. A towering wave – taller and fiercer than those already battering the ship and sweeping its decks – engulfed him.

'Oh, heavens. No!!' cried one of the sailors. 'I can't see him. We've lost him! He's gone!'

2

THE SPECTRE

As Sam stood by the window of the study at 22lb, checking that Tiger De Ville had not followed him, Watson talked about his recent visitor – James Wilson Booth Senior.

'His friends call him JW – he is a man of indescribable wealth.' Watson explained that Booth had invested massively in the fast-expanding telephone industry at just the right time, earning the contract to lay the first transatlantic cable, creating direct telephonic contact between England and America. Hence the name of his new company, the Anglo-American Trans-Atlantic Cable Company, of which he was the sole owner. 'JW,' Watson continued, 'is furious with Holmes because he fears for the safety of his cable-laying boats. Holmes undertook to protect them.' Watson sighed. 'If only he knew Holmes like I do.'

Buffeted by the sea, Holmes disappeared from view more than once, but just when hope was lost, he would emerge from the waves, clinging to his rope with superhuman tenacity. Finally, his labours were rewarded. He managed to lever the ticking limpet bomb from the side of the ship. It tumbled into the foaming waters, and from the bowels of the sea came the dull thump of an explosion – Holmes had removed the bomb in the nick of time.

Holmes's three helpers, tired themselves, hauled the exhausted hero up. Willing hands reached out to help him aboard and drag him over the rails. Above the clamour of the wind and the crash of the water, their voices could just be heard.

'Thank God! The ship is saved!'

'You have saved the *Arcadia*, sir.'

'*We* are saved!'

The drenched figure, no longer in immediate danger and now on the relative sanctuary of the deck, was still roped to his three fellow helpers, who competed with each other to shake his hand.

'And thank God *you* are safe.'

'God bless you, sir.'

'God bless you.'

Some time later, when Holmes was in dry clothes, he and the Captain were enjoying a well-earned moment of relaxation in the Captain's cabin. Holmes rested his tired legs on a footstool.

'I am not only grateful, Mr Holmes,' said the Captain, 'I am astounded by your bravery.'

'I detected the limpet bomb in the nick of time, Captain. But the storm outside still rages.' Indeed, the *Arcadia* was pitching violently, for the wind was blowing unabated and the sea was high. The Captain, however, detected some darker meaning in Holmes's words.

'I am not sure that I fully understand you, sir.'

'We may have won the battle, Captain, but the war is by no means over,' was Holmes's ominous reply. 'I have an unusual sensation of impending doom,' he went on. 'I am afraid. Deeply afraid. For you. For your crew. And for myself.'

'You shock me, Mr Holmes. Do you imply there have been threats against your life?'

'There have, but I also have an intimate understanding of our adversary.'

As Holmes did not offer more information, the Captain was obliged to ask, 'Do you know then who was responsible for the limpet bomb?'

'The man I suspect is a most unusual criminal. A so-called professor, his abilities are truly remarkable, but he is driven by demons. I believe he is presently formulating a plan that will have serious repercussions for the whole of Europe.' The Captain looked dubiously at Holmes. 'But as I have no concrete evidence, this sounds like a plot that would shame a boys' penny comic. I am grateful to you for concealing my identity from your crew, Captain. Please continue to do so. It is essential that I work anonymously. And I would ask you a further small favour.'

'Of course. Honoured.'

Holmes took his watch from his waistcoat pocket and detached it from the fob. 'This half-hunter belonged to my grandfather. It is a Breguet – Swiss – exact to the second. It is engraved with the initials "S H" as you see – my grandfather's name was Silas. If anything should happen to me, I would ask you to see that it is given to a lad by the name of Sam Wiggins. My friend Dr Watson will guide you to him.'

'You may rely upon me, Mr Holmes.'

'Also, allow me to return your copy of the *Complete Works of William Shakespeare*. It has been of great comfort.'

The Captain placed Holmes's beautiful timepiece

in the ship's safe. The safe door closed. The dials clicked reassuringly. 'No harm can come to it there, Mr Holmes.'

As he spoke, the Captain saw a look of such profound concern on the Great Detective's face that he decided not to interrupt his troubled meditations. He moved discreetly towards the cabin door, but before he could leave the cabin Holmes leaped suddenly to his feet.

'Forgive me, Captain. I have been remiss. I need to search the lower hold.'

'Just speak to the purser, Mr Holmes. When would—?'

'Now, sir. Now! This very instant! The limpet bomb will not, I fear, be an isolated incident.'

And before the Captain could say another word, Holmes pushed brusquely past him and shot out of the room!

Still with half an eye on the street, Sam informed Watson and Billy that he had seen not only Tiger De Ville at the Tower but also the evil Professor Moriarty.

Watson considered his response carefully. 'Mr Booth's fear of sabotage, combined with Sam's alarming information, suggests to me that Holmes was right – Moriarty is up to something.'

'Wow!' exclaimed Billy.

'You know what Mr Holmes said to me the other day?'

'Tell us, Sam.'

'He said, "I fear that Moriarty intends to realise his title – the Napoleon of Crime." I thought he was just going on, like, the way he does about the Professor, but maybe . . .'

'What did he mean by the Napoleon of Crime?' Billy asked.

'Well, Billy, Napoleon attempted to dominate Europe,' replied Watson. 'He had England shaking in its shoes!'

'Wow!'

'Moriarty. Emperor of Europe,' Watson mused. 'I fear we are in for a torrid time.'

'Hey, Doctor,' cried Sam in surprise, 'we got another visitor.'

'At this hour? I don't believe it. What *is* happening tonight? Billy! Would you – Oh!' Billy was already on his way to greet their latest caller. 'Sam, you had better make yourself scarce. Nip in there.' Sam dived into an adjacent room, leaving the door slightly ajar. Almost immediately, Billy admitted a short, smart, elderly man, white with shock. His manner was formal and soldierly. In words barely audible but articulated with military precision, he asked for Mr Sherlock Holmes. Watson mumbled his now familiar excuses.

'I *must* see him, Dr Watson, on a matter of great, I might even say national—' He broke off, seeming to regret what he was saying, but then continued. 'It is true, it is a matter of national importance.'

Watson wondered if *he* might be of assistance. In response, the visitor turned slowly and left the room shaking his head, muttering, 'What will they do to me, now? What *will* they do?'

'Billy will show you out,' Watson called helplessly, and slumped, baffled, into his armchair.

Sam ran to the study window, adjusting the curtain so that he could observe the stranger's departure.

'Who on earth was that?' asked Watson.

'The Constable of the Tower, at a rough guess,' replied Sam.

'Come now, Sam. Only one man we know can make such extraordinary deductions.'

'Look at the evidence, sir. There was a gunpowder burn on his cheek. That, plus his manner of speech and the missing forefinger on his right hand, suggest that he was a military man. The Constable of the Tower is a retired soldier.'

Watson could barely believe his ears. 'I'm impressed, Sam.'

'That's not all, though, sir. Mr Holmes said there was some history between the Constable and De Ville. And you heard what he said as he went out.'

'"What will they do to me?"'

'Right. He wanted Mr Holmes's help on a matter of national importance – you saw how he tried to cover that up. Somebody's threatening him. And who's behind it?'

'Moriarty?'

'And De Ville.'

Watson was used to being outthought by Holmes, but to be so bettered by Sam Wiggins was a humiliating novelty. 'I am *very* impressed, Wiggins,' said Watson, caught between admiration and pique. 'I think we should go straight to Scotland Yard.'

'I hate to disagree, sir. Mr Holmes wouldn't go to Inspector Lestrade for this one. He would summon the team.'

'The Irregulars? You know I worry about your involvement in Holmes's cases.'

'I'm already working on this one, sir.' Watson did

not speak, but Sam could see the Doctor was on the point of giving in. 'You know I'm right, sir. Call the Irregulars. It's elementary!'

The doll's house at which the Duchess of Albion was gazing belonged to her mother, Queen Victoria. With its genuine marble flooring, handmade furniture and a fully mechanised, chiming grandfather clock, it was a thing of wonder. The Duchess of Albion's daughter, Princess Alice, adored it so much that Queen Victoria had loaned it to her granddaughter on the occasion of her eighth birthday, which had been celebrated a little over a month ago.

Leaning heavily on her husband's arm, the Duchess stared in desperation at this object of priceless beauty. Next to it, Alice's white satin bedroom slippers – embroidered with a burgundy-coloured 'A' – added to her torment, because the owner of the slippers was nowhere to be seen. Princess Alice had disappeared. She had been missing for twenty-four hours.

'There is no word of her, my dear,' said the Duke, 'she has simply vanished. The people behind her kidnapping must have motives other than a ransom, for they have left us no way of making contact. We shall find our daughter, have no fear, but I am very much afraid that the Queen must know.'

'Is there no alternative?' the Duchess cried.

'I have done everything I can think of. In the morning, we *must* go to Her Majesty.'

At this, the Duchess cried openly. Her daughter had gone. Her husband was being businesslike. And now she would have to face the wrath of her mother, Queen Victoria.

Somewhat against his better judgement, early next morning Watson summoned the Irregulars. Sam and Titch arrived together, and Potts brought Edie McArdle. She was responding well to Watson's treatment, but her sight was gradually deteriorating and, unfortunately, her condition could not be halted. She disliked feeling that she was a burden but Potts tended her with real care, knowing just when to help her and when to leave her alone. As soon as they were all assembled, Billy closed the study door and Watson began.

'You know how fond I am of you all. I fear for what might happen to you. Some of Holmes's cases are matters of life and death, as you know from bitter experience. However . . . in Holmes's absence there has been an unprecedented escalation in clients, which is most disturbing – there may even be connections *between* these cases. Let me tell you exactly what the problems are, and then we can decide if there is anything we can do without Holmes to guide us.'

With Sam's help, Watson filled the others in on Tiger De Ville, Holmes's work for Mr J.W. Booth, and the late-night visit from the man they deemed to be the Constable of the Tower. The Irregulars listened in silence as Watson warned them that behind all these cases there lurked, as in the Case of the Dragon Tattoo, the threatening spectre of Professor Moriarty.

3

MISSING PERSONS

Billy Chizzell, Potts, Edie McArdle, Titch Simpson and Sam Wiggins were sitting in the kitchen of 22lb, as Mrs Hudson prepared Dr Watson's lunch. After their meeting, Watson had gone off to his Paddington surgery, and they had gravitated to Mrs Hudson's quarters belowstairs, as they nearly always did. But there was an air of gloom about them, because their meeting with Watson had been inconclusive. There was nothing they could do to pacify Mr J.W. Booth. Tiger De Ville was clearly in London – but what they were to do about him, they had no notion. They suspected some connection between De Ville's presence at the Tower, the Constable's late visit and Moriarty's plans – but they needed Holmes. Although Watson knew where Holmes was, he was unable to contact him. They were helpless.

'You get a body down, you lot,' said Mrs Hudson, as she rolled some pastry. 'Mr Holmes'll be all right.'

'It ain't just Mr 'Olmes!' cried Potts.

'No,' said Titch. 'There's something real odd going on.'

'There's too much happening,' Billy stated flatly. 'That's what it is. Usually, there's just *one* thing. Mr Holmes concentrates on it till it's sorted. With this, there's lots of what you might call threads: first the guv'nor himself is gone – in total secrecy as usual, according to the old Doc . . .'

'Dr Watson to you, Billy my lad,' said Mrs Hudson, brandishing her rolling-pin. 'You show some respect.'

'Sorry, Mrs Hudson. Then second, there's this American chap . . .'

'And don't forget De Ville – who clobbered Sam at the Tower,' said Titch – ever mindful of Sam's status.

'I *haven't* forgotten, Titch – hang on!' Billy protested. 'De Ville is the third thing . . .'

'And the Constable,' added Sam.

'Give me a break,' said Billy. 'I was coming to that. Anyway, there's *four* threads at least!'

'Billy's right,' Potts chipped in. 'This one don't feel normal. Know wot I mean, Mrs H?'

Mrs Hudson had given up trying to instil respect into Potts. She flicked him round the ear with the tea towel that she kept tucked into her pinafore when she was cooking.

'Beggin' yer P, Mrs H,' said Potts, grinning. 'Wot do *you* fink, Sam?'

There was a tendency to defer to Sam as the leader of the group. They all respected his skill in working things out, and if there was a decision to be made, it was usually Sam who made it.

'Billy's spot on,' agreed Sam. 'And there's something else that I didn't mention before, because I didn't reckon it was important at the time, but I've been thinking about it. When Mr Holmes went away, I fancy he was worried.'

'That's not like him,' said Billy. As page-boy at 221b, he knew Holmes better than any of them.

'That's what I mean,' said Sam. 'He said something *nice* to me before he sent me off to the Tower, and he never does that.'

'Wot did 'e say?' enquired Potts.

'He told me to take real care of myself. Only he was a bit upset, you know? Like he felt something might go wrong.'

'Funny,' said Billy. 'That's *not* like 'im.'

The Irregulars thought about this for a moment. Mrs Hudson lifted one of two large rounds of pastry from her floured wooden board and placed it over an enamel plate, ready for the spiced apples that were stewing in a saucepan on the hob. They all watched as she raised the plate on one hand, and with a couple of deft twirls, spun it round, removing the overhanging pastry with a bone-handled table knife.

'Nice one, Mrs H,' said Potts.

'There's something else, too,' said Sam. 'Mr Holmes said he might have a present for me.'

'He *might* have?' asked Titch. 'What did he mean by that, Sam?'

'I don't know, Titch. It's weird. *And* he said, "The time would come."'

'The time would come? I don't get it,' said Billy.

'Perhaps he's going to give yer a watch,' grinned Edie sweetly.

'Don't be daft, Edie.'

'Don't you speak to Edie like that, Billy ol' son.' Potts always jumped to Edie's defence. 'When Edie says stuff like that, you orter know by now, that all you 'ave to do is sit back and wait fer it to 'appen!'

'Sorry, Edie.'

'That's all right, Billy me old turnip!' grinned Edie.

'Turnip?! Please do not allude to my chubbiness in that unkind way.'

'Sorry, I'm sure.'

'I've got big bones. My mum says I'll grow out of it.'

'Not if you always eat my leftovers, young man,' said Mrs Hudson with a wink.

''Ang on! We're losin' track 'ere,' said Potts. 'Wot d'*you* reckon's goin' on, Edie?'

'Sure, I've only just come in on this, but it does feel different,' said Edie thoughtfully, flicking away a strand of her long auburn hair from the side of her mouth. 'It's like . . . there's *too much* goin' on.'

'That's just what I said!' Billy remarked indignantly.

'We wasn't listenin' to you, Billy,' said Potts, 'cos you're just a chubby ol' turnip. Aincher?'

They all laughed at Billy, who stuck his bottom lip out miserably. Then they all went quiet.

Sam broke the silence. 'Trouble is . . . there's nothing we can do,' said Sam. 'I hate that.'

The small group was silent again as Mrs Hudson put the apples – smelling sweetly of cloves – on to the pastry. Covering them with a pastry lid, she shaped the rim with her finger and thumb, poked a hole in the centre, splashed it with beaten egg and slipped it into the oven. As the Irregulars sat licking their lips, there was a gentle knock at the front door.

''Ere's anuvver one,' said Potts.

'Too much happening! What did I tell you?' said Billy.

'Well go and see who it is, Billy Turnip,' said Mrs Hudson. 'And don't get your hopes up. Mr Holmes and the Doctor have said I can have my room repapered, and that might just be the decorator.'

When Billy opened the front door, he could see instantly that it wasn't the decorator. A grandly dressed woman, short and slim but imposing, was holding the railing for support.

'Wow!' thought Billy. 'She's not poor.'

The lady, wearing a large black hat with the veil down, asked quietly if she might see Mr Holmes. 'Please come in,' said Billy. He could tell that she was in a state of real anguish, although she displayed remarkable self-control. He led her upstairs to the study, and managed to ease her gently into a chair before she fainted.

Billy fetched the smelling-salts, wafted them under the lady's nose and waited calmly for her to come round. His growing awareness of people's needs was really down to Watson. Billy's mum had always wanted her son to run a hotel, and although Billy had resisted the idea at first, Watson had introduced him to a patient who worked in the hotel trade, and now Billy regularly did part-time jobs for him. His innocence and optimism made him instantly likeable. He was especially good with anyone in distress, which often came in handy at 22lb – as was the case now. When the woman stirred, he leaned forward and asked her gently, 'Would you like a glass of water, ma'am?'

'No, thank you.' All she required, she said, was a moment to regain her composure, and Billy gave her time. Eventually, she said, 'I must see Mr Holmes.'

This could have been a difficult moment, but Billy took it in his stride. 'I'm afraid he's not available this exact minute, ma'am. But if you care to wait, his colleague will be here very soon.'

'Thank you.'

'And you're sure there's nothing I can get for you?'

'No, thank you, young man. I will rest here. If it is not inconvenient.'

'Not at all, ma'am. You sit tight, and I will bring Dr Watson up the minute he gets back.'

Billy crossed his fingers and hoped that Watson would not be held up at his surgery. He bounded down to the kitchen where the Irregulars quizzed him about Holmes's latest client.

'Why did she have her veil down?' asked Titch.

'Because she was crying,' said Billy. 'Really discreet, though, know what I mean?'

'She sounds like a nob!' said Potts.

'She is,' replied Billy. 'Dead smart clothes. And a lovely way of speaking.'

'A lady of the aristocracy, then,' Edie chipped in, smiling, 'who doesn't wish to be recognised.'

'In a nutshell, Edie,' said Potts.

'And it's all part of the pattern we were talking about,' added Sam. 'Another case for Mr Holmes.'

'I wonder who she is,' said Titch enthusiastically.

'D'you reckon it's safe to leave 'er up there on 'er tod, Billy?' asked Potts.

'I'll nip up in a minute and check, but I'm sure she's genuine.'

'It could be Irene bloomin' Adler, couldn't it? In disguise, and come to get 'er own back!'

'Don't get larky, Potts.' Edie slapped him playfully on the arm with the back of her hand. 'Anyways, Irene Adler's still inside.'

'She might 'ave escaped!'

'I wouldn't put it past her, Potty!' said Billy. 'Flipping heck, I hope Dr Watson won't be long.'

Mrs Hudson was quick to agree. 'So do I! This apple pie is ready!'

'Don't worry abaht that, Mrs H,' said Potts. 'If the old Doc don't turn up, us lot'll knock it off for you.'

Once again, Potts had to duck Mrs Hudson's flicking tea towel.

Billy popped back up to the study. The lady was still seated in the armchair. And at that very moment, by good fortune, Dr Watson returned. To her considerable displeasure, Mrs Hudson's lunch had to be kept waiting while Watson talked to Holmes's latest client.

'Perhaps you would care to tell *me*, dear lady,' said Watson, at his most courteous and charming. 'I am Dr Watson, Sherlock Holmes's friend and colleague.'

'I know very well who you are, Dr Watson,' replied the lady.

Watson felt rather flattered. 'I shall of course relay everything to Holmes the moment I see him.' The lady was still hesitant. Watson was aware that Billy was waiting by the door, but in the light of their theory about Moriarty he was keen to know what had brought a third client to Holmes's door within twenty-four hours. 'I assure you, madam, that your case will be treated with the utmost confidentiality.'

Suddenly the lady cracked. 'My daughter is missing,' she blurted out. 'She has not been seen for a day and a half.'

'May I ask your name, madam?'

'I am embarrassed to tell you. This should never have happened to a family such as ours. No one else knows I am here. Not even the Duke, my husband.'

Billy was stunned – Edie had been right – she *was* a lady of the aristocracy who didn't want to be recognised!

'Would I know your name, dear lady?' Watson enquired sympathetically.

'I am the Duchess of Albion.' Watson's heart stopped. 'Princess Alice has been kidnapped.' The Duchess had no need to inform him that the missing girl was Queen Victoria's granddaughter. 'I was hoping,' the Duchess continued, 'Mr Holmes might help.'

She was so close to tears that Watson's heart went out to her. 'Would you like to tell *me*, Duchess?'

The Duchess was relieved at the possibility of sharing her burden with so kind a listener. She told Watson readily what little there was – that Alice had been playing with her godfather at Albion House when she was snatched from under their very noses in broad daylight. The kidnappers had left not the slightest clue as to their identity.

'Holmes is right,' breathed the troubled Doctor.

'Only Moriarty could have done this!'

Contemplating the Duchess of Albion's story, it occurred to him that this was an ideal opportunity for the Irregulars to help. He looked at Billy, whose thoughts were clearly running along the same lines – Billy could always be relied upon to spot a chance for heroics! The Irregulars were bursting for something to do, and Watson thought that by the time Holmes returned, they might well have gathered some crumbs of information for him to work with. He took his courage in his hands. 'Duchess,' said Watson in his best bedside manner, 'I think there *may* be something we can do to help trace your daughter – even without Mr Holmes.'

The Duchess departed, greatly relieved. Watson despatched his lunch, and the gloom that had prevailed in the kitchen evaporated. At last they had something to do!

The Atlantic lay calm, spent, after the storm. The *Arcadia* had resumed cable-laying, and Sherlock Holmes climbed, this tranquil sunset, up to the crow's-nest – the high lookout post – way above the deck of the ship. He scanned the scene below through a telescope. Lying ahead, barely visible, was the coast of

Ireland. Holmes observed a rowing boat, which had just left the *Arcadia* and was approaching one of the accompanying service boats. The very fact of this boat leaving the *Arcadia* made Holmes feel vaguely ill at ease. His troubled thoughts drifted to his futile search of the lower hold.

What little breeze there was dropped to a gentle whisper, and an unusual, brooding stillness prevailed. The only sound was the purr of the ship's motor. Suddenly, the ocean heaved and stirred. The ship listed and swayed violently. The Captain, on deck, concerned that the exaggerated impact of this turbulence on the crow's-nest might throw Holmes into the sea, raised his loudhailer.

'Come down, sir! On deck immediately!'

Holmes was clinging on for dear life as the masthead swung viciously to and fro. All his remaining attention was focused on the rowing boat – which was now unmanned and floating free. This further alarmed the Great Detective. The service boat, on to which the three men from the rowing boat had been transferred, was turning away from the *Arcadia*. Holmes ignored the Captain's cry and through the eerie silence he bellowed, 'Captain! Abandon ship.' The Captain was astounded. Holmes repeated his cry from on high.

'Abandon ship with all speed!'

Awaiting orders, the dumbfounded crew looked to their captain, who remembered all too well, from their conversation in his cabin, Holmes's words of warning. The *Arcadia* settled back into the still water. This tranquillity was shattered by a series of thunderous explosions from the bowels of the boat. The *Arcadia* rose upwards, like a toy. She was almost clear of the water before she fell back, lying at an alarming angle. Flames belched from the funnel and engine-room. Smoke poured from her exposed side. A series of blasts had holed the ship in so many places that she was sinking fast. Holmes was catapulted into the boiling sea, but his fate was unnoticed in the panic, as those men who had not been blown to pieces strove desperately to save their lives. Some scrabbled for the lifeboats, but because the ship was lying on her side, these could not be launched. Those who were able to jumped into the water, and swam as hard as they could towards one or other of the service boats.

All the surrounding boats bar one, which was now heading away at speed, looked on, stunned and helpless, as the *Arcadia* smoked and spat in the seething water. They could not get too close or they would be sucked under as the ship sank, and it was clear to all of them that she would not be afloat for long. At the last, she righted herself and then slid swiftly into the sea. The crow's-nest, where Holmes had been perched, was the last thing they saw, disappearing beneath the water, picked out by the blood-red rays of the dying sun. It was empty. Rescue boats were launched, but it was nothing more than a futile gesture, for in the minds of all those watching, there was but one thought: they would never again see their friends and colleagues who had been on board.

4

A PRIVATE TRAIN

When the Duchess of Albion left Baker Street, the Irregulars set out, full of optimism, to begin their search for Princess Alice. After a long day contacting their friends, asking a lot of questions and wearing out much precious shoe leather, they had got precisely nowhere. Potts decided to talk to his dad.

'Can you 'elp us, Dad? We was at it yesterday, and most of today, and nuffing to show!'

Potts's father – the tough, wiry man of whom Potts asked his question – was a Bow Street Runner, a policeman; a far cry from his younger days when he had kept company with some of the more unsavoury characters of the Soho underworld.

Father and son were seated at the bar of The Silken Garter, the pub in Soho below their home.

There were only a few regulars there: evening trade had not got under way. Potts and his dad had tucked themselves into one corner of the bar. Potts's mum, Lily, a barmaid who played the piano, was polishing the brass foot rail. She could see that whatever they were talking about, they did not want other people to overhear.

'Give us a song, Lil!' came a raucous cry. 'Liven things up a bit!'

'Later, love. Let me get this dump cleared up. Get rid of some of the riff-raff.'

'Like that dog-eared old 'usband of yours?' The regulars greeted this remark with jeering laughter.

'You watch your tongue, young man,' said Lily. 'I'm under no obligation to serve you.'

'No offence, Lil!'

Potts's dad ignored this banter, lit a cigarette, scratched his thinning hair and turned to his son. He was fond of Eli. He'd been just like him: larky and with one eye always open for a quick shilling.

'Why don't you get your Mr Fancy Holmes on the case?'

''Aven't you 'eard, Dad? 'E was off on some big job like, and yesterday evenin', the ship 'e was on got blown up.'

'What?'

''E's dead. The old Doc knew 'e were at sea, and cabled the owner of the shippin' company – some filthy-rich Yank. Then the papers got 'old of it. It was in *The Times* this mornin'.'

'*The Times*? Stone me, Eli . . .'

'Don't call me Eli, Dad.'

'Sorry, son. But where d'you get such notions as reading *The Times*?'

'It was Doc Watson wot told us – "Sabotage at sea," it said. "Great Detective missin'." 'E was thrown overboard in the explosion, like, and 'e's drowned.'

'You'll perhaps spend a bit more time on your proper job now then.'

'I never once let Mr Dyke down, Dad. I was running for 'im jus' this lunch-time – payin' out. An' I always give mum my share, don' I?'

'Yeah, you do, son. You're not a bad lad.'

'Will you 'elp me on this then?'

'Yeah. I'll tell the boys.'

'Discreet like tho', Dad. Young gal missin'. Not the 'ole truth, eh?'

'Course.'

'Fanks. Bye.' Potts leaped off his stool. 'See ya later, Mum.' Lily, seated at the piano, was now singing for the regulars – their favourite – 'The Boy I Love is up in the Gallery'. Potts ran over, dodging the spittoons, skidded to a halt in the sawdust and gave her a peck on the cheek. She smiled at him, and he set off for Baker Street Railway Station, where he was due to meet the others, at the spot where Edie sold her violets.

Billy and Titch were already with Edie, waiting for Potts. They were tired and depressed. As evening drew on, the temperature had dropped, and they were cold. In addition, their search had been unfruitful and the news about Sherlock Holmes had affected them all badly. Titch was trying to cheer them up, bragging about Beaky, her pet pigeon.

'He's the most incredible pigeon ever. I know he looks a bit plain, but he can find his way home from anywhere. If I was to take him to India even, to see my uncle, he'd get back to Baker Street.'

'Where did you get him from?' Edie asked.

'You know I work at Sclater Street sometimes?' Titch replied.

'Sure. Selling songbirds.'

'Ay. They're real popular right now. I picked up Beaky from one of the other stalls.'

'Where d'you keep him then?' asked Edie.

'On the roof at 22lb.'

'He's been up there for some time now,' said Billy. 'I look after him if Titch isn't around.'

'Sure, you're a quiet one, Titch. I had no idea.'

'And look – I've made this little pouch, see, that ties on to his leg, so he can carry messages back. It's Dr Watson that lets me keep him on the roof,' said Titch proudly. 'I don't think Mr Holmes knew there was a hutch up there!'

'He never *will*, now,' Billy added glumly.

'No.'

They were all quiet for a moment, contemplating the death of the Great Detective.

'Hey look,' said Edie. 'Here's Potts!'

They all greeted Potts warmly.

'Where's Sam?' panted Potts.

Titch was suddenly overcome with gloom. 'He's gone off to Holyhead harbour with the Doc.'

'Cheer up, Titch,' said Billy. 'You see, Potts, there's a few personal possessions that have been collected from the wreck, and the police invited the Doc to go and see if any of them belonged to Mr Holmes. He was so down, Sam went with him.'

'I can't believe he's dead,' said Edie. 'Sure, I thought he was indestructible.'

'We all did,' said Billy with a lump in his throat. 'It's the first time I've ever known someone well who died.'

'No mopin'. We need to talk.'

'We oughtn't to use Baker Street,' said Billy, 'with the Doc away, and Mrs Hudson real low about Mr Holmes.'

'Sure. Will we go to my place, then?' Edie asked. 'It'll be a bit crowded.'

'The more the merrier!' Potts offered Edie his arm, and the four of them set off down Marylebone Road towards her home in the 'rookeries' of Lisson Grove.

'Anyone got any news on the Princess, then?' asked Potts jauntily.

'I talked to a couple of mates down by the river,' said Titch.

Billy chipped in that he'd been spreading the word with the lads in the hotel trade. 'They've got to keep her somewhere. Might be in a hotel. You never know.'

'I got my dad on the job,' said Potts. 'Just now. 'E's gonna get the Bow Street boys to listen out.'

This met with general approval.

As they neared Marylebone Station, an unpleasant fog began to form.

'Cor blimey! It's lookin' grim tonight,' said Potts.

'Not in there it's not,' murmured Edie, gazing

wistfully at the Station Hotel.

Following Edie's gaze, they watched an elegant young couple being helped out of a hansom-cab. They stared enviously as the pampered pair went into the glowing warm, escorted by a liveried doorman.

'I've worked in there!' said Billy. 'It's dead posh. But it doesn't half cost! Money – that's all you need!'

'Sure, I'd rather have a good friend than a purse full of cash,' said Edie, squeezing Potts's arm.

'I fancy both,' said Potts. 'A chum *and* a bit of dosh.' Uniformed boys ran out to unload smart leather cases. 'When Billy and I 'ave our 'otel, Titch, you can all come and stay! Eh, Billy?'

'Dad still wants me to be a porter, like him.'

'Leave it out. We're gonna own a chain of 'otels. Including this one! We shall run the biz from our rooftop suite. They 'ave their own barrooms. Right, Billy?'

'Yeah. They're brilliant. Bigger bathrooms than the *whole* of your place, Edie!'

'Sure that wouldn't be difficult!' said Edie. 'You could fit our place on a pinhead!'

'I wish Sam was here,' said Titch quietly.

'No more mopin'!' cried Potts, digging Titch in the ribs.

'He'll be back later, Titch,' added Billy. 'Hey, look! If we pop through the station, we could have a word with my dad. Get him and his mates to keep an eye on the trains for us.'

They moved into the station concourse.

'Sure, I can *hear* your dad, Billy,' said Edie.

'You're kidding.'

'I am not, Titch! That's him, whistling. Listen.'

They all held their breaths and listened. None of them could hear anything above the noise and bustle of the station, but sure enough, Billy's dad appeared, whistling, pushing a trolley piled high with cases and bags.

'It's just like Billy's whistle,' Edie remarked.

'Your hearing's incredible,' remarked Titch.

'Makes up for the dodgy minces, don' it, Edie?'

'Not really, Potts.'

'I know. It does a bit, tho'.'

'What are minces?' Titch asked.

'It's rhymin' slang: mince pies – eyes – minces.'

Mr Chizzell breezed up. 'Hallo, you lot! Let me get this load on the six thirty and I'll be with you. Gotta shift, I don't want to lose me tip!'

He returned, moments later, with an empty trolley, spinning a sixpence.

Billy explained why they had all come to see him. 'Well, I never. I'll tell the lads, and if there's any news, we'll report back to base. Where are you all off to now?'

'Edie's, Dad.'

'Good. 'Scuse me, there's a customer.' Eying Potts, he added, 'Don't take that short cut through the sidings. It's dangerous. Besides, there's a private train in there tonight. Ta-ta!' With that he was off.

Billy turned towards the main entrance.

'I wouldn't mind 'avin' a gander at a private train,' said Potts. 'You know that actor bloke – 'Enry Thingamy – wot runs the Lyceum Theatre – *'e's* got 'is own train! Wiv 'is name on the side!'

'Wow!'

'We might see 'im down there, wiv all the uvver turns, practisin'! Free show!'

'Don't get larky, Potts.'

'Come on, turnip,' said Potts.

'No, Potty, no,' Billy objected. 'Dad can get real sore. And don't call me that.'

'We won't come to no 'arm, Billy. You up for it, Titch?'

'I'm game, but what about Edie?'

'I myself will take personal care of Miss McArdle!'

'I'll meet you round at Lisson Grove,' said Billy

shamefacedly. Shoulders drooping, he left them.

'Poor ol' turnip!' said Potts. 'This way, team!'

Just before the platform sloped down to the level of the track, they hid behind a pillar to avoid the suspicious eyes of a wheel tapper. When it was all clear, the three kids ran across to the buffers at the end of the sidings, where the private train Billy's dad had mentioned was puffing steam gently. Their aim was to get on the other side of the train and up a metal ladder on the embankment wall. This would bring them out a couple of roads away from Edie's. Potts had done it loads of times. It wasn't much quicker, but it was great fun.

They scooted past the signal, crossed the line and rounded the end of the train, which consisted of a plain wagon and two ornate carriages, attached to a small engine.

'Take a butcher's at that train, you two,' Potts observed. 'That fancy little balcony on the end. Bloomin' dandy.'

Passing the steps up to the balcony, they slipped into the gap between the train and the wall. Potts was about to help Edie on to the ladder when she suddenly stopped.

'Wot's up?' asked Potts.

'Quiet,' said Edie.

It was impossible to achieve anything like real quiet anywhere near a railway station. One train was arriving in the main station, another was departing, but Potts knew Edie was on to something. He got Titch to stand on one side of her, and he stood on the other. Edie crouched down between them, her eyes closed, hands cupped around her ears, listening.

'You won't believe me.'

'Course we will,' said Potts.

'I can hear a child crying.'

Neither Potts nor Titch could hear anything.

'Where, Edie?'

Again Edie listened intently. 'It's a girl, and she's crying.'

'Where tho', Edie?' asked Potts.

'That's what you won't believe. She's in the train.'

'This one 'ere?'

'This private one?' asked Titch.

'Yes.'

'Wot you sayin', Edie?'

'Sure, what do you think I'm saying?' said Edie firmly.

They stood a moment, taking their discovery in.

'If that's Princess Alice in there, we 'ave to get 'er out,' said Potts.

'How?'

'We need to distract 'ooever's got 'er.'

'Hang on, Potts,' said Titch. 'We don't know it's her!'

'You're right, Titch. Let's 'ide by this coal bunker 'ere. See if Edie can pick anyfing else up.'

They took cover beside the coal bunker. As they were hiding, a station guard came down the platform and began crossing the tracks towards them.

'Keep down,' said Potts.

The guard, carrying a lantern and two small flags, walked along the side of the train, raised himself on to the carriage steps and knocked on the door. Shortly, it was opened. After a few brief words the guard made his way back towards the station, calling, 'Evening, Major,' over his shoulder. The carriage door slammed shut.

'Major! Did you 'ear that?' whispered Potts. 'Could you make out wot they said, Edie?'

'The train has to leave in the next ten minutes. The guard came to tell them.'

'Who was he talking *to*?' Titch enquired.

'Big bloke wiv a 'uge moustache. Wot 'e addressed as Major!'

Voices were now coming from the engine, and they

could hear coal being thrown on the fire. The driver and fireman were clearly building up a head of steam, prior to departing.

'We've got to act fast,' said Potts. 'Edie, nip up the ladder and get Billy. All right?'

'Give me a hand up.'

Potts and Titch lifted Edie up so she was safely on the bottom rung of the ladder, but she was uneasy about leaving them.

'Go *on*, Edie. Get Billy. Titch, you get on that little balcony fing at the back of the train, and when I tell you, make a lot o' noise. I'll get in fru that carriage door, and see wot I can find inside.'

'This is crazy, Potts.'

'We can't just let the train go wiv 'er on it, can we? 'Ooever she is!'

They were all agreed. They had to do something.

Titch crept towards the balcony at the rear of the train, while Potts urged Edie to go and fetch Billy.

'Up you go, Edie. Go on.' Reluctantly, Edie began climbing the ladder.

Potts ran to the carriage steps. 'All right, Titch,' he hissed.

On the balcony, Titch started yelling and banging. Potts jumped on to the carriage steps and reached out to open the door. To his surprise, it was opened for him, from inside the train. Potts leaped down and hid himself beneath the train. He could see a man's legs coming down the steps. A voice from inside the train called out. 'What is it, Major?'

'Kids,' replied De Ville.

Alarmed by what was happening to Potts, Edie had come back down to the bottom rung of the wall ladder. From beneath the train, Potts watched in terror as De Ville moved towards her. With the speed of light he yanked her down, catching her in his huge arms. At that very moment, the engine let out a violent hiss of steam, and the whole body of the train shuddered and clanked.

'I'll soon sort you out, young missy,' said De Ville, as he threw Edie on to the train, which had already begun to judder forwards. De Ville leaped on to the carriage steps and jumped in, slamming the door.

Potts crawled swiftly between the slowly moving wheels. Titch jumped clear of the balcony and joined him.

'What shall we do?'

'I dunno,' said Potts. 'They've got Edie! They've got Edie!'

'Pull yourself together, Potts.'

'I promised 'er she'd be all right, Titch,' cried Potts. 'Wot shall I do?'

'Get Billy. Get any info about the train you can from his dad. I'll stick with the train. I've got Beaky. I'll be in touch.'

As Titch spoke, the end of the train eased past them. Titch jumped on to the balcony – the gate was still swinging open. Potts watched, frozen with shock, as the train gathered momentum.

'Will you be all right, Titch?'

'Just GO!' yelled Titch, working her way underneath the balcony looking for a place where she could hang on.

Potts watched the train nosing out of the sidings in mute horror. The clank of the wheels was deafening. Potts was afraid that Titch would fall on to the sleepers, inches below, but Titch was small and lithe. She could climb anything, however steep, and the difficulties of this underworld did not hold the same fears for her as they would have done for Potts. Once lodged with her feet on the axle cover and her back on a supporting beam, Titch felt secure. Lowering her head, she spoke to Beaky. 'Sorry about this, old boy.' From inside her jacket came the reassuring sounds of Beaky cooing.

As the train clattered over the points on to the main

line, Potts felt sick with shock. Edie was now *on* it –
held captive by Tiger De Ville! Titch was underneath it.
It was all his fault. He gripped the sides of his bowler,
pulled it hard on to his head and said miserably, 'And
there's nuffing I can do. Not one single flippin' thing.'

The carriage in which Edie had been unceremoniously
dumped, in which she was being held prisoner, was
comfortably furnished. Edie had never imagined that a
train would be like this – carpeted, with a comfy chair
and a small bed, which she presumed was intended for
the other occupant of the carriage, a grandly dressed
little girl. This girl sat motionless, curled up in the
chair, with her arms round her knees and her back to
Edie, whom she ignored completely.

Edie tried to see out of the windows on either side of
the carriage, but they were firmly shuttered. She
glanced back at the girl, who kept her face turned away.
All Edie could see was her beautiful, curly, golden hair.

'My name's Edie,' she said. 'Hallo.' Edie could not
understand why the girl rejected her friendliness. 'If
you don't speak to me soon I shall give up,' she said.
The girl still did not respond. 'I don't feel like talking
either,' said Edie, 'but it'd make life easier if we got
along. Don't you think?'

The girl shrugged.

'My name's Edie. Hallo.'

'Hallo,' said the girl haughtily, without looking at Edie.

'You're Princess Alice, aren't you?'

The girl seemed mildly surprised. After a lengthy silence, she drew breath. 'Yes,' she said grandly, although she still didn't look at Edie. 'I am granddaughter to Queen Victoria.'

'Sure,' said Edie. 'That's why I'm here.'

Alice ignored this remark, asking imperiously, 'Who told you my name?'

'Ah, well,' said Edie. 'That's for me to know. And you to find out.'

And for the first time in the two hours they had been together, Princess Alice looked at her. Her eyes were red and blotchy. She had been crying.

The train rattled on into the foggy night.

5

HIDDEN MEANINGS

The first moments of Titch's journey under the train were uncomfortable. As she manoeuvred herself into a large toolbox slung under the fancy balcony, she muttered a fervent prayer that Edie would at least find Princess Alice on board! She managed to get tolerably comfortable, and then she checked Beaky. Titch loved Beaky. Like Sam, he was family. To her relief, being under a train didn't seem to worry him in the least!

It was too dark to see where they were going, so as the train clattered on through the night, Titch curled up, using some rags wrapped around the tools for comfort. They stopped only once, in a wood, when the fireman jumped out and changed some points. Shortly after that, everything went pitch-black. The track sloped gently downhill, and Titch felt the temperature drop sharply. They had entered a tunnel and were going underground.

As the train drew to a standstill, Titch became aware of a strange, eerie light. She crept out of the toolbox and lowered herself cautiously to the ground. The train above her breathed and sighed like a mighty animal, sensing her presence underneath its body. On one side, Titch could see nothing. On the other, there was a wall. Looking between the underside of the train and the top of the wall, Titch was astonished by what she saw: they were in a vast cave – a cave that had been turned into an underground station.

From her vantage point, Titch could observe what was going on without too much risk of being spotted. She nursed her bruises, comforted Beaky, and watched. The station was gaslit, and in the dim, wavering light, Titch could see armed, uniformed guards running about. Two of them had guard dogs on leashes. Guards ran to the front carriage door and opened it. A very large man descended. Titch couldn't see his face, but he was thickset, his long arms swinging strangely by his side. Titch had overheard De Ville's name in the sidings, and remembering Sam's description, she was certain this was him – Tiger De Ville. She also recalled that Mr Holmes regarded him as the second most dangerous man alive. He was clearly important, because the guards seemed afraid of him. He indicated the rear carriage – where Edie and the Princess were imprisoned – and then strode up the platform in the company of another official, who trotted beside him, checking things on a clipboard.

Four more guards ran up at the double. Two of them entered the train. After a few moments they emerged with Edie – who looked very pale – and the other girl. It was the first time Titch had seen her. She had on a pretty white dress, over which she wore a burgundy velvet half-cloak, which one of the guards ripped from her. Her patent shoes were shiny and her golden hair was in ribbons. She looked out of place in this subterranean railway station. She was whimpering. It was definitely Princess Alice. The guards roped the Princess and Edie to each other. One man drew a gun and hustled them into a wide, arched opening in the cave wall, the only exit from the platform.

After the prisoners had been dealt with, supplies were unloaded from the wagon behind the coal tender and wheeled on handcarts to a storeroom at the head of the platform. Titch was staggered by the place – not just a station deep inside the earth, but a complete world, hidden away.

Peering back along the rails, all Titch could see was darkness and the tunnel, stretching up and away towards freedom. At least, she thought, her tasks were clear: to find out where the girls were being kept prisoner, discover where the caves were situated – which would probably be the hardest job of all – make a plan, and send the information back to Baker Street via Beaky. But first things first: she and Beaky had to eat.

'The captain of the *Arcadia* drowned,' said the officer, in answer to Sam's question. 'Mr Holmes, as you know, disappeared without trace.' He was cold and snooty. He showed no sympathy whatsoever to Dr Watson, who was in shock at the sudden loss of his closest friend. Nor did the man seem in the least affected by the sinking of the ship and the tragic loss of its crew. He continued coolly, unemotionally. 'Everyone below decks and most of their fellow men were blown to pieces. Little survived the blast. The ship's safe was recovered by sheer chance. In it were found some unidentified objects which you see here – a pretty sorry collection.' It shocked Sam that this callous remark was directed at Dr Watson with a degree of malice.

The contents of the mangled safe had been labelled and laid out on a long table. 'As you observe, they are mainly documents slightly damaged by the water. And a few . . . unimportant items up that end—' the officer dismissed them with a wave of the hand, '—items of a personal nature.' Sam couldn't wait to get away from this horrible man. He moved off up the table.

'These . . . few items,' Watson asked lamely, 'is this the full extent of—'

'Dr Watson,' called Sam urgently, examining the contents of the safe.

'Don't interrupt,' said the officer curtly.

'Actually, my good man, I wish to speak to him,' said Watson. 'Excuse me.' He turned pointedly away from the officer and joined Sam, who was increasingly animated. 'What is it, Sam?'

'I think this is Mr Holmes's watch, Doctor.'

'What would it have been doing in the ship's safe?'

'Perhaps he gave it to the Captain on purpose, like. Look at it, sir. Look properly. It *is*, you know. It's Mr Holmes's half-hunter.'

Watson picked it up. 'It does look familiar, Sam.' He turned it over and gazed at the initials 'S H' engraved upon the back. 'You are right, Sam,' said Watson, his voice thick with emotion. 'This . . . *is* Holmes's watch. It belonged to his grandfather.'

Sam took Watson by the arm. 'Remember I told you he said he might have a present for me?'

'Yes indeed.'

'He also said that "*the time* would come . . .". Edie made a joke about him giving me a watch.'

Watson's mind was numb with grief. 'I don't quite follow, Sam. What—'

'Excuse me.' The officer intervened. 'Will you be much longer? I am rather busy this afternoon.'

'We shall not detain you unnecessarily,' said Watson mechanically. The officer tutted angrily.

Sam continued, undaunted by the officer's interruption. 'This is Mr Holmes's watch, Doctor. And the time *has* come . . . I'm sure this is what he meant,' he said, indicating the watch. 'Can you open it?'

Watson fiddled with the delicate mechanism. The back sprang open, and out fell a small piece of paper, not much bigger than a postage stamp. Sam unfolded it.

'Look, Dr Watson . . . look at this.'

'Holmes's writing! I would know it anywhere.' Watson's eyes misted over. 'I don't have my reading glasses with me, Sam,' he burbled. 'What does it say?'

Sam stared at the small piece of paper.

'On one side it says *Hamlet*, and on the other, *Look to the Queen there, ho*.'

'Shakespeare,' Watson observed. 'What can it mean?'

'Do you mind if I ask you to move on?' said the officer. By now, Sam had had enough of this unfeeling official. He looked up to him.

'Actually, sir, I do mind. We have just recovered a precious possession that belonged to this gentleman's closest friend. Who's dead. We have *not* finished. And we will not be moving on until we have. Right, Doctor?'

Watson was touched by Sam's thoughtfulness and courage. 'Quite right, young Sam. Quite right!'

The Duke of Albion had been brought up with strict military discipline, and he found it hard to be naturally warm.

'How is the Queen today, my dear?' he asked.

The Duchess sighed. 'Given how unemotional Mama can be, I would say she was distraught.'

'I wish I could give you good news about Alice. A major operation has been mounted by the police but there is not the smallest breath of rumour to lead us to the criminals who have done this terrible thing.'

The Duchess did not dare confess to her husband

that she had initiated moves of her own to try and find their daughter. The Duke slightly misread his wife's silence. 'We shall find these villains, my dearest. We shall find Alice, too,' he added. 'Somebody, somewhere, knows where she is.'

Nothing could have been further from the discomforts Titch had endured than the luxurious First Class compartment of the Holyhead to London express in which Dr Watson was sitting. Opposite him, Sam was feeling really sorry for the poor Doctor, who was shattered by Holmes's death. The officer's unpleasantness had made him even quieter. He was not at all his usual lively, considerate self, but was gazing vacantly out of the train window, clutching Holmes's watch.

Sam was also silent – puzzled by Holmes's note. Perhaps, Sam pondered, Holmes's death was part of Professor Moriarty's plan. It even crossed his mind that the officer who had been so rude to Watson might be in the pay of the evil Professor – according to Holmes, his operatives infiltrated every corner of life. Sam was also suspicious of the businessman reading a newspaper in the far corner of the carriage. Was he too one of Moriarty's men? Princess Alice must have been kidnapped by

inside agents. How else could she have been taken so easily? Perhaps the Constable had come to Baker Street to warn Holmes that she was to be abducted.

Look to the Queen there, ho! Holmes's note gnawed at Sam's mind, repeating endlessly, like the rumbling of the train as it sped towards London. He couldn't wait to get back to Baker Street to see what Titch and the others had found out. Little did he know that, when he returned, he would find only Potts and Billy waiting for him.

When they had been bundled into their cell, Alice and Edie's ropes were removed. Their prison was bare in the extreme. They had a mattress each, nothing more. A candle provided the only light in the windowless cave. There was a hole in the ceiling. Listening hard, Edie could hear the swell of the sea.

The Princess didn't understand what was happening to her. She hated the cold and desperately missed the luxuries of home. She longed to see her mother. She was intrigued to know why Edie was on the train – but she was confused. She didn't like Edie's shabby clothes or her unfamiliar Irish accent, and unused to being addressed as an equal.

In spite of herself, Edie was just as intrigued by the

Princess. She had never met anyone so far removed from her own class, but she was too proud to make all the effort, so she left Alice alone, hoping she would eventually come round. The omens, however, were not good, and Edie knew that before too long, thrust together in this isolated cell, a timeless world without day or night, things would pretty soon come to a head.

Underground, life followed a well-regulated routine. From her vantage point between the train and the platform wall, Titch calculated that there were two dogs and about a dozen guards. She studied the pattern of their patrols. She observed the food store into which she had seen men wheeling supplies at the time of her arrival. It was unguarded, but it was locked.

Above the storeroom door, there was an air vent. Most children would have thought it impossible to get up that high, but Titch could climb anything. Leaving the safety of the rails for the open platform would be dangerous, but Titch was patient. She waited and watched. From the platform to the interior there was only one exit, through an arch. When the patrolling guards turned into it, the station was deserted. This was Titch's chance. She nipped up on to the platform, raced towards the storeroom door and jumped, landing with her feet on the door handle, gripping the frame above the door. Heaving herself up, she deftly transferred her grip to the bottom of the air vent, pulled hard until her toes were on the frame, pushed with her feet and squeezed through the vent into the store. It took seconds, and Titch made it look easy.

Inside, boxes and crates were piled high – which made it simple to climb down, and more importantly, easy to get back out. And *in* the boxes – there was food! Tins. Bottles. Chocolate! Treated carefully, this was an unlimited supply. When Titch and Beaky had eaten, and Titch was loading stores into her pockets, a gust of wind made her aware of a round hole in the ceiling. The air coming through it smelled odd and musty, but Titch also detected the salty tang of the sea. It would make sense, she thought, if the caves were near the coast.

Examining the network of caves was very risky, but cautiously, Titch explored. It was a question of waiting for the guards to pass and making a dash for it. Luckily the cave walls were uneven and offered plenty of cover. The layout turned out to be quite simple. The passage that led through the arch from the platform soon split in two. Titch crept past an unmanned guard post, along the right fork. Here she discovered service quarters – an empty kitchen, a deserted dining room and washrooms. Peering cautiously through the round window of one of the doors, she saw a dormitory. The men were sleeping.

The last door opened into another storeroom. Titch slipped in. Identical wooden crates were stacked high. Titch levered open one of the lids. The crate was packed with straw, in which lay sticks of dynamite. Titch knew nothing about explosives, but you didn't have to be an expert to see there was a massive amount of it.

Off the left fork Titch discovered a passage leading to a room with a massive, steel door. A sleepy guard sat on a box, his rifle leaning against the wall beside him. Titch worked out that this was Alice and Edie's prison. Seeing this stronghold she instantly forgot all hopes of an easy rescue. Tiptoeing past the turning to the cell, Titch saw another door, which was also guarded – two men here.

Titch concluded that this was Professor Moriarty's headquarters. She reckoned she would have to get inside it if she was going to find out where the caves were situated. Until she knew that, there was no point in sending Beaky to 22lb for help. Titch wondered if the Professor himself was here. She was on the point of leaving when a voice from inside the office brought the guards smartly to attention. A man with a huge handlebar moustache and a distinctive black V in his hair stuck his head round the door and demanded some papers – Tiger De Ville. One of the guards handed over a list that was hanging on the wall – some kind of timetable – clicked his heels and saluted. Through the open door, De Ville growled orders, which Titch could not quite hear. Before the guards moved, she bolted silently back to her hidey-hole.

Shortly after Titch had crept back under the train, a strange handcar appeared on the line, coming down the tunnel driven by two men pumping away in a seesaw motion. They came noisily to a halt, dismounted and disappeared through the arch. Titch heard voices. Then they began to trolley the wooden crates from the explosives store on to the platform. They stacked them there. A couple of guards helped them transfer the crates on to the handcar. Titch overheard snatches of their conversation . . .

'There's masses here. He'll sink the boat!'

'He's already got enough to blow up the whole island!'

So Moriarty's caves *were* near the coast.

'How does he shift it on his own?'

'He's a big man!'

'He'd have to be.'

'Typical Irish navvie!'

Eventually one of them said, 'Come on. Let's get this stuff out of here.' Piled high with dynamite, the handcar, worked by the two men, ground slowly off along the rails and disappeared back up the tunnel. With all this activity, Titch sensed the whole place was gearing up to something, that Moriarty's diabolical scheme, whatever it was, was nearing its climax.

Titch now had a complete mental picture of the Professor's subterranean kingdom, but she needed to get into Moriarty's office to discover where the caves were. And then came the moment she had been dreading – preparations began to move the train. Time was running out.

Billy and Potts walked slowly along busy Marylebone Road on their way to Edie's home in Lisson Grove – no thought today of taking the dangerous short cut. They were dragging their heels because they dreaded what they had to do. Every day since Edie's disappearance, the two lads had made their way to the McArdle household. Every day they hoped they would have good news, but as time passed and Beaky did not return, their task became bleaker. The

McArdles were a close family, and they were increasingly desperate about the loss of their little Edie, the youngest of the girls.

'I 'ope 'er dad ain't there, Billy.'

'Don't worry, Potts. He understands,' said Billy, putting a brave face on things, and trying to make Potts feel better.

'We ain't got nuffing new to tell 'em, tho', 'ave we?'

'No. But we have to do this, Potts.'

'I know,' Potts admitted.

A horse-drawn omnibus passed them going the other way. 'If I 'ad the fare,' Potts joked grimly, 'I'd get on that.'

The flats where Edie lived were so crowded they were known as 'the rookeries'. Edie had three sisters. With their mum and dad, they lived in two small rooms on the second floor of a grisly tenement block. The stairways were narrow and grubby and smelled of urine. A pair of foul-mouthed tramps were arguing over a sleeping space in the hallway. Thinly clad, grimy children were playing games, shouting. In a doorway, a well-dressed couple, holding a bible, were caring for a girl of twelve who was drunk. She was yelling at them to leave her alone.

'I dunno 'ow Edie copes wiv this dump, Billy,' said

Potts under his breath. 'It's 'orrible.'

'Well, when we find her and Princess Alice,' said Billy enthusiastically, 'Queen Victoria will give us such a huge reward, we'll be able to get her out of here into a decent pad.'

'That'd be good. In the meantime . . .' They trudged up to the McArdles' front door. Potts banged hard with his fist. The door was eventually opened by Edie's mum. It was obvious to both of them she had been crying.

'Any news?' she asked.

They shook their heads glumly.

'Ah well. Come in, why don't you? Mr McArdle's not here.'

With some relief, but heavy hearts, Billy and Potts went in.

'I'm sick of this,' said Alice, jumping to her feet. 'I need to speak to Daddy. He will tell the Queen, and she will see to it that the nasty people who are keeping us here are punished.' Only just eight, Princess Alice had been surrounded by servants from the day she was born. She snapped out an order. 'Girl. Call the guards.'

Edie was three years older than Alice. She had been earning her own living for almost as long as the

Princess had been alive. She had learned to survive, and she was not one to be bossed about. 'And you think the guards will bring your dadda along for a nice wee chat, do you?' she enquired, trying to get Alice to face the reality of their situation.

The Princess did not like it. 'You're not supposed to ask royal personages questions.'

'Your royalty won't get you out of here.'

'I am the daughter of the Duke of Albion, granddaughter to Queen Victoria.' She stomped up to Edie. 'You will address me as *Princess* Alice.'

'Sure, you may be a princess, but it won't cut here . . . *Alice*. We're in the same boat, and like I keep saying, we'd best try and get on.'

'Don't lecture me, you little peasant, or I—'

'Alice! Be quiet!'

Alice recoiled in shock. 'No one addresses me like that.'

'Sure, if you call me a peasant again, I shall slap your face. Say you're sorry.'

Alice stamped. '*You* should say sorry to *me*!'

Edie's blood was up. She forced Alice into a corner. 'Say you're sorry!' she said threateningly. 'I mean it.'

Like a sulky three-year-old, Alice mouthed the word, 'Sorry.'

'Well if you can't do better than that . . .' said Edie, raising her hand.

'Sorry,' said Alice. The word came out low and mean-spirited. But she said it.

'That'll do,' Edie snarled. 'Just. But don't try your luck. Sure, we shouldn't quarrel. We should put our minds to getting out of here.'

'The police will find me,' said Alice haughtily.

'I reckon my friends have got a better chance of finding out where we are than your police,' retorted Edie. 'I've got a feeling . . .' She stopped. She was on the point of saying that she sensed her friends were quite close, but she decided against it. 'Never mind. You wouldn't believe me.'

'I *don't* believe you. Even if your friends *do* find us, what could they do?'

Edie glared at the lost, boastful little girl cowering in the corner. 'It would surprise you, Princess Alice, what my friends can do.' She sat down on her mattress, and her tone changed. She spoke calmly, deliberately. 'I have to tell you . . . I sometimes get the shivers. I see things, and mumble. There's nothing I can do. You mustn't be frightened. Just try and remember what I say. Do you follow?'

Alice hadn't got a clue what Edie was talking about.

'Why do you say this?'

'Because,' said Edie, reaching for her blanket, 'I'm feeling a bit odd. And the time may come quite soon . . . when I am going to need your help.'

Alice gulped. She knew she had been behaving badly, and she knew it was because she was frightened. Edie's strange warning unnerved her even more.

'What will I have to do?' she asked anxiously.

'Wrap me up and keep me warm. Can you do that?'

'Of course.'

'But most important . . .' Edie continued, '. . . listen to what I say.'

'Why?'

'Because sometimes what I say when I'm feeling funny can be useful. It might even help us get out of here. I know it sounds weird, Alice, but please . . . however cross you are with me . . . listen to what I say. Just listen.'

6

THE SPIDER IN HIS WEB

Titch was growing increasingly anxious. She was no nearer contacting Edie and Alice, and lacked answers to all her questions. Was Moriarty here? What was he planning? What was the purpose behind the movement of the crates of dynamite? Titch was sure the answers were held in Moriarty's office – but it was so closely guarded.

Titch decided she would have to take a calculated risk. When it was quiet, she edged past the passage leading to Alice and Edie's cell, using the niches in the rock face for cover. She looked out along the corridor leading to Professor Moriarty's headquarters. Suddenly, the guards snapped to attention as the office door opened and De Ville appeared. Without stopping, he turned back and called into the office, 'The train is ready, Professor.'

'So,' Titch thought, 'Moriarty, the mastermind, *is* here, and *that* is his lair.'

'You may leave whenever you require, sir,' De Ville continued. 'At a moment's notice.'

Titch flattened herself into a cranny in the rock face as De Ville strode past. He was preoccupied, reading some papers. She caught the strong whiff of cigar. Titch felt more strongly than ever that she had to get into Moriarty's office. But how? And when? One thing was obvious – there was no point in trying to get in this way. She would be caught.

The only possible way into Moriarty's lair might be the 'chimney' Titch had spotted in the ceiling of the food store. At the earliest opportunity, she got back into the store, where she silently organised the boxes so that she could climb up and explore. The chimney was not an inviting prospect – just a dark hole.

Titch managed to worm her way in. The blanket darkness made it hard to breathe. She stopped to steady her nerves, and then began to lever her way up. The tunnel rose vertically, and then began to level out, until Titch could crawl. She could smell the sea more strongly.

The tunnel also widened until Titch could actually sit up. She relaxed a bit, and took Beaky out of her jacket. He strutted about, relishing the freedom. Titch felt her way forward cautiously, on all fours, passing another tunnel branching off into obscurity. She reckoned she had found her way into the ventilation system for the whole of Moriarty's underground network. It would certainly serve as a temporary home. If Titch was right, and the purpose of this system of tunnels was to air the rooms below, it might even give her access to Alice and Edie's cell.

When Billy wanted to find Edie, he whistled. Gathering her courage, Titch whistled, quietly, but high-pitched like Billy, wondering if Edie's acute hearing might pick it up. She listened, in the hope of a reply, but heard nothing.

Edging forwards, Titch came across another, much shorter 'chimney' than the one she had struggled up. Looking down it, she could see a room. An oil lamp dimly illuminated a huge desk on which lay a magnifying glass, on top of a map. Behind the desk was a chair. Peering into the room, Titch could see there were two long windows, carved out of the cliff-face, although it was too dark outside for her to see anything through them. By one of the windows was an enormous telescope. Titch sensed that she had stumbled on Moriarty's office. As her eyes explored the room, she

realised with a start that it was occupied.

The man was seated in shadow in the corner, facing away from Titch, gazing out of the window, deathly still. He was dressed in black. Titch stared down at the back of his large bald head. His elbows rested on the arms of a voluminous black leather chair. His thin legs were stretched out, crossed, unmoving. His breathing made no sound. The very sight of this figure — cold, impassive, contained — turned Titch's blood to ice. She knew without question that she was looking at the mastermind, the legendary, the evil . . . Professor Moriarty.

Edie was in a deep trance, mumbling incoherently.

'You're frightening me, Edie,' said Alice. It was the first time she had used Edie's name. She knew she needed Edie, having learned, after several attempts, that it was useless to demand attention from her captors. Touching her, Alice discovered Edie was ice-cold. Somewhat gingerly, she tucked up Edie in the blankets, and then sat on her mattress and cradled her. Edie calmed a little. Alice felt relieved.

Edie spoke, in a clear voice. 'I know, Titch, I know.'

'What?' Alice was confused but excited, bravely doing as Edie had told her.

Edie became unintelligible, although Alice again made out the word 'Titch'. Edie suddenly went rigid as a board.

'Don't,' whispered Alice, frightened again. 'Don't. What are you trying to say, Edie? Who's Titch?'

'Not Titch . . . Billy,' Edie murmured through clenched teeth.

'Billy?'

Edie was still stiff, cold and trembling. 'Billy's nrrr-nrryyy-nrrying . . . He's trying to ree . . .'

'Read?'

'Reach.'

'Reach?'

Edie was trembling, struggling to speak. 'Billy's . . . trying . . . to reach us.'

Alice had no idea who Billy was. She put her ear to Edie's mouth. Edie was whispering something about a train leaving the rails. Then the word 'crown', which she repeated.

'Crown . . . crown . . . Down . . . rolling down, downhill.'

'What, Edie?'

Edie was making a huge effort. 'Crowns . . .' she said loudly, her body stiffening. 'Downhill . . . rolling.' Then suddenly she went limp. She lay in Alice's lap, breathing very deeply, but relaxed now. Alice stroked her forehead, as her nanny did to her when she was ill. Edie's eyes were still fluttering, but she had stopped shaking and was quite calm. After a few minutes, she spoke. 'Alice. I warned you this might happen. Don't be scared. I'll be all right soon.'

'Thank goodness.' Alice breathed a sigh of relief.

'I think a friend of mine is close.'

'That's not possible, Edie.'

'It is, Alice. His name's Billy and I think he's nearby. I think I heard him whistling to me. My friends know where we are.'

'How can they?'

'They can, Alice, believe me.'

Alice wanted to believe, but couldn't. 'Even if they know where we are, Edie, what can they do about it?'

Edie smiled. 'It would surprise you, Alice, what my friends are capable of.'

The friends of whom Edie spoke so proudly to Princess Alice were seated around the kitchen table at 22lb, a sadly diminished group. Potts had not cracked a joke since Edie's capture. Sam was worried about Titch – the hoped-for message via Beaky had not arrived. And Billy was low because he couldn't make things better. Inspector Lestrade had informed Watson that the police were out in full force trying to locate Princess Alice but had found not so much as a hint of her whereabouts. The private train Billy had reported via his dad had disappeared without trace. Nearly a week had passed since Holmes's death, and the Irregulars were depressed because they felt so utterly helpless.

'I shall want you lot out of my way very soon,' said Mrs Hudson. She made a great fuss getting the ironing-board out. 'The Doctor will be back from his rounds very shortly for his lunch.'

The miserable trio decamped to the study.

'I'm sure that note of Mr Holmes's means something,' said Sam, trying hard to be positive.

'*Look to the Queen there, ho?*' said Billy.

'What can *that* mean?'

'Flippin' Shakespeare!'

'Maybe Mr H knew sumfing abaht Princess Alice's kidnap.'

'Exactly, Potts. I'm sure it's got some connection with the Constable of the Tower. I've been thinking . . .'

'Not like you, Sam.'

'Don't get larky, Potts.'

'. . . we've got to find out more about the Constable. And Tiger De Ville.'

'Let's get Dr Watson's military books out,' Billy suggested.

From the shelves, they took down Watson's Army Lists and several of his history books. They sifted through the index for references to Major De Ville and the Constable.

So involved were they in their labours that they didn't hear Watson drift into the room. Life had lost all meaning for him. He ignored the three boys, and waited numbly for Mrs Hudson to carry his lunch up. When the lads realised he was sitting there, slumped wretchedly in his armchair, they felt guilty.

'Sorry, Doctor.'

'Didn't see you there, Doc!'

'I beg your pardon?' replied Watson in a daze.

'We're just looking through some of your army books, sir.'

'Good, Sam, good,' Watson commented without enthusiasm or understanding.

Seeing the Doctor so downcast, Billy asked, 'Can I get you a nice restorative glass of port, sir?'

'Drinking at lunch-time, Billy? No thank you. Bad medicine.'

'You know wot, Doc?' said Potts. 'Billy's right. You're in need of a tonic. Come an' 'ave a butcher's at this stuff abaht the war in Afghanistan.'

'You were a soldier up there, weren't you, sir?'

'I was, Billy,' sighed Watson. 'I was. I still have a Jezail bullet in my leg.' Rubbing the wound, he stood, and crossed the room to where the three boys were working. 'Show me.'

'That's more like it, Doc! Pull up a chair, and join the club!'

For the first time since Holmes's death, Watson actually smiled.

Titch was startled by the barking of the guard dogs. She peeped out from under the train. Guards were running along the platform, the water tank was being checked, and coal shovelled on to the fire. There was a sense of urgency and fuss, and then *he* appeared – Professor Moriarty – walking purposefully towards his personal carriage. With him was De Ville. What a terrifying pair they made, the evil Professor and his villainous henchman. They boarded the train. Doors slammed, the whistle sounded, and almost immediately the train began to move.

For Titch, this was the most dangerous moment

since her arrival. Crawling swiftly between the wheels of the departing train she flattened herself at the base of the platform wall and waited. As the train pulled out – the wheels clanking and grinding inches from her face – she covered herself with the old sack that she had been using as a blanket. She would wait until all was quiet. Then she would go and hide in the ventilation tunnels. And she prayed that, with Moriarty and De Ville out of the way, she would be able to explore the Professor's office. She wanted to examine the map on his desk, and take a look through the telescope to discover what it was pointing at.

Edie and Alice were sitting cross-legged on the floor, eating their lunch. Alice pushed the metal plate away with disgust.

'Eeeurgh. I don't know how you can eat this filthy stuff.'

Edie didn't like it either, but she was used to humble fare and was grateful that they were at least fed regularly. 'Try and finish the potatoes,' she said. 'You must eat something.'

'I've eaten them all. They're the only things I can swallow. Everything else is vile,' Alice sobbed. 'I'm so hungry.'

'Sure. Tell you what, Alice – I was saving my spuds till the end. *You* can have them, and I'll eat your stuff that you don't like. Be like a thank-you for looking after me earlier.'

Alice stopped crying. She wiped her eyes with a delicate lace hanky. But she didn't speak.

'Well?' Edie asked. 'Do you want them or not?'

Alice clearly longed for them. She stuck her hand out and said sharply, 'Give them to me.'

Edie eyed her contemptuously. 'They obviously didn't teach you manners in that palace of yours.'

'Give,' Alice snapped.

Edie put her plate down. 'Alice . . . don't speak to me like that.' Alice whimpered and began to cry again. 'Sure, you have no sense at all, do you?'

'I'm not used to being treated like this.'

'D'you suppose I am?' Edie replied, unmoved by Alice's tantrum. 'I have to share a bed with three sisters, but I tell you this: if I offered to share my *grub* with them, they'd be nice about it!' Edie picked up her plate, took the spoon, scooped up a potato and raised it tauntingly to her lips. She licked her lips. 'Well?'

'Sorry,' said Alice.

Edie was surprised. 'What?'

'I'm sorry,' Alice repeated.

Edie lowered her spoon. 'That's more like it. Give me your plate.'

Alice passed Edie her plate. Edie spooned the mush of cabbage and gravy which was their regular fare onto her own plate and transferred her potatoes to Alice's. She held it out. Alice took it, but said nothing. Edie cupped her hand behind her ear. 'What was that I heard?'

'Thank you,' said Alice.

'My pleasure.' Edie watched.

Alice wolfed the spuds and wiped her mouth. 'Thank you.'

'Sure. That's all right.' Edie grinned and set about her own meal.

To her surprise, Alice had more to say. 'That was most thoughtful of you, Edie. Thank you.'

'Well,' said Edie, smiling, 'now we're getting somewhere. Princess Alice.'

Looking down from her chimney tunnel, Titch could see that Moriarty's office was deserted. Feeling confident, she worked her way out of the opening, feet first, until she was hanging by her fingertips from a lip of rock, and then dropped down on to the desk. With her shoes in her pockets, she landed quietly, splaying her feet to avoid the map. She jumped swiftly down on to the floor, ducked down behind the desk, and waited. Nothing. She was safe.

The map on the desk was an Ordnance Survey map of the south coast of England. There was a line under the name Stokes Bay – an area overlooking the River Solent and the Isle of Wight. Titch immediately spotted a series of caves marked out with names and dates – Drake's Hole (1803), Nelson's Eye (1804), Wellington's Way (1814) – disused, man-made coastal defences that had been taken over by Professor Moriarty. This was the information that Titch had been longing to get hold of. Quickly, she found a small piece of paper and a pencil and traced a map of the whole network, showing the railway line, the concealed points, the tunnel, the subterranean train depot, the HQ, the guardroom, the dynamite store and the cave where Edie and Alice were imprisoned.

As Titch worked, Beaky cleaned up a few crumbs of sandwich from a plate on Moriarty's desk. Stroking his neck brought back fond memories of when she had first seen him at the bird market. It was so quiet, Titch was sure she would hear any of the guards. Uninterrupted, she completed the map, and at the top of the paper she wrote the name Stokes Bay – the location of Moriarty's brilliantly concealed and superbly equipped underground kingdom.

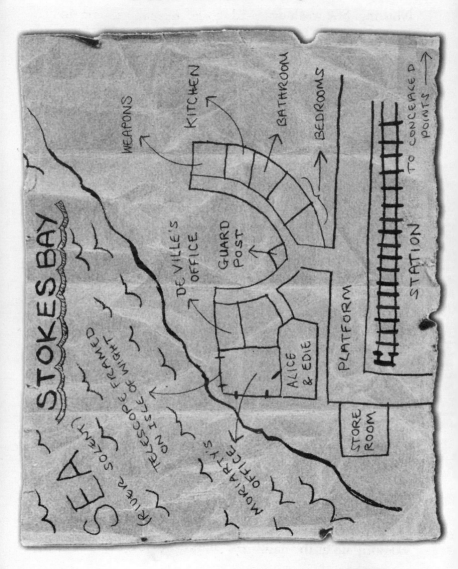

The windows of the Professor's office looked out over water – the River Solent. The sea. Titch wondered why the evil Professor had gone to such trouble to create this extraordinary complex here. Was the Isle of Wight the island to which the dynamite was being shipped? Was there something *on* the island in which Moriarty was interested? Before Titch sent Beaky back to Baker Street, she looked through the telescope in the hope that it might give some clue to Moriarty's intentions. It took a moment for her to get used to the huge image in the lens, but what came into focus was a railway tunnel. Titch wondered if it was perhaps the entrance to another underground kingdom of Moriarty's on the Isle of Wight. She moved the telescope sideways. Through the late-afternoon light, she could just make out a railway station – Ryde Pier Head. Carefully replacing the telescope at its former angle, she went back to the desk, turned over the paper and drew on it the River Solent, the Isle of Wight, Ryde Pier Head Station and the railway tunnel mouth. She then loaded the paper into the small leather tube attached to Beaky's leg. It was time for Beaky to fly home, and for Titch to get out.

She stood on the desk, holding Beaky lovingly. Looking up at the chimney, she tried to work out how

she was going to climb out, when she heard a key turning in the lock of the door. 'Off you go, Beaky,' she whispered. She gave him a kiss on the head, and launched him upwards. Beaky flew up and perched in the opening of the 'chimney'. Titch jumped down from the desk and looked frantically about. The room was bare – there was nowhere she could hide properly. She slipped into the corner and burrowed down behind Moriarty's black leather armchair. The door opened. In came a guard. He went straight to the desk and gathered up the dirty plate. He looked round to check the room before leaving. Glancing up, he caught sight of Beaky. Startled, he dropped the plate, which shattered on the stone floor. Titch watched, horrified, as he drew his gun. She covered her eyes in fear as he aimed directly at Beaky.

7

A CHRISTMAS PRESENT

rincess Alice's father, the Duke of Albion,
leaned over the latest stack of documents to be
delivered to his desk. His office in Imperial
Place was an enormous, brown, gloomy room, peopled
by grandly dressed footmen, busy with tasks for the
royal household.

The Duke was checking Queen Victoria's plans for
Christmas and the anniversary of Prince Albert's death
on 14 December, only five days away. Her Majesty had
expressed a desire that this year she should be joined for
both occasions by her many European relatives at
Osborne House on the Isle of Wight.

In spite of Princess Alice's kidnap, it was important
for royal life to carry on as normally as possible, so the
Duke was checking travel details for a guest list
featuring the Saxe-Coburgs, the Hohenzollerns and the

Princes of Schleswig-Holstein. They were travelling to England to enjoy a short stay in Osborne House.

The Queen had refused to go to the Isle of Wight on Friday the thirteenth. She was going down on Thursday 12 December, with all the royal children, their nannies and staff. Next day, their parents would join them, taking the train to Stokes Bay, and from there the royal ferry to the Isle of Wight. The royal train would then carry them from Ryde Pier Head Station virtually to the doors of Osborne House. The Queen's private railway had been the brainchild of her husband Prince Albert.

Even thirty years after his death from typhoid fever at the age of forty-five, the anniversary was precious to Her Majesty. If the Duke's arrangements all went smoothly, at least twenty-five members of the royal families of Europe would be at Osborne to commemorate Prince Albert Day, this coming Saturday, which was scheduled to include a memorial service in the local church, and fireworks.

As if he needed more to worry about, the Duke had one other thing on his mind. The Queen's family had decided, as a Christmas surprise for Her Majesty, to install the very latest example of modern technology at Osborne House – a lift. Its purpose was to help the

Queen, who was not a young woman, by transporting her from the main hall at ground level up to her bedroom on the first floor. Building work was nearing completion, but the Duke was apprehensive because Queen Victoria resisted strongly the slightest suggestion that she should take life more easily with increasing age. She also detested surprises. The lift would have to be very carefully presented to Her Majesty, or the royal visitors would be in for a very unhappy Christmas.

Terror-stricken, Titch watched from behind Moriarty's chair as the guard took aim at Beaky. His finger on the trigger, he was about to fire. Titch couldn't bear it.

'No!' she shouted, jumping from cover. 'Please don't shoot him! He's only—'

But it was too late. The shot rang out, echoing horribly in Moriarty's office. Titch's cry had distracted the guard, and the bullet pinged off the rock face just beneath Beaky and ricocheted back into the room. Ducking, instinctively, Titch yelled, 'Go for it, Beaky! Home! Home!' Startled, afraid, Beaky disappeared up the chimney. The guard did not know whether to take another shot at Beaky or cover Titch. He fired up the chimney again. As the noise subsided, Titch watched in horror as a few feathers drifted slowly down from the black hole in the ceiling. Pointing the gun at Titch, who was cowering behind Moriarty's chair, the guard backed towards the door and pulled a lever on the wall. Bells began to ring outside the office.

Another guard arrived within seconds. Titch moved slowly towards the two of them, feinted, dived between them and shot out of Moriarty's office but with the alarm sounding, the walls seemed to grow guards – they were everywhere. The corridors were narrow, and although Titch did what she could to evade capture – deceiving one, dodging round another, outrunning a third – it was not long before she was trapped, each possible getaway blocked, the guard dogs straining at their leads, growling ferociously at her. Conceding there was no way out, Titch stood, awaiting capture. The man that had tried to shoot Beaky came forward.

'Come with me, sonny,' said her captor. He pushed her arm up high behind her back. 'I'll take care of you.'

Mrs Hudson didn't like to see Billy miserable, he was normally so cheery. She could see that he was carrying all the Irregulars' cares on his shoulders.

'Billy.'

'Yes, Mrs Hudson?'

'Turn the lamp up. Give me a hand with this laundry.'

Billy did as he was asked. Presenting him two corners of a damp sheet, Mrs Hudson held the other two. As they stretched and folded, she asked, 'Where's Sam?'

'He's gone up to the roof to see if there's any sign of Beaky. He doesn't think of anything else and he's missing Titch like mad.'

'I'm sure he is.'

'And he's been searching through Mr Holmes's books.'

'Why?'

'Something to do with the Queen.'

'According to the newspaper the Queen's going to celebrate the anniversary of Prince Albert's death at Osborne House. On the Isle of Wight. And the family's staying on there for Christmas as usual.'

'You know a lot about the Queen, Mrs Hudson.'

'I know almost everything there is to know about our beloved Queen, Billy.'

Mrs Hudson bustled over to him holding out her bit of the sheet. 'Here – you take both ends, now. Hold it nice and high. Keep it off the floor while I do the rack.' She unhooked the rope from the wall by the range and lowered the rack. 'And young Master Potts? What's he up to?' said Mrs Hudson, narrowing her eyes. She wasn't at all sure about young Master Potts. They began folding the sheet.

'He's running for Jacky Dyke this evening. There's a big boxing match on.'

'Disgraceful. Betting? On fighting?'

'He's missing Edie, Mrs Hudson.'

'Poor, dear Edie. What a mess! Well, you've gone too far this time, you lot. It was bound to happen. Dr Watson's always warning you.'

'I'm worried about *him* as well. I've never seen him so low.'

'That's to be expected, Billy.' As they hung the folded sheet on the clothes rack, Mrs Hudson explained that they were unable to hold a proper funeral because Holmes's body had not been recovered. 'And a funeral,' she added, 'would help.'

'How do you mean?'

'It would help the Doctor, and all of us in fact, come to terms with the shock of Mr Holmes's death.'

Billy pondered this. 'He was my hero,' he said quietly. 'I wish he was here now. To help sort this mess out.'

'We're bound to miss a man as remarkable as Mr Holmes, Billy, but it'll get easier with time. It took me five years to get over my husband's death. I still miss him every day. But it's bearable now.' She patted Billy on the shoulder. 'Come on, dear. Do these pillowcases with me.'

Not showing how upset he was, Billy began folding the large squares of damp white linen.

The guards frogmarched Titch down the corridor, dogs yapping at her heels. She wondered where they would take her, and was relieved when they unlocked Alice and Edie's cell and slung her in. The huge steel door slammed to. The heavy bolts were shoved into place. The key grated in the lock.

Alarmed, Princess Alice jumped up and moved as far away from Titch as the confines of the cave would allow.

'Titch!' cried Edie, squinting through the half-light. 'Is that you?'

'Are you all right, Edie?'

'How did you get here?'

'I followed you.'

'How?'

'Jumped the train.'

'No!'

'Ay. How *are* you, Edie?'

'I'm alive! This is Alice.'

From the far corner, Alice corrected her: 'Princess Alice.'

'Don't start that again, Alice,' Edie warned gently.

Alice looked down her nose at Titch and enquired, 'Who are you?'

'He's a pal of mine. Sure, didn't I tell you my friends knew where we were?'

'Did you hear me whistling, Edie?'

'Sure. I thought it was Billy.'

'At least you knew there was someone here.'

'Sure. It's great to see you.'

Titch turned to look properly at Alice, who was still in the far corner of the cave. 'Hallo, Princess. I'm Titch.' Titch held out a hand. She looked filthy after travelling under the train and living rough. Alice hesitated, then, catching a beady look in Edie's eye, stepped forward and put her hand limply in Titch's, as if she expected it to be kissed rather than shaken.

'Hallo,' she said, hardly opening her mouth, and withdrawing her hand quickly as though to avoid contamination. Titch was transfixed.

Edie broke the silence. 'Sure, don't mind Alice. She's scared, but she's all right, really. Does Potts know where we are?'

'Not yet, no.' Edie was disappointed. 'But Beaky's on his way now, I hope,' Titch added, to cheer Edie up. 'I'd just made a plan of where we are and put it in his pouch, when all hell broke loose.'

'Where are we, then?'

'On the south coast.'

'I thought I could hear the sea. We'll just have to hope Beaky makes it, then,' Edie said staunchly.

'He'll make it,' cried Titch 'He's an amazing bird. What do they treat you like?'

'They're pigs.' Alice stamped her foot angrily.

'Sure, they don't treat us that bad. But there's only one of them has any kindness.'

Titch could see Edie was putting on a brave face.

'They're pigs,' repeated Alice sourly. 'My father will put them in their place. Just you wait and see.'

Titch was surprised by Alice's attitude. Edie smiled wryly. It was obvious that she had had a difficult time, locked in with this snotty little eight-year-old. Titch wondered what it was going to be like now there were three of them.

Frustrated and desperate, Sam visited Inspector Lestrade at Scotland Yard to try and persuade him to bring the Constable in for questioning.

'We've got nothing to do, so we've been keeping an eye on the Tower, Inspector, and Tiger De Ville is back in London. Believe me – he's the man who grabbed Edie. And he's got Princess Alice. There's a history between him and the Constable, you see. They served together in Afghanistan with the First Bangalore Pioneers – the Jowaki Expediton of 1877.'

'Where on earth do you get this stuff from, Wiggins?'

'Dr Watson's Army Lists, sir.' Sam reminded Lestrade that the Constable had made an attempt to talk to Sherlock Holmes over a week ago. 'The Constable also served alongside Alice's father, the Duke of Albion. They're friends, and De Ville's got a hold on him. I know it. It's all linked, Inspector – the sabotage of the *Arcadia*, Mr Holmes's death, Princess Alice's disappearance, the Constable, De Ville. It's linked.'

'Linked? By what?'

'Not by what. By who.'

'Who then?'

'Professor Moriarty.' Lestrade looked sceptical. 'Inspector, Mr Holmes told me he was afraid. He was never normally afraid.'

'Did he say what he was afraid *of*?'

'Of what the Professor is up to.'

'And what that might be?'

'Well . . . becoming the Napoleon of Crime – dominating Europe, sir.' Even as he said it, Sam knew how unlikely it sounded. He felt powerless. 'Don't forget the note Mr Holmes left in his watch,' he pleaded.

'Jog my memory, Wiggins.'

'Look to the Queen there, ho!'

'This is not evidence, Wiggins,' Lestrade said dismissively.

'I admit that, sir, but Mr Holmes was working on this case before he died. We owe it to his memory.'

Lestrade had learned a degree of sullen respect for Sam during the case of the Rose of Africa. He put his hand on Sam's shoulder.

'Well, Wiggins, if you can provide me with a scrap of *proper* evidence I will haul the Constable in for questioning.'

'Thank you, sir,' said Sam. But he knew Lestrade was losing patience and he would have to find the answer fast.

The Queen's surprise Christmas present from her children – a lift at Osborne House – had been satisfactorily installed. With Her Majesty's arrival on the Isle of Wight imminent, the royal staff were under strict instructions from the Duke of Albion that there should be no trace of building work. Thus it was that when most of the workmen had finished for the day and set out for the estate cottages where they were lodged, two of them stayed behind late. To all appearances, they were checking the mechanics of the lift and tidying away anything that might alert the Queen's suspicions to the fact that her home now boasted this very latest technological addition.

The area beneath the lift cage was surprisingly spacious – with room to house the motor, as well as the counterweights and the drum round which the cables that raised and lowered the lift cage were wound. One of the two workmen, who were both Irish, watched his companion closely. 'What d'you reckon, O'Hare?' he asked timidly.

O'Hare, the man addressed, was laying an electric cable. He was a thoughtful man of few words. He did not reply but concentrated on stripping back the end wires of the flex. The man watching, who was bagging up rubbish in a sack, was a burly ex-navvy with a red face and a shock of ginger hair. He was physically powerful, but nervy. He did not like silence. 'Where shall we run the wire, O'Hare?'

'The wire's not the problem, Reilly. It's the point of contact. When the lift comes down to the ground floor, contact has to be made.'

'Or it won't go off, will it?'

'Leave it to me, Reilly! I'm the brains. You're the brawn. And keep your voice down. We don't want anyone to hear.'

'I tell you who I don't trust: that Spooner feller. He's always poking around.'

O'Hare snorted. 'Spooner! He's an eejit.'

Reilly continued to pile rubbish into his sack, watching intrigued as O'Hare fixed the cable high on the wall of the lift shaft, lining it up with a protrusion at the back of the lift cage. When he was satisfied, he turned to Reilly. 'You can try it now.'

Reilly was relieved to have something positive to do, and lumbered up the stairs to the lobby off the main hall, from where the lift was operated. On O'Hare's instruction, he sent it up to the Queen's bedroom on the first floor, then brought it back down to ground level. O'Hare's voice echoed up the shaft 'Take it up again. All the way! Give me five minutes.'

While Reilly was waiting by the lift, he became aware of a presence close behind him. He whipped round.

'Mr Spooner!' It was the man they had spoken of earlier. Spooner was long and thin, but he was bent, suffering from curvature of the spine. His hair was lank and stringy, his manner oily. He shuffled closer to Reilly. 'I am intrigued by this newfangled machine,' he remarked. 'How exactly does it work?'

Reilly was suspicious. 'Why should an artist feller like yourself be interested?' he countered somewhat clumsily.

'I am fascinated by the march of technology, sir – the pedal cycle, the automobile, the telephone. This.' With a spindly finger, he indicated the lift. 'Do tell me how it works.'

'Well . . .' said Reilly unwillingly, 'there are wires which hold the lift cage. They go up high over some pulleys at the top of the tower. That's six floors, right?' Spooner nodded enthusiastically. 'The wires are attached to big counterweights, like, that balance out the . . . er . . . heaviness of the lift and its passengers. The motor is situated down below, and it winds or unwinds another set of wires round a big drum, that take the lift up or down, like.'

'Mmmm . . . very simple really.'

'I suppose.' Reilly was disconcerted. He found it rather complex.

'And the machinery is all down below, is it?' said Spooner, nosing still further forward.

Reilly was keen not to discuss what was going on 'down below'. He dodged the question, calling out to O'Hare, 'How's it going?'

'Nearly there,' came the reply.

In order to prevent Spooner questioning him further, Reilly asked, 'And how is your painting going? A portrait is it not?'

'Indeed. A portrait of Her Majesty. It is well-nigh complete, although I myself do not do the actual painting you understand. That is done by Maestro Edmund Leinster. I am his humble assistant,' Spooner grovelled, 'allowed to flesh out a little of the background, do you see? A modest contribution,' he added with a shrug. 'I am preparing things for the final sitting. Her Majesty will be arriving very shortly, as I am sure you are aware.'

To Reilly's relief, they were interrupted by O'Hare's cry. 'Try her again.'

Spooner watched as Reilly operated, making him increasingly uncomfortable. Reilly summoned the lift back down to ground level. The process was repeated until O'Hare was satisfied. Reilly then had the excuse he was looking for to get away from Spooner and rejoin

O'Hare in the lift shaft.

'That Spooner feller is sniffing around,' he whispered.

'If he sticks his nose in too far, I'll take care of him,' O'Hare replied. 'All I have to do now is join the cable to the dynamite.'

'It's standing by for when you want it, O'Hare.'

'Good. You can bring it over in the next couple of days. I'll complete my work at the last moment. We don't want it blowing up too soon, do we? We're done here.' O'Hare gathered his tools together. 'Well?' he said. 'Have you not got something to show *me*?'

'I have, O'Hare. It's all ready. I just said.'

'Look at you with that axe handle. Can you never be without it?'

'I like it, O'Hare. It makes me feel safe.'

'Aaah. Like a kiddy's comforter,' said O'Hare, locking the lift-shaft door.

To add to the Irishmen's concerns, Spooner was still hovering as they informed a member of staff that the lift was in perfect order, and that when they had disposed of their rubbish sack they would be leaving. Spooner watched as they walked down the drive. He waved an overfamiliar goodbye.

'I really don't like that feller,' said Reilly, halfheartedly returning the wave.

O'Hare did not look back 'Stop fretting, Reilly. I'll deal with him. With that axe handle of yours. Forget him. Show me the tunnel.'

O'Hare set off. Reilly, somewhat reassured, followed him.

'So tell us about this place, Titch,' Edie urged. 'Where are we?'

'It's Professor Moriarty's underground kingdom,' said Titch.

'Who's he?' Alice demanded.

'He's an evil—'

Edie nudged Titch. 'Sure, Alice,' she said, 'he's the man who had us brought here.'

Titch realised it was important not to scare Alice. 'Ay. He's . . . not very nice.'

Alice's neck straightened. 'Wait till my father gets hold of him,' she said royally.

'Sure, I look forward to it. Carry on, Titch. Alice, come on and listen.'

Nervously, Alice joined them.

'It's the most amazing place,' Titch went on. 'Brilliantly concealed. There's food, fuel, and a stack of dynamite – they've been shipping it out at night.'

'But where are we?' asked Edie eagerly.

'On the south coast. Place called Stokes Bay. I've got a feeling they're based here to keep an eye on the Isle of Wight.'

'The Isle of Wight? Sure I've never heard of it.'

'It's an island in the River Solent,' said Alice.

Edie and Titch looked at each other in amazement.

'Do you know it then, Alice?' Edie enquired.

'Yes. I go there every year.'

'Do you, now?'

'Yes,' Alice replied confidently. 'For our holidays. We all go.'

'Do you?'

'Yes. The others will be going there any time now – to remember my grandfather's death. It's rather dreary. I shall join them as soon as I get out of this horrid place. We always go there for Christmas. You can come too if you're still nice to me.' Alice looked at Titch. '*You* might have to have a scrub, but you can both stay with us. My grandmama has a house there.'

'Oh.'

'It's called Osborne House. It's very nice. Much more homely than Buckingham Palace.'

Titch and Edie were speechless, but Alice's tone was so matter of fact that they were inclined to believe her.

'Are you telling the truth, Alice?' Titch asked cautiously.

'Of course,' Alice protested. 'I'm not allowed to tell fibs.'

'I know you're right about the River Solent. It was on the map,' said Titch. 'And thanks for inviting us to stay.'

'Nanny gets extremely annoyed if we don't tell the truth.'

'All right, Alice. We believe you.' Edie patted her arm.

Titch was thinking hard. 'You know, Edie, what Alice is saying makes real sense. If Professor Moriarty is up to something, it could have do with . . . with *her* . . . Alice's gran. Know what I mean?'

Edie pondered the disturbing thought that Moriarty's schemes might be aimed at Queen Victoria. Alice raised her eyebrows. 'Well I hope this Professor . . . Thingamy is not going to upset Grandmama. She wouldn't like that at all. And when she's angry, she can be scary. I mean – absolutely terrifying.'

When Beaky flew up the chimney tunnel from Moriarty's office, narrowly dodging the second bullet which grazed his breast, he paused and listened. He could hear the pandemonium below – alarm-bells sounding, guards running to and fro, yelling, shouting, the dogs barking. He waited in the dark, taking stock of the situation. His breast was sore, but he was well fed and watered. He had recognised Titch's cry of 'Home!' He could smell briny air, and flew towards it, heading for a growing pinpoint of dim light. With a huge flap of relief, he reached the mouth of the passageway and perched, looking down at the sea below, relishing the fresh night air. He took a deep breath and soared out into open sky. He headed out over the water, flying upwards until he was level with the top of the cliffs, then he turned and headed inland.

Seeking to provide Inspector Lestrade with the evidence he was demanding, Sam, Billy and Potts continued to keep an eye on the Tower. One evening, when Tiger De Ville left on foot, some little way behind him there followed a ragged street urchin with a wooden leg. De Ville might not have been surprised to know he was being trailed, but he would have been astonished to learn that his pursuer was Billy Chizzell. Billy had learned the art of disguise by observing his master, his hero, Sherlock Holmes.

De Ville made his way past St Katharine's Docks and

entered a maze of tiny cobbled streets that ran like a honeycomb through the riverside area close to the Tower. Billy almost lost his man when he doubled back as a precaution, but clinging to De Ville's trail – and fully aware how dangerous it would be if he was caught – he pursued his quarry to a small dilapidated boathouse. And there he waited. Darkness fell, providing better cover, but nothing happened. Billy began to think De Ville had given him the slip.

After some time, the boathouse doors giving on to the river began to open. Out of the darkness of the swirling river, a small craft glided in noiselessly. The doors closed. Still nothing happened. Billy wondered if De Ville intended to leave in the boat. He eventually concluded that a meeting must be taking place *inside* the boathouse – *on* the boat maybe! Who could De Ville possibly be meeting in such carefully orchestrated secrecy? Was it perhaps Professor Moriarty?

Billy imagined what Sherlock Holmes would have done in the circumstances. Removing his false leg, and flexing his knee, he moved quietly to the side of the boathouse, where he climbed easily on to the low roof. Getting on was straightforward enough, but the wooden roof tiles were old and worn. Some were loose, and Billy was a touch overweight. He crawled gingerly towards a hole in the roof – where one of the tiles had rotted through. Praying that the ancient structure would hold, he put his ear to the gap and listened.

When Reilly and O'Hare were out of sight of Osborne House, beyond the prying eyes of Mr Spooner, artist's assistant, they marched through the darkening night in the direction of the Queen's private railway line. Reaching the line, they walked along it for a couple of miles until they came to a tunnel. Ensuring they were unobserved, they entered it. Reilly lit a flashlamp he had secreted inside the tunnel mouth. Halfway along, he took a key from his pocket and inserted it into the lock of a door set back in the tunnel wall.

'Does anyone know what's in here, Reilly?'

'Course not, O'Hare. I've been doing it at night. It's taken me weeks. A little boat delivers crates of it from the mainland, and I have to ship it all the way here on my own. It's not been easy.' O'Hare grunted dismissively. 'Wait till you see inside, O'Hare.' Keen to impress his brainier companion, Reilly opened the door and shone his lantern into a small room piled high with sticks of dynamite.

O'Hare smiled and said, 'Bang!' under his breath. 'Have you got cable?'

'Miles of it. Look.'

'Good. Where's the plunger?'

'Behind you.' O'Hare bent down to examine it. 'Will it do?'

'Yes.' O'Hare smiled maliciously.

Nervously, Reilly indicated the dynamite. 'Is there enough?'

O'Hare smiled. 'You don't know about explosives, do you, Reilly?'

'No.'

O'Hare patted his workmate patronisingly on the back. 'Good work, Reilly. You've done really good work. There's enough here to blow up the whole island.'

Back at Baker Street, Sam, Potts and Dr Watson – desperate for information to give Inspector Lestrade – debriefed Billy in the study.

'Are you sure De Ville met Moriarty, Billy?'

'Definitely. No doubt at all.'

'I told the Inspector De Ville would lead us to Moriarty!' Sam punched his hand in frustration.

'You're wasting your time trying to outwit the Professor,' remarked Watson gloomily. 'Evil man. Holmes grappled with him unsuccessfully for years, as you well remember from the Case of the Dragon Tattoo.'

'You must 'ave 'eard *sumfing*, Billy.'

'Just odd words. And they didn't make sense.'

'Wot d'you mean?'

'Well, I can't believe they were making plans for Christmas.'

'Christmas?!' said Sam.

'All that palaver over Chrissmas? It don't seem likely, do it?'

'There was talk of a present, too – a *Christmas* present, I suppose.'

'Chrissmas *present*?' quizzed Potts.

'That's what I heard,' said Billy. 'A Christmas present . . . for her.'

'For her?' They were all baffled.

'Hang on,' said Sam, 'what if *her* was the Queen? *Look to the Queen there, ho.* Right?'

'Mrs Hudson said the Queen's going away for Christmas,' Billy remembered.

'Maybe it's Chrissmas wot joins everyfing togevver.'

'Exactly, Potts,' cried Sam.

'Christmas is just the week after next,' Billy exploded.

'But what can we do?' said Sam miserably. 'We still haven't heard from Titch.'

'Have you been up to the roof recently, Sam?'

Sam nodded. It was clear from his downturned mouth that his journey to the rooftop to check Beaky's hutch had been unfruitful. Potts, too, was depressed. He was longing for news of Edie, and the lack of information increased his guilt. As for poor Dr Watson, he was again locked in a world of his own, musing over the loss of his closest friend.

'Cheer up,' said Billy, trying as ever to be positive. 'Titch'll send us news as soon as there is any!'

Sam nodded, but he was beginning to fear that something terrible had happened. Maybe Titch had been captured, like Edie. Or even worse . . . perhaps she had been killed under the train. Why else had Beaky not brought back the information without which they could do nothing? Most of all, he feared that Lestrade would lose patience and the entire operation would fall apart.

8

OFF THE RAILS

'When you had your vision, Edie,' enquired Titch, 'were you real bad?'

'You know me, Titch.'

'Did they take care of you?'

'They didn't know. Alice was very nice to me.'

Titch looked at Alice doubtfully. 'Was she talking in her sleep, like, Alice?'

'Yes. I was very frightened.'

'What did she say?'

'Something about you and Billy. It was hard to follow.'

'What exactly?'

'Something about a train.'

'A train?'

'It sounded like . . . a train . . . was coming off the rails.'

'Was that all?'

'No. She mentioned crowns rolling down a hillside.'

There was a moment's silence while they considered this disturbing image.

'Moriarty's train came back last night,' said Edie.

'I didn't hear nowt.'

'You were both asleep. I have this instinct that Professor Moriarty's back,' Edie went on. 'And sure, the train left again later.'

'There's a lot going on, isn't there?' Alice stated in her direct way.

'Ay, there is,' said Titch, brooding. 'A hell of a lot. Something's going to happen.'

Edie's brow puckered. She looked at Alice.

'Are you getting pictures in your head again, Edie?' asked Titch.

'Sure. I sometimes see this group of children, like.'

'You mean Sam and the gang?'

'No. They're dressed in posh clothes.' She glanced at the Princess. 'Like Alice. They're all having a good time, except one little girl who stands on her own, away from the others, looking sort of miserable.'

'That sounds like Eleanor,' Alice remarked.

'Who's Eleanor?'

Alice looked as though she might burst into tears.

'Don't fret, Alice,' said Edie kindly. 'Tell us. Who's Eleanor?'

Alice's lip quivered. 'Eleanor . . . is my baby sister.' Titch had not really considered that Alice, being a princess, might be prey to the same simple emotions as ordinary people, like missing her kid sister. 'She sulks when I'm not there,' Alice continued. 'She's the one I miss the most. After Mama.'

'Alice,' Titch asked, 'you know you said you were all going to your gran's place – Osborne House, was it? – for Christmas?'

Still upset, Alice nodded.

'Is . . . Eleanor going 'n' all?'

Alice was still fighting her tears. 'Everyone's going. All our cousins, too. Lots of them are coming over from Germany, specially.'

'To your gran's house on the Isle of Wight?'

'Yes.'

'For Christmas?'

'Yes. And Grandpa's anniversary.'

'And you were all going there on the train?'

'*Our* train. Yes. The royal train. And the royal ferry of course. Why?'

'Oh . . . not to worry,' Titch replied, not wanting to upset the Princess unnecessarily.

Later, when Alice was not listening, Edie asked Titch quietly, 'What are you thinking?'

'I'm not sure, Edie. But I'm beginning to think it's really important for Beaky to get back to Baker Street fast. *Really* important. Something big is going to happen.'

Under cover of night, Reilly and O'Hare ran a cable from the cache of explosives in the tunnel along the railway line towards Osborne House and up the embankment to a small copse some fifty yards from the tunnel mouth. This is where they secreted and camouflaged the plunger. They buried the cable and walked back towards the tunnel.

'O'Hare.'

'Yes?'

'D'you reckon the cable's well enough hidden?'

'Yes.'

They entered the tunnel. After a few paces, Reilly spoke again. 'O'Hare.'

'Light the flashlamp, will you?'

He did. 'Where's the flare?'

'Reilly, you're like a kid with your questions.'

They continued in silence, their feet crunching on the gravel, passing the cache in the middle of the tunnel. Reilly could bear it no longer.

'Well, where is it?'

'It's there. Have *you* put the dynamite in the lift shaft?'

'Exactly the amount you told me. In place. Well hidden. All you've got to do is connect it.'

In the dark, O'Hare smiled. They were nearing the Ryde end of the tunnel, and stopped walking.

'O'Hare?'

'Yes?' said O'Hare through pursed lips.

'Is it the right time?'

'Yes, Reilly. It's the right time. That's why we're here.'

'O'Hare?' O'Hare did not reply. 'Will *he* be watching?'

'That's the whole point, Reilly. Will you shut up?'

O'Hare found the hidden flare and stuck it under Reilly's nose. He lit it and stood in the mouth of the tunnel, waving it slowly back and forth above his head.

Watching the flame through his telescope, Professor Moriarty felt a glow of contentment. This signal from the Isle of Wight meant that the lift and the tunnel were dynamited and all was ready. Moriarty glided like a phantom to his desk, where he pressed a button. A distant bell rang in the guardroom, and before the Professor had resumed his seat in the voluminous black leather armchair, there was a knock on his office door.

'Is everything set for our evacuation?'

'Yes, Professor.'

'Good. When we leave, this place must be bare. Not a trace, not a hint, not a clue.'

'Understood, sir.'

'You are in charge, are you not? In the absence of Major De Ville.'

'No, sir. I'm second-in-command. But the place is already as good as empty. Only me and the chief left now. And yourself of course, sir. There's your few things in here, and the Princess – plus the two prisoners. Has a decision been reached about them?'

Moriarty made a cathedral with his long, thin fingers. His response was calculated.

'The Princess has served her purpose. The two interfering urchins have never been of interest. They can all be eliminated.'

The guard was surprised by Moriarty's coldness. He understood the Professor's desire for power, but this ruthless indifference to the fate of three innocent children shocked him.

Moriarty snapped at him. 'Why are you waiting?'

'I beg your pardon, sir.' The guard clicked his heels, and left the room at the double.

Moriarty allowed his fingers to relax and intertwine. He rubbed the palms of his hands together with an almost malicious relish. Holmes was dead. The police, led by Inspector Lestrade, were searching frantically, fruitlessly, for Princess Alice. The main thrust of Moriarty's diabolic scheme – the assassination of the crowned heads of Europe – could proceed, perfectly, and on time. 'If all goes according to plan,' he thought, 'in less than two days' time there will be such chaos in Europe that, out of it, I shall emerge supreme, powerful.'

In Imperial Place, Thursday 12 December dawned chilly and bleak. The Duke of Albion, who was up early, looked as grey as the fogbound skies. 'Are the children ready for their journey?' he asked his equerry.

'Carriages leaving for Waterloo Station in fifteen minutes, Your Grace. Barring accidents, they will be at Osborne within four hours. With Her Majesty, of course.'

'Tomorrow?'

'A simple family day. Culminating in your arrival with Her Majesty's relatives.'

'Good. And plans for Prince Albert Day?'

'Everything is in order for Saturday, Duke.'

The Duke once again checked the schedule in front of him. 'I'm not superstitious like the Queen, but I wish we were not travelling on Friday the thirteenth.'

The equerry nodded.

'One more matter – Princess Eleanor. Never a happy child, and quite lost since Alice . . . disappeared. She will travel today, with all the other children as planned, but I thought it wise for her to be accompanied by her mother in addition to her nanny.'

'My very thought, Duke. Shall I . . .'

'Not necessary. I have already made the extra arrangements. I would go myself, but I am obliged to chaperone the Queen's relatives tomorrow as planned.' The Duke stopped rubbing his eyes and enquired wearily, 'Have you been through the latest despatch box? Is there any news of this wretched lift?'

'It is, apparently, a huge success. They have to stop the servants playing with it.'

'The children must not give the game away! The Queen doesn't miss a trick.'

'If I might be so bold, Duke, perhaps the *children* should present it to the Queen, shortly after their arrival, when high tea is concluded. In order to . . . soften the blow, as it were.'

'Excellent idea. The Queen does have a sentimental

side, although,' the Duke observed dryly, 'few of us are privileged to witness it. See to that, please.'

'Certainly. The *official* . . . inauguration of the lift will take place tomorrow, when Her Majesty descends from her bedroom chamber to greet you and all her guests on *your* arrival at Osborne. It will, I am sure, be a triumph. On a personal note, it is the Saturday evening, Prince Albert Day, when I wish I could be with you. I love fireworks.'

The Duke's mind had reverted to Alice and Eleanor, and their distraught mother, the Duchess of Albion. 'Indeed,' he commented distractedly, 'I am sure it will be a thrilling show.'

In the continued absence of any news from Titch, Sam sat with Billy and Potts, his head in his hands, thinking. Holmes's half-hunter and the piece of paper it had contained, with the words *Look to the Queen there, ho!* lay before them on the kitchen table.

'Look to the Queen there!' said Billy, as if saying it out loud would help them understand.

'Look to the Queen there, *ho!*' Potts repeated, carefully sounding the 'h'.

Sam looked up and spoke deliberately. 'I have a theory. Let's consider what we have so far . . . 1. The

Arcadia goes up. Mr Holmes is killed. 2. Princess Alice disappears. So . . .' he pointed at the paper, *'Look to the Queen there, ho!'*

'Don't follow tho', do it?'

'That's my point,' said Sam.

'Wot?'

'1. Mr Holmes is out of the equation. 2. Mr Lestrade and the police are running round like headless chickens looking for a hostage. So . . .' said Sam decisively, 'Look to the Queen . . .'

'I'm still not wiv yer.'

'Who's looking after the Queen?'

'You tell us, Sam.'

'No one, Billy. That's what I'm driving at.' It took a moment for this to sink in. 'Everything's linked . . . by the Queen.'

'I get it, Sam! Distract everyone, then pop the Queen off!'

'Wow! A plan to kill Queen Victoria.'

'A Christmas present . . . for *her*,' Sam concluded.

'It makes sense.'

'It's just a bit 'ard to believe.'

'Except for this,' said Sam. 'Mr Holmes suspected that Moriarty was working on something really big.'

'Knockin' off ol' Queen Vic is big all right!'

'Exactly.'

'Wow! Who shall we tell, Sam? Lestrade?'

'I'm not sure, Billy.'

'Wot we gonna do, Sam?'

'I don't know, Potts. I'm thinking.'

'Well, fink fast, Sam,' Potts urged, 'cos I got a feelin' you're right. In which case . . . we're runnin' out of time!'

Bright afternoon winter sun broke through the coastal mist to greet the Queen and royal children on their arrival at Stokes Bay Station. From there, the royal ferry carried them over a calm sea to the Isle of Wight. At Ryde Pier Head Station stood the Queen's private train, green and gold and gleaming, waiting to take the royal party direct to Osborne House. It looked like a big toy, the most perfect train a child could ever have imagined.

The royal party walked along the thin red carpet that traversed the platform, led by Queen Victoria and Mr Perkins, the station-master, looking grand in his top hat. Mr Perkins seated the Queen in her personal compartment, then aided the children as they climbed the carriage steps. They dived into the deep-padded, cushioned seats, thoroughly enjoying themselves. All, that is, save one small girl, who mounted the train clinging nervously to her mother's hand.

'You will stay with me, all the way, won't you, Mama? I am still feeling a bit sick from the ferry.'

'Of course I shall stay with you, Eleanor.'

'All the way to Osborne?'

'Don't worry, dearest.' For the Duchess of Albion to say this was ironic. Since Alice had been snatched from under their noses, she had been *so* worried she had barely let Eleanor out of her sight. The Duchess and her youngest daughter found seats in the quietest of the three carriages, with the nannies, where the Princess sat gripping her mother's hand with both of hers.

'Can you answer me a question, please, Mama?'

'I can try.'

'Do we go through any tunnels on this trip?'

'We have to go through one, but it's not very long.'

Princess Eleanor did not like the thought of a tunnel, and snuggled closer to her mother. Through the carriage window they saw Mr Perkins nod to the guard, who waved his green flag. A whistle blew. The engine snorted. 'I wish Alice was here, Mama.'

'So do I, Eleanor. So do I . . .'

'I hope she's all right.'

'She is. I think we shall see her very soon.' The

Duchess's words hid her deepest fears, but she could not disguise from Eleanor that something was seriously wrong.

The train pulled out of Ryde Pier Station and began its short journey to Osborne House.

Edie, Titch and Alice stared at the retreating form of the guard. Their cell door closed. The bolts were shut, the key turned. The mood was calm, ominous.

'He was quite nice just then,' said Titch. 'What's up?'

'He's always been nice,' Alice noted.

'Sssh!' Edie was making signs. They stopped talking, and listened.

'I can't hear anything.'

'Quiet, Alice. Edie's listening,' whispered Titch.

Edie listened intently. Her eyes still closed, she spoke slowly. 'I heard that guard – the nice one – say that it wasn't time to get rid of us yet. The head man apparently wants to shoot us *now*.'

Alice started to whimper.

'Stop it, Alice. Sure, it won't do any good.'

'We've only got one real hope then, haven't we?' said Titch.

'We haven't got any hope at all,' Alice responded miserably.

'We have, Alice. We've got Beaky.' Titch noticed that Edie had gone very pale and still. 'Edie. Are you all right?'

'I've got this queer feeling, like you had, Titch. Something's about to happen.'

'Like what?'

'Like . . . to the children I told you about. I can see them clear as day.'

'Eleanor?' asked Alice.

'A little girl with straight brown hair. And ribbons like yours.'

'That's Eleanor.' Alice began to moan loudly. 'What's happening?'

'It's like my vision when I was sick. They're on a train.'

Titch went over to Edie and held her. She began to tremble. Alice was sobbing. Without warning she began to stamp and scream. Edie went rigid and cried out: 'The train. It's the train.'

Alice screamed again. With her hands over her ears, stamping, she echoed Edie's cry. 'The train. It's the train. Eleanor! Eleanor! Eleanor!'

Reilly's mouth was dry. Nervously he watched the smoke from the approaching train. When it came into view round the bend in the line, he tensed. He was waiting for the moment when the engine disappeared into the tunnel. In the nearby copse, where O'Hare was listening for Reilly's cry, looked at his watch, and smiled.

9

LOOK TO THE QUEEN

'Assassinate the Queen?' cried Dr Watson. 'It's a fascinating theory, Sam, but you need proper evidence to support it. As it is, no one will believe you.'

'You're right, Doctor. The Inspector said the same.' But Sam was like a dog with a bone. He could not let go. 'I am sure that's what Mr Holmes meant by his message, though.'

'I know, I know, but Holmes – rest his soul – would only ever act on evidence. You have none! Now stop sulking and listen to this.' Watson opened his *Times* and read to Sam:

'At a gathering of the gentlemen of the press yesterday, Mr James Wilson Booth Senior, owner of the Anglo-American Trans-Atlantic Cable Company, announced proudly that, in spite of severe setbacks, including the sinking of his cable-laying vessel, the *SS Arcadia*, in which many innocent lives were lost . . .' Watson's voice faltered, but he soldiered on, '. . . the project for the laying of the Atlantic Cable had been completed on schedule. "It is planned," proclaimed Mr Booth proudly, "for the President of the United States, Mr Grover Cleveland, to inaugurate the line by telephoning your British Prime Minister. He desires to convey his own and the American people's Yuletide wishes to Her Majesty Queen Victoria and her subjects." The Queen will be at Osborne House, where she will commemorate Prince Albert Day with the largest gathering to date of her family, including many of her European relatives. The royal family is holding with tradition and staying on at Osborne to enjoy the festive season.'

Watson lowered the paper. 'Isn't that extraordinary?'

'You mean the coincidence?'

'What coincidence, Sam?'

'The Queen. Mr Booth. Christmas. Everything.'

'No. I was referring to the astonishing strides in modern technology, Sam. Being able to *talk* to people in America.'

'There *is* the coincidence, too, though, Dr Watson. And . . .'

'What, Sam?'

'There's something in this article I can't quite put my finger on. Mr Booth. The *Arcadia* . . .'

'You're getting worse than Holmes, Sam. Obsessive. Obscure.'

'I know you don't believe me, Doctor. But I'm sure I'm right.'

'Holmes was stubborn, too, Wiggins – one of his less admirable traits. Forgive me, but I must get off. I have an appointment at the surgery. Take my lunch tray down to the kitchen, will you? Save Mrs Hudson.'

Sam picked up the tray, but he was riled. 'It's not right, Doctor. Nobody's doing anything. No trace of Princess Alice. No interest in Edie. Titch gone. You lot can give up if you like, but I won't.'

Reilly joined O'Hare, and together they watched the train carrying the Queen and the royal children chug round the final bend of the line before Osborne House Station.

'Did you hear my shout, O'Hare?'

'I did.'

'So did you get the timing?'

'I did.'

'And?'

'You're like a kid, Reilly. Tomorrow, the engine will pass the explosives cache twelve seconds after it enters the tunnel.'

Reilly considered this. 'There won't be much of it left, will there, O'Hare?'

'No, Reilly. There won't be more than a splinter.'

'And when will you connect the dynamite in the lift, O'Hare?'

'I told you. As late as I dare before we come out here to blow the royal bastards sky high.' O'Hare examined his huge, tense companion. 'For heaven's sake, Reilly, relax, will you? The tunnel is wired and now we have the timings for tomorrow. The lift will take care of itself.'

But Reilly was incapable of relaxing. He gripped the wooden shaft of his axe tighter than ever, as though O'Hare was going to take it off him.

'O'Hare.'

O'Hare was losing patience. 'What?'

'When you blow the cache in the tunnel, everyone on the train will go sky high.'

'Right.'

'And there won't be much left of the Queen and her lift, will there?'

'Hopefully not!' replied O'Hare with evident glee.

'The punishment for treason is death, O'Hare. And us being Irish there won't be a lot of sympathy about if we're caught. Think what happened to that Fenian feller who tried to blow up the Tower. Penal servitude. And he didn't kill anyone.'

'That eejit! He was caught trying to light the fuse! Relax. The plans for our getaway are very neat. Professor Moriarty will take proper care of us. Not that I require remuneration. Getting rid of that smug bunch of nobs will be its own reward. I can't wait to see them in bits all over this hillside!'

'Yes,' mused Reilly, considering this image carefully.

'If only they had all been on the one train,' muttered O'Hare. 'Kids and all! We could have got the lot of them, then! Never mind. Not long to go now.'

It was the Queen's wish that the children should see her portrait as soon as they arrived. She had one final sitting for the fashionable artist Sir Edmund Leinster, whose painting was one of which she was quietly proud.

Accordingly, shortly after their arrival, the Duchess of Albion guided the children into a small private chamber where the Queen was sitting on a dais with a

sceptre in her hand. Every trace of the childish anticipation of the train journey evaporated instantly in the awesome presence of Her Majesty. She greeted them as best she could without upsetting Sir Edmund, who combined an arrogantly artistic temperament with extreme gravity – a combination deadly to children and fun.

After several minutes of strained silence, during which Sir Edmund flicked his brush impatiently at the canvas, the maestro asked the Queen if his assistant might remove the children as they were distracting him. The Queen gave her consent unwillingly. She felt a twinge of disappointment, as they had not really had sufficient time to admire her portrait.

Sir Edmund's assistant, Mr Spooner, led the Duchess and the children from the chamber. Spindly Mr Spooner alarmed them. He was tall but slightly stooped, and as he leaned down to ingratiate himself with his royal charges, strands of his long, lank hair were in danger of brushing their faces.

'Come this way, children,' he said in a thin, weaselly voice. They followed him into the main hall. 'Perhaps the Duchess would like to show you to your bedrooms – I know you have not yet had a chance to see them.'

The Duchess disliked Mr Spooner, and she

thought it extremely impertinent of him to make this suggestion. 'Come, Eleanor,' she said, snubbing Mr Know-it-all, 'shall we show your cousins where they are sleeping?'

As the children went up the Grand Staircase to their rooms with the Duchess, young Prince Edward burst into the hall. He had avoided the viewing of the portrait, because he knew he would be bored. Instead, he had nipped out into the vast grounds of Osborne House to see if the secret den he had made on his last visit was still intact.

'Ah! Prince Edward!' Spooner positively gloated. 'I wondered where you had got to. I am Sir Edmund's assistant – my name is Spooner.' He placed his hand on Edward's shoulder. Edward shuddered. 'I have a special treat in store for you.' Spooner was bending over the young Prince, his stringy hair dangling down. He reminded Edward of a daddy-longlegs. The Prince hovered reluctantly at the foot of the stairs, extremely uncertain about accepting treats from spooky Mr Spooner.

'This way.' Mr Spooner moved his hand to the small of Edward's back and steered him in the direction of the newly installed lift. 'Now, young man,' he confided, 'can you keep a secret?' Prince Edward nodded. He was teased in the family for his closeness in guarding secrets. 'This is a secret that must be kept from the Queen until after tea. It is the latest addition to Osborne House – a lift.'

The Prince was still far from sure how he felt about Mr Spooner, but he was absolutely sure how he felt about lifts. 'Oh yes,' he found himself saying, 'that would be really really interesting. Thank you.'

The lift had been situated most discreetly at the base of the tower, just off the main hall. When they reached it, Spooner greeted an uncouth figure lingering by the lift doors. Edward did not recognise him, but fancied that this man had seen Spooner approaching and done his best to slip away. Spooner called after him loudly, 'Still here, Mr O'Hare?'

'Last check on the shaft,' said O'Hare resentfully. 'Don't want anything to go wrong tomorrow.'

'Might I detain you a moment, Mr O'Hare? You see, I think this young gentleman here would be fascinated to see how a lift works, wouldn't you, Prince Edward?'

Edward was still unsure about Spooner, and very worried by surly Mr O'Hare, but his boyish curiosity again got the better of him. 'I would just love to see the motor and stuff, please.'

'I need to get away,' O'Hare protested.

'Come, come, Mr O'Hare. It is a great piece of good fortune for us to find you here, and you don't want to let the young Prince down, do you?' Spooner raised his voice uncomfortably loud, and O'Hare did not want to attract attention.

'What do you want to see?' he asked the Prince grudgingly.

Edward knew quite well what he wanted to see but spooky Spooner got in first. 'Why, the shaft and the workings is what a young prince wants to see, Mr O'Hare!'

O'Hare had just checked the dynamite that Reilly had concealed beneath the motor, so that he had nothing left to do but connect the wires. The last thing he wanted was strangers inspecting the machinery, but he had little option. He led Spooner and the Prince downstairs and unlocked the small door that led into the strange world beneath the lift. 'Interested in machines?' he asked as he ushered them in.

'Loves them, don't you?' said Spooner, again sneaking his answer in first. 'In we go. Don't be afraid.' Spooner was so keen for the young Prince to follow O'Hare, that it crossed Edward's mind he was the victim of some strange conspiracy. He was so preoccupied with the notion that he might be in danger that he did not realise O'Hare had already begun explaining the purpose of the wires and the weights. He began to listen. He was fascinated. He relaxed. He was usually treated like royalty, and this novel experience was exactly the sort of opportunity he longed for. Mr Spooner winked at him. The truth was that, in spite of his odd companions, Prince Edward was beginning to enjoy himself.

In the absence of Dr Watson, who had gone to a road-planning enquiry at Paddington Town Hall, the three downcast Irregulars were holding yet another troubled meeting in the study of 22lb. They were helpless. Sam's theory was nothing more than a theory and there was still no word from Titch.

'What can we do, Sam?' Billy asked.

'I keep trying to think what Mr Holmes'd do.'

'I wish we 'ad some news of Edie,' said Potts miserably.

'And Titch,' added Sam. 'Trouble is, Dr Watson's right,' he added bleakly. 'All we've got's our instinct, and when did grown-ups ever listen to that?'

At this moment Mrs Hudson came into the study, all of a flurry.

'Billy, Billy. Come quickly.'

'What is it, Mrs Hudson?'

Mrs Hudson was in too much of a rush to answer. She was already trotting back along the landing. Led by Billy, the Irregulars set off in hot pursuit. 'You were so quiet I thought you'd gone out,' Mrs Hudson called as she sped downstairs. 'Come quickly.'

They had never before seen Mrs Hudson *run* anywhere!

'You all right, Mrs H?'

'You seem in a right pother.'

'Follow me and you'll see why.' She led them down to the kitchen and indicated a small damp bundle, lying in a large towel, near her stove.

'Wot is it, Billy?' called Potts, bringing up the rear.

'You won't believe it, Potts! Sam! It's Beaky.'

Beaky was hardly recognisable – soaking wet, with feathers missing, and blood oozing from his chest.

''E looks like 'e's been shot.'

'Poor old Beaky,' said Billy, kneeling to look at him closely.

'If Beaky's hurt,' said Sam, stroking Beaky's head with the back of his fingers, 'it'll break Titch's heart.'

'It'll break mine,' said Billy. 'Get Titch's *message* out, Sam. That's what we really need.'

Sam moved Beaky gently and saw, rather worryingly,

that the leather cap which sealed the tube in which Beaky carried messages was hanging loose. Sam's fingers probed the tube. 'It's empty.'

'What?'

'Nothing. There's nothing here.'

'Oh no. No. Nooo!'

'Calm down, Potts.'

'Sorry, Mrs H, but that's wot we need to rescue Edie.'

They all looked at poor bedraggled Beaky and contemplated the implications of Titch's lost message. The gloom that had been gathering around them in the study was now palpable.

'When did he get here?' asked Billy.

'I don't really know,' replied Mrs Hudson. 'Before tea, I was in the top room, tidying up after the decorator, when I heard this scrabbling at the window, and there was Beaky.'

'I'll go up and take a look in his hutch,' said Sam. At that very moment, they heard the front door closing. 'Dr Watson'll know what to do for him.'

They all ran upstairs. Sam carried on up to the roof, while Billy and Potts greeted the Doctor. They dragged him down to the kitchen, not even giving him time to put down his dripping umbrella. Watson could see that poor Beaky had clearly had a narrow escape. He staunched the blood and dried him down tenderly. He was feeding him with a pipette from his Gladstone bag when they heard Sam's cry. They looked at each other – fearing the worst.

'Doctor! Billy! Potts!' Sam came bounding down the stairs. 'Look! Look what I found in Beaky's hutch,' he yelled.

'What is it?' Billy called up the stairs.

'You won't believe it.'

'Wot?'

Sam tore into the kitchen, ran to the table and placed before them a small piece of paper.

'What on earth . . .?' exclaimed Mrs Hudson.

'They're from Titch,' said Sam. 'They were in Beaky's hutch. They're wet, but you can still read them.'

And there, on the table before them, was Titch's plan of the caves, and her map showing the Solent and the Isle of Wight. Somehow, like Beaky, they had survived! The trio poured over the small drenched scrap of paper.

'Well,' said Billy, 'at last we know where they are.'

'We can get Edie out now!' cried Potts.

'That'll be the easy bit,' Sam observed. 'The question we have to ask *is*, what connection there might be between Titch's information and Mr Holmes's message – *Look to the Queen there.*'

'*Ho!*' cried Potts.

'You never give up, do you, Wiggins?'

'No, Doctor. Sorry.'

'It's admirable, Sam, if a little wearing.'

'Be fair, Doc. Sam's been sayin' for ages that there's a link between all these goin's on and 'Er Maj.'

'The Queen to you, young Master Potts.' Mrs Hudson was all ears. 'What on earth has our Queen got to do with Beaky?'

'We're not sure, Mrs Hudson,' said Sam. 'I've got a bee in my bonnet about a note Mr Holmes left.'

'Well, the Queen is on the Isle of Wight,' Mrs Hudson chipped in proudly. 'Went there this afternoon.'

'Eh?'

'She's always there for the anniversary of Prince Albert's death.'

'Wot!?'

'Her favourite house is there.'

'WOT?!'

'Osborne House.' It was rare for Mrs Hudson to be the centre of attention and she was enjoying herself. 'She spends Christmas there—'

'That's it!' cried Sam. 'You know that article in *The Times* that you read to me, Doctor?' Watson nodded. 'There was a reference in it to Prince Albert's death, and all the royal family being at Osborne House.'

'Indeed, Sam, I remember.'

'She always goes to Osborne for Christmas.' Mrs Hudson was in full flow. 'Longstanding tradition—'

'Just a moment, please, Mrs Hudson.' Sam turned to Billy. 'What did Professor Moriarty say to Tiger De Ville in the boathouse?'

'That something would make "a nice Christmas present for her".'

'For 'ER!!!' bellowed Potts.

'For *her*,' said Billy. 'You're right, Sam. It's all about the Queen.'

'Mr H's message is abaht the Queen, Doc!'

Sam was sitting in the chair by the stove. He leaned forward, his chin on his hands, reminding Watson of Holmes. 'Where is the Queen now?' he asked.

'At Osborne 'Ouse.'

'And where is that?'

'On the Isle of flamin' Wight!!'

'And what was Holmes's final instruction to us?'

'*Look to the Queen there!*' said Billy.

'*HO!*' cried Potts with huge emphasis on the 'H'.

Speaking with great intensity, Sam reiterated his theory that Moriarty's crimes had been intended to create a distraction. He pointed out that, according to Titch's diagrams, the centre of Moriarty's current operations was on the south coast, overlooking the Isle of Wight. 'His aim,' he concluded, 'is to assassinate the Queen.'

'Wiggins, you're a genius,' exclaimed Watson in wonder. 'Holmes would be proud of you.'

'When is the actual anniversary of Prince Albert's death, Mrs Hudson?' asked Billy.

'You don't know anything, do you?'

'When is the flippin' anniversary?' enquired Potts, increasingly agitated.

'You young people.'

'WHEN?' yelled the three of them.

'All right, all right. No need to be hasty,' replied Mrs Hudson. 'It's December the fourteenth,'

'December the fourteenth?'

'Yes.'

'Good Lord!' cried Watson. 'That's the day after tomorrow.'

10

OSBORNE

Sam, Billy and Potts were in the kitchen at 22lb, nursing Beaky back to health, waiting eagerly for Dr Watson's return. When the good Doctor finally appeared, arriving at breakneck speed in a hansom-cab, he was out of breath and deeply frustrated.

'I have been unable to make contact either with Lestrade or Princess Alice's mother,' he grumbled. Billy took his coat and hat, and Watson paced backwards and forwards before the range. 'The Duchess, from what I can gather, is already at Osborne House.'

'Wow!'

'Mrs H was right!'

'Heaven knows where Lestrade has got to.'

'Still lookin' for Princess Alice, I shouldn't wonder.'

'Like everybody else, Potts,' Sam remarked. 'Just as

Professor Moriarty intended.'

'What are we going to do?' Billy asked.

'Well . . .' Watson took a chair at the head of the table. 'On my way here, I was thinking, and this is what I propose. We need to act immediately, and we should divide our resources,' he stated firmly.

''Ow d'you mean, Doc?'

'What you said earlier is quite right, Potts. If we rescue Princess Alice – *and* Edie of course – we would gain immediate access to the Queen. We could then warn her of any impending assassination attempt. My problem with that is, we don't know how *long* a rescue attempt might take. It might not be that easy.'

'No, sir. I see wot you mean.'

'But that need not prevent *you* making a rescue bid with Billy or Sam, whilst I attempt to contact the Duchess at Osborne House. Divide our resources, eh? What do you all think of that suggestion?'

Sam nodded his agreement.

'I fink we should crack on wiv it right away, Doc.'

'Brilliant,' said Billy. 'Who's going with Potts, then, to rescue Edie?'

'Let's deal with the details later, Billy, on the train.' Watson was beginning to seem much more like his old self. 'You go and order us a cab for Waterloo Station.

Where are we headed, Sam?'

Sam was pensive. 'Stokes Bay, sir.'

'Well, we can finalise our plans en route to Stokes Bay. We should get moving. It'll be dark by the time we get there, as it is.' The Doctor reached for his coat, which Billy had put on a chair by the range.

'Look out, Moriarty!' cried Potts.

Dr Watson waved his hat jauntily. 'We're on our way!' The Irregulars had not seen him this positive since Holmes's death.

'I fancy a knight'ood for you, Doc! *Sir* Doctor Watson. Wot about that? That'd pull the patients in.'

'Don't let's count our chickens before they're hatched, Potts. Moriarty is a vile foe. If we apprehend him, it will be more than dear Holmes ever achieved.'

'Cab on the way, sir.'

'Good lad, Billy.'

'Buck up, Sam. What's the matter?'

'I'm thinking.'

'You can think on the train. Come on!'

''E finks everywhere, Doc. *Sir* Doc, I should say. Come on, Sam. Look lively! I'm all excited. We're gonna rescue Edie and find Titch. And . . . guess wot? I ain't never been on a train before.'

* * *

Before high tea, the royal children were *all* told about the Queen's lift, and they decided that as Princess Eleanor was so upset, *she* should be the one to present the surprise gift to Her Majesty. They hoped it would cheer Eleanor up, and dilute the Queen's anger, should she be displeased. At tea, the Queen was in unusually good humour because Sir Edmund Leinster's completed portrait had met with universal praise. The verdict was that it had captured not only the regality of queenhood and the importance of Empire, but also the softer, gentler side of the Queen's nature – a remarkable achievement.

Throughout tea, as Welsh rarebit, chocolate cakes and blancmange were consumed by the ravenous army of children, Queen Victoria was positively radiant. When tea was over, as the moment for Eleanor's 'surprise' drew nearer, there was a lot of nudging and suppressed giggling amongst the younger children, which the Queen could hardly fail to notice. Her contented look changed. She became stern, raising her voice just enough to silence all other conversation. 'What, might I enquire, is going on?'

The children looked pointedly at Princess Eleanor who was immediately overcome by a fit of shyness. Her mother, the Duchess of Albion, came to her rescue.

'Eleanor has something she would like to show you, Mama.'

'You may get down from the table, Eleanor,' said the Queen. 'Don't hide behind Edward. Come here where I can see you properly. Edward! Elbows *off* the table. How many times must I tell you?'

With a deal of whispered encouragement, Eleanor was persuaded to approach the Queen. Still holding the large cushion she needed to help her reach the table, she made her way gingerly to the Queen's chair at the head of the table, where she stood looking at the floor.

The Queen spoke kindly to her. 'What have you to say to me, my dear?'

Eleanor mumbled something into her cushion. The Queen reached out and gently raised Eleanor's head, until the little Princess was looking at her. 'Give your cushion to me, my dearest – thank you. And speak so that I can hear you, like a grown-up girl.'

Eleanor tried to speak sensibly, but the occasion was too much for her and again she mumbled indistinctly. The Queen leaned forward and said sweetly, 'Don't be shy. Come, whisper in my ear.' Princess Eleanor stood on tiptoe and did as she was told. The Queen listened. Then, suddenly, she sat bolt upright. She glowered.

Her eyes swept round the table. Very, very slowly, she said, 'A surprise? You have a surprise for me, Eleanor? You know I dislike surprises.'

Prince Edward put his hand up. 'May I speak, please, Grandmother?'

The Queen's fierce gaze fell upon the game young Prince. 'You may.'

'Nelly's got a very *nice* surprise for you, Grandmother,' said Prince Edward with a hopeful smile.

'I presume you mean Princess Eleanor.' The Queen turned threateningly back to Eleanor. 'Tell me, if you please, what this . . . surprise is.'

At this further darkening of the Queen's tone, Eleanor lost her nerve completely and ran to her mother, burying her face in the Duchess's dress.

The Queen commanded the table. 'I suspect that I am the only person in this room not to know of this surprise. Am I correct?' Her demeanour intimidated all the children save one. Edward was too excited to notice that he was about to put his head in the lion's mouth.

'It's a really really *fantastic* surprise, Grandmother, and you'll love it. *I'll* show it to you, if you like. Eleanor's too shy, and she's missing Alice.'

The Queen, too, was missing Alice. But her way of

coping with the loss was not to mention Alice's name. She was irritated by Prince Edward's casual allusion to her beloved granddaughter.

Edward ploughed on, unabashed. 'Anyway, Nelly can't reach the buttons.'

'Buttons?' muttered the Queen, horrified. 'I trust you are not going to surprise me with anything so grotesque as that cardigan you gave me earlier this year!' There was a stunned silence. The Queen had not hitherto hinted that the cardigan, which Prince Edward had given her for her last birthday, had been found wanting. Again the Duchess saved the situation.

'Why don't you let Edward show you, Mama? He's very keen and he knows all about how it works.'

'How it works?' The Queen considered the implications of the phrase. She lowered her eyebrows. 'Is this ghastly surprise to be some repellent gadget?' she demanded, peering sternly at Prince Edward.

Unperturbed, Edward cried, 'You're getting warm!' Jumping from his seat at the table, he ran to the Queen and offered her his hand. 'Come on, Grandmother. You'll love it. Really you will.'

Prince Edward was beaming at her so beguilingly, and the Queen was so flattered by her portrait, and so pleased to be surrounded by such delightful, happy children, that she relented. 'When you have wiped all trace of chocolate from your mouth, Edward, you may . . . surprise me.'

'Yippee!' cried the Prince. The table held its breath. Surely young Edward had gone too far this time. To their relief – and surprise – the Queen smiled. To Her Majesty's surprise, the family clapped and cheered. And to her further surprise, the Queen found that she rather enjoyed it.

'Do you think we're on the right track, Potts?'

''Ard to say, Billy. Let's 'ave anuvver gander at Titch's plan.'

The two boys were walking along the railway line from Stokes Bay, looking for the hidden points that would indicate the fork in the line leading to Moriarty's underground kingdom. They jumped off the rails and sat on a large boulder. Potts took Titch's map from his pocket and they examined it closely.

'Can't tell in this light. But Titch obviously didn't know where the main line runs *to*.'

'Nope. But on the map, the sea is over there, Potty, on the left, so we're going in the right direction.'

'Some trip this. Never been on a train before. Never seen the sea before! Amazin'!'

'We can't have missed the points, can we?'

'Don't seem likely. We've been walkin' for ages, tho'.'

Billy began struggling up the embankment.

'Where you goin'?'

'Just to have a dekko.' He scrabbled to the top and peered about. 'There are some trees on Titch's map, aren't there, Potts?' he called.

'It's too dark to see much, innit, Billy?'

Billy slid and scrambled back down the bank, and joined Potts on the boulder. He took the map and pointed at the trees Titch had drawn on either side of the line.

'I can just make out a forest up ahead. Quite a long way up the line, but I'm pretty sure we're doing the right thing.'

As they started off up the line, Potts suddenly stopped. ''Ey listen, Billy. There's a train comin'.'

They ducked down behind the boulder and waited in the dim evening light. The rumble of wheels grew rapidly louder and closer. In a flash the little train shot by. When the noise subsided and the smoke had cleared, Potts said to Billy, 'I've seen that train before.'

'They all look pretty much the same to me, Potts.'

'Not that one. That was the one wot took Edie.'

'What?'

'That was the train wot Titch was under. *That*...
must be Moriarty's private train.'

'Are you sure?'

'Dead certain. Did you spot that fancy little balcony
on the back?'

Billy nodded.

'Moriarty's train.'

'We're on the right track then, Potty.'

'We sure are.'

'Wow!'

'Come on!'

'It'll be good to see Titch and Edie, won't it?'

'Dead right it will! I 'ope they're all right.'

'Course they are.'

'Come on then.'

They set off again in the wake of Moriarty's train
which they could still see and hear, steaming along the
line ahead of them. They now felt positive. Keen to get
on with the rescue.

'Wow, Potts. This is exciting.'

'Ain't it just?!'

'Wow! I mean ... Wow! Wow! Wow!'

From their cell, Titch heard the hiss and clank of
Moriarty's train arriving. She was aware of a deal of

activity outside the cell door – rushing of feet, slamming of doors, cries of 'Sir! Tiger's here!' Evidently, Tiger De Ville had returned. After a huge fuss, there was a deadly calm. Now *he* was back, Titch thought, a decision would probably be taken about their being shot.

Titch looked back into their gloomy cave and observed a surprising, rather touching scene: Alice was bathing Edie's eyes. This was one of the things Watson had advised Edie to do at least twice a day to keep her eyes clean. Before the pandemonium, the one guard who was nice to them had brought a bowl of warm water, bicarbonate of soda and some cotton wool.

'Sure, Alice, this is real sweet of you. One of my sisters usually does it for me. It's very soothing.'

'I'm sorry I was horrid to begin with,' Alice said, dabbing the cotton wool right into the corners of Edie's eyes. 'I was frightened.'

'Course you were,' Edie replied. 'So was I.'

'And I was shy. Because I never get to meet ordinary people. Being a princess.'

'Sure,' Edie smiled.

Alice chattered on happily. 'Although there's nothing ordinary about Titch, is there? Coming here under a train. Having a pet homing pigeon. Nothing ordinary at all. How long will it take Beaky to get back to London, Titch?'

'I must have been in here for nigh on two days, right? He should be there already.'

'Really? Jolly good.'

'Ay. In fact, with any luck, Sam and the others will be on their way to find us. If they can understand my diagrams.'

'I do hope so. If they shoot us before your friends get here, my daddy won't know who to punish.'

'Ay,' Titch commented wryly. 'That would be annoying, wouldn't it, Alice?'

To Titch and Edie, Alice seemed younger than her years. She had been protected from real life by her birth and upbringing, and she spoke innocently and openly, without any real understanding of what was happening. Nevertheless, the sudden mention of being shot gave all three captives pause for thought.

'Sure. They'll be here in time to save us,' said Edie, trying to lower the tension. But with the return of De Ville, they all sensed that events outside were coming to a head.

'What sort of a person is your dad, Alice?' Titch asked. 'Do you like him?'

'Well, I love him very much of course,' Alice replied

in her frank way. 'But . . .' she chewed a bit of her loose golden hair, 'Papa is always busy. You see he was a terribly important soldier, so he is frightfully strict. I shouldn't really say this, but I'm not altogether sure about *liking* him. What about *your* father, Titch?'

'I hate my father, Alice. I left home to get away from him.'

'Goodness. Why?'

'He were . . . he were cruel to me.'

'Why didn't your mama stop him?' asked Alice.

'She left home when I were a baby. Same reason as me, I shouldn't wonder – to get away from my dad. I never even seen her. Well, I don't remember her.'

'How awful for you,' said Alice gravely. 'I like my *mama*. She would never leave us. You'll like Mama, too. And you, Edie. Titch, was your papa horrible to you because you pretend to be a boy?'

Edie held her breath. She knew quite a lot about Titch, and suspected a good deal more. She knew about her background on the canals, and her uncle in Calcutta, but she would never have had the nerve to put questions to her in Alice's blunt way. She could not imagine what Titch would say. She and Potts both went along with Titch's pretence: if Titch felt safer disguised as a boy, that was fine by them. Titch was caught off guard. She assumed that as people took her for a boy, her appearance and manner were convincing. She decided to bluff it out.

'Don't be daft, Alice. By the way, I've got something to tell you about your ma that you don't know.'

'What?' asked Alice, slightly taken aback by Titch's change of tack. She stopped bathing Edie's eyes for a moment.

'This'll surprise you, Alice,' Titch carried on quickly, relieved that Alice had been sidetracked, 'but I've seen your ma.'

'Have you? When?'

'Well, when you first went missing, she visited a friend of ours to ask for his help.'

Alice was intrigued. 'A friend of yours?'

'A grown-up. A detective.'

'Sure. A very clever detective,' Edie affirmed. 'We work for him.'

'Where is he now then, if he's so very clever?' Alice asked pertly.

Titch didn't want to tell Alice that Sherlock Holmes was dead. 'He had to go to sea on another case,' she mumbled. 'Anyway, it's cos of her – your ma – that we're here. She asked him to find you. And as Edie said – we sort of work for him.'

'That's very like Mama,' Alice exclaimed.

Titch stole a glance at Edie, but her eyes were still covered with pads of wet cotton wool. 'What do you mean, Alice?'

'Mama always knows just the right person to go to.' Titch found it hard not to smile. 'When we're all out of here – as long as they don't shoot us, of course – I shall see to it that you both receive a proper reward. And your friends.'

Now they had got to know Alice better, Edie and Titch were becoming rather fond of her. She looked at things in a way they could never hope to, but she was straight as a die. You knew where you were with her.

'Tell you what, Alice,' said Titch, 'for a princess you're not a bad sort.'

'Not at all,' Edie added, grinning. 'And not a bad nurse either.'

'Thank you,' said Alice. Unusually, she was lost for words. 'I like you both, too.'

'Then we'd best get out of here. Hadn't we?!' said Titch.

'Sure,' said Edie.

'Oh. Definitely,' Alice added emphatically.

'Cos I don't half like the sound of that reward!'

When Watson, Sam, Billy and Potts had taken the train from Waterloo to Stokes Bay, Watson and Sam had been given the responsibility of contacting the Duchess of Albion on the Isle of Wight. They were eager to tell her that the Irregulars knew where Alice was being held prisoner, but their principle purpose was to warn her about a possible assassination attempt on the Queen. When they arrived at the ferry port their plans were scuppered by the news that, for security reasons, there were no more public ferry crossings to the island until the royal party was safely ashore next day.

They asked around the harbour, and Watson managed to persuade a fisherman to take them to the island in his boat, under cover of darkness. The old man was jumpy at first, but the sea was calm, the sky was clear, the moon was bright and his nerves settled. In his rich Dorset accent, he remarked, 'You can steer by them stars tonight. All the way to France, if you want. Beautiful.'

They made the crossing without difficulty, landing in a secluded cove, where Watson paid the old boy handsomely. He told them to walk straight inland, up the shallow beach, to follow the cliff path up through the trees, and they would come to a railway line.

'Turn left, you'll end up in Ryde,' he explained. 'Turn right, you'll get to Osborne House in no time! Her Majesty's in residence tonight. I'm sure she'd be right pleased to see ye!' They thanked him and jumped ashore.

As they walked through the woods above the beach, Sam remarked to Watson that the fisherman was righter than he knew – that if the Queen knew what they knew, she would be extremely glad to see them. Watson agreed. They reached the railway track with ease, and set off along it in the direction of Osborne, Watson observing that it all seemed to be going rather well. 'Rather *too* well, Sam.'

'There's plenty of time for something to go wrong, sir.'

'Quite right. You see that flag in the distance, Sam? Might that be Osborne House?'

'I think it is, Doctor. But look.' They stopped walking. Sam pointed. 'There's a tunnel ahead. There's a tunnel on Titch's map.'

'Why would Titch have shown a tunnel, Sam? Come to think of it, how did Titch even know about it?'

'It must have something to do with Moriarty's plans, Doctor. Or Titch wouldn't have bothered.'

'Good point, Sam,' Watson whispered. 'We'd best proceed with care. Sshh.'

They moved cautiously along the lines, treading carefully on the sleepers. The moon was so bright that it cast shadows, but when they reached the tunnel, they could not see a yard into it. It was pitch-black. They ventured slowly in, but the darkness was so impenetrable that it unnerved them. They stood, wondering whether to follow the rails through the tunnel by touch, or go back out and over the embankment, picking up the rails at the other end. Intimidated by the opaque blackness, they opted for the less frightening route over the top. As they were retracing their steps, a beam of light from inside the tunnel shattered the gloom. A loud voice broke the silence of the night.

'Do not move. Stay right where you are,' came the stern command. It was a voice Sam felt sure he knew, but he couldn't think straight, because the light was so dazzling. He and the Doctor shaded their eyes from its brilliance. Neither of them could see clearly, but they could hear two figures walking urgently towards them.

'I don't like this, Doctor,' Sam murmured as the men approached, their footsteps crunching on the heavy gravel at the side of the rails.

Watson ignored both Sam's warning and the man's

threatening tones. 'Ah, my good man,' he called amiably, 'how very fortunate . . .'

'Have you got your service revolver handy, Doctor?' Sam whispered.

'Don't worry, Sam. These men are probably security guards from Osbor—'

'Who are you?' The menacing voice cut Watson off, echoing in the tunnel.

Watson looked into the advancing beam of light. Shielding his eyes, he replied, 'My name is Watson. *Dr* Watson. It is imperative—'

'Watson? Did you say Dr Watson?'

'Indeed I did, my good fellow.'

The two men carrying the lamp were now running fast towards Sam and Watson. As they ran, the light beam sprayed over the rails and tunnel walls, catching Sam and the Doctor fleetingly. Watson was beginning to think Sam's concern was well-founded, and shifted his hand towards the revolver in his overcoat pocket.

'Do not move!' The voice was fiercer this time. 'Stay right where you are! I have you covered with a gun.' Sam and Watson froze. The two men were now close enough for them to see that the speaker was telling the truth. The light beam glinted on the barrel of a very large revolver which was pointing straight at them.

Watson moved in front of Sam to protect him physically from this threat. 'I think you'll find that's quite unnecessary, my good man.' He held out his open, empty hands, in an attempt to calm things down.

Some light reflected back from Watson's outstretched palms, and in it Sam glimpsed the two strangers. The speaker was holding both the gun and the flashlamp. It was difficult to see his face behind the harsh beam, but something was gnawing at Sam's memory. He struggled to remember where he had heard the man's voice and those words – *Do not move! Stay right where you are!* – not very long ago. He could make out more of the other man, who was large and burly, and over whose shoulder he detected the shaft of an axe.

The voice came again. 'What the hell are you two doing here?' Sam caught sight of a large bushy moustache. 'This is royal land.'

Then for a brief moment, Sam saw the man's hair, and his blood turned to ice. Running from the middle of his forehead, clear against his thick grey hair, was a black V. It was unmistakeable – the mark of the tiger. 'Doctor,' Sam breathed, 'it's *Tiger De Ville*!'

De Ville heard. The light swung directly into Sam's

eyes, blinding him. De Ville recognised him instantly. 'You!' his voice snarled. 'I warned you, kid, that I would always have one eye open for you.' He held the lamp out to his companion. 'Hold the lamp.' Reilly took it. 'This time, kid, you won't get away.' Like lightning, De Ville's free hand flashed out, aiming to grab Sam by the collar. Sam jumped back, evading De Ville's grasp, but this further enraged him, and he tried to barge Watson out of the way in an attempt to collar his young enemy.

'Leave the boy alone,' interjected Watson, fending De Ville off. De Ville shoved Watson angrily aside and took another swipe at Sam. This time Sam was ready for him. Ducking, he yelled, 'The light, Doctor!' At the same time, he kicked out hard at De Ville's gun hand. His foot landed viciously on the underside of De Ville's wrist as Watson dashed the lamp from Reilly's hand. Reilly swore as it clattered to the ground, extinguishing the flame. Sam was pleased to hear a growl of fury as De Ville's gun flew through the darkness, hitting the tunnel wall before landing with a harsh clang on the rails.

'Run for it, Doctor!'

Sam turned, and was off. Watson followed, more slowly, feeling in his pocket for his trusty revolver. They could still hear De Ville scrabbling around, fuming, looking for *his* gun, but he gave up with a howl of frustration when he saw Sam emerge from the tunnel into the moonlight. He started after him, keen not to give his young foe too much of a start.

'You,' he snarled at Reilly, 'take care of the Doctor.' Reilly was trying to relight the damaged flashlamp as De Ville stumbled out of the tunnel mouth, barking commands. 'I'll get the kid. Lock *him*,' he waved his arm at Watson, 'in the cache.'

De Ville quickly gained a steady footing and scrabbled up the steep embankment after Sam. Sam was well ahead but he was concerned about Watson. He glanced downwards looking for the doctor. At the same time, he caught sight of De Ville, pursuing him ferociously up the slope, and below, on the track, he glimpsed Watson backing away, holding Reilly at bay with his revolver. 'Shoot him in the leg!' thought Sam as he reached the top of the embankment. 'Shoot him,' he prayed, tearing off in the general direction of Osborne House. The last, very worrying thing Sam saw, before he headed for the cover of some trees, was Watson catching his foot on a sleeper, losing balance and being felled by a colossal blow from Reilly's axe handle.

Sam ran on, but he was torn – should he make his own bid for safety and keep alive their hopes of getting a message to the Duchess of Albion? Or should he return to help Watson? He could hear De Ville prowling through the trees behind him. In panic he pressed forward, his nightmare gradually becoming a reality.

In his dream, when he was being chased, he occasionally had the advantage of knowing where he was. Now he was completely lost. He ran headlong, with De Ville hard on his heels. At one point, he burst out of a copse of trees and found himself on a road. Open space was dangerous – if it came to a straight race, De Ville would catch him easily, and Sam could hear the man growling angrily behind him. Sam charged across the road, avoiding some sheep that loomed up at him in the moonlight, and into the bushes on the other side. He cut himself on some sharp brambles, he bruised his hand when he stumbled and fell, and he nearly lost an eye when he ducked late to avoid a protruding branch. He dodged round trees, he jumped ditches, he crawled through a hedge, and all the time Tiger drew closer. As in his nightmare, Sam came to a wall. As in his nightmare, his pursuer grabbed his leg but Sam managed to kick De Ville away as he clambered over. He jumped down, and then, briefly, he was out of his pursuer's sight while De Ville mounted the wall.

Sam noticed that the greenery was less wild on this side of the wall. It felt more like a garden, less like a wood. He plunged between two large bushes, glancing back at the same time to see if De Ville had got over the wall yet, and saw him on top of it! A shaft of moonlight split the trees, illuminating the distinctive black V in his hair. His face seemed all hair – shaggy eyebrows, bushy moustache, the striped mane. There was a glint of teeth as he jumped down roaring, 'I'll kill that kid. Kill him. Kill him!'

In an instant Sam lost his footing, his ankle twisting as he fell. He expected to hit the ground and stuck his hand out to soften the blow, but found himself brushed by leaves, tumbling down a slope. He rolled over twice, flailing about, and came to a dead halt on his back at the bottom of a hollow. His ankle hurt, his whole body felt scratched, but his landing was soft. He looked up and could see nothing. Darkness. A flash of moonlight through the thick leaves above him. He felt beneath him. Not the rough touch of soil and greenery, but something soft, firm and strong – cloth of some kind.

Sam was mystified. He was trying to work out where on earth he was, when he became aware of De Ville prowling among the bushes, cussing and threatening. If he made a break for it, De Ville would see him. He tried to still his breathing, desperate not to give himself away. De Ville scoured the area all around him. He swore and kicked the ground in frustration. A shower of stones sprayed into Sam's hideout. Sam knew Tiger was out there, hunting for him. He remained on his back, terrified, listening, as De Ville lit a cigar. Sam heard the match strike. He could smell the harsh tang of the tobacco. Eventually, De Ville's footsteps withdrew. Sam heard his curses growing fainter. He identified grunting and scraping sounds as De Ville scaled the wall, and then everything was quiet. Sam rubbed his sore ankle and considered his situation. De Ville was gone. It was the middle of the night. He could not wake people up at Osborne House until daylight. He considered that he had been fortunate to evade De Ville and that the best place for him to spend the night was exactly where he was. It was too dark for him to see where that was, but he was relieved to be safe, and did not want to risk being captured.

He felt around his hideout and found some books, although he couldn't make out what they were. There was a jar of pencils, a cushion, a mug, a plate, a rug and some chocolate. Not having eaten since before they set sail, he could not resist the chocolate. His thoughts drifted to Billy and Potts, Edie and Princess Alice. He longed to see Titch again. And he was worried about Watson – De Ville's last instruction to his companion had been to lock Watson in 'a cache'. What was that? *Where* was that? His ankle was sore, and he was weak with fatigue. Using the cushion as a pillow, he wrapped himself in the rug. Before long he fell into an exhausted and, for once, dream-free sleep.

Dr Watson's fate was a great deal less pleasant. When Reilly hit him with the axe shaft, he passed out. Reilly took Watson's revolver, recovered De Ville's gun, then dragged Watson into the tunnel. It wasn't long before he decided it would be easier to carry him. Discarding his axe shaft, he slung Watson over his shoulder. The Doctor drifted in and out of consciousness as Reilly lugged him along the tunnel, unlocked the door of the dynamite cache, dumped him in a corner and trussed him up like a turkey. Watson had been so stunned by the initial blow that he was hardly aware of what was happening to him. By the time Reilly closed the door on him, he was just able to identify the sound of the key in the lock. When he recovered his senses more fully, he could smell oil and coal and smoke – the scent of railways – but he was unable to move or see. He wondered, painfully, how Potts and Billy were getting on. His neck hurt miserably. The blood pounded in his head. He hoped Titch and Edie were still safe. He thought fitfully about Sam – was there still a chance that he might get their message to the Duchess and the Queen? Every bit of him ached, and he slid into a dark and painful slumber.

11

SPOOKY MR SPOONER

As he locked Watson into the dynamite cache, Reilly's nerves told him he was not alone. Swinging the flashlamp round, he demanded, 'Who's that?'

'Don't be daft, Reilly.'

'O'Hare! Where have you been? Major De Ville's gone chasing after some kid. And I've just tied up the bloke he was with. In here.'

'Ha! He won't survive long in there, will he? Let's go find Tiger.'

Walking along the tunnel, Reilly asked, 'How's the lift?'

'I told you. I'm doing it last thing in the morning. But instructions have been issued that the lift is not to be touched until the Queen uses it tomorrow. So unless one of those spoilt brats plays with the blasted thing, on that great occasion, the Queen and whoever is nearby will go sky high. Praise the Lord.'

'I shall be glad to be getting out of here.'

'Let's finish the job first, shall we?' said O'Hare, firmly. He didn't like the signs of weakness he detected in Reilly.

By the time they reached the tunnel mouth, De Ville was sliding back down the embankment. He landed awkwardly by the track and slipped to the ground. Reilly and O'Hare ran and helped him to his feet. Humiliated, he pushed them away. To have been outfoxed by a kid was galling enough, but that it should have been *that* kid, and that it had happened on the eve of the momentous coup that the Professor had been planning for years, not only angered but troubled him. He was also disturbed by Dr Watson's presence. How could *he* be involved? Sherlock Holmes was dead!

'Where's that meddling Doctor?' he growled.

'He's in the cache, sir,' replied Reilly. 'As you asked.'

'The lift?'

'In hand.' O'Hare smiled.

'Right. Did you find my gun, Reilly?'

Reilly handed it over. 'Good man.' De Ville sounded confident, but he remained perturbed. Everything else had gone so smoothly – the sinking of the *Arcadia*, the kidnap of Princess Alice, the death of Sherlock Holmes. Had word somehow got out about the planned assassinations? 'I shall stay till the morning, then I must get back to the mainland to inform the Professor everything is under way. *Your* boat will be waiting on the south side, as soon as the train job is done. Clear?'

'Yes, sir.'

'Keep your eyes peeled for that blasted kid. I lost him in the grounds of the house. God knows where he got to.'

'Is he dangerous?'

'He might be. I've seen him before. Let's get some sleep.'

'Shall we go look?' O'Hare enquired. 'See if we can track him down?'

'No. Just keep an eye on the Doctor. The kid'll come back for him. When he does, pick him up.'

Billy and Potts ran along the rails until they found the concealed points where the track forked. Excited, eager, they followed the line deep into the forest, as far as the tunnel. From here they progressed carefully. When they reached the station platform, they could see no one, apart from the driver and fireman on Moriarty's train. There was no sign of Titch. They were thrown. They had been relying on Titch's knowledge of the place. Without it, they were not quite sure how to proceed. After watching for a long time, they counted only two guards. The caves felt deserted, abandoned. The food store door was swinging open, creaking eerily, and the store itself looked empty.

They studied Titch's plan, and when things were quiet, they made a swift recce into the interior to confirm the location of Alice and Edie's cell. They saw at once – as Titch had done – that they stood no chance at all of getting the girls out – if indeed they were still in there. They didn't like the atmosphere. It disturbed them. They withdrew along the tunnel, to the safety of the woods, to discuss it.

'This isn't good, Potts.'

'Nope. It feels empty. Like it's all over. Like we're too late.'

'And Titch. Where's Titch, Potty?'

'Exactly. Where's Titch?' They had been so optimistic. Their disappointment now was intense.

'I've got to find Edie,' Potts burst out. 'I promised 'er mum 'n' dad. I 'ope nuffing's 'appened to 'er.'

'We're going to have to think carefully about this,

Potts. One of those guards had a gun. If we're going to get Titch and Edie out . . .'

'*If* they're in there.'

'We're going to have to be patient, Potty. And plan. Like Sam would.'

'Yeah.'

'Not rush into it like before.'

'I guess. But, Billy . . .'

'What?'

'If we're right, tomorrow is the big day. Friday the firteenth. Yeah?'

'Or Saturday.'

'So if we're patient for too long . . .'

'Yes?'

'We'll be too flippin' late. Won't we?!'

With the threat of death over their heads, none of the captives slept well. Alice spent most of the night crying. Edie was troubled by a recurring dream. She was standing on the edge of a ravine. On the other side of it were two small figures. They were calling to her, but she couldn't make contact with them. Titch comforted Alice, and kept an eye on Edie, so she didn't get much sleep either.

When the kind guard brought a snack in at

daybreak, they asked him if he knew what was to happen to them. He looked uneasy and left hurriedly, shutting the cell door without a word. It was locked and bolted.

'I don't like this,' said Alice.

'No,' said Titch. 'He knows. And doesn't want to say.'

They all felt that the moment of their execution was drawing nearer.

Edie tried to be positive. 'If Beaky got back to 22lb all right, one of the others'd be here by now, do you not think?' Titch agreed. 'And this dream I've been having, is like they're trying to reach us, but can't.' Titch and Alice nodded hopefully. 'I think the next time they open our door, we have to make a dash for it. We may not get far, but if Sam or Billy or Potts or even the Doctor is here, they could help and ... who knows?'

'Be better than sitting here waiting ... to be ...' Titch didn't like to finish the sentence.

'And then we could find Papa, and he can tell them off,' said Alice with finality.

Edie eyed Titch. 'Sure, Alice, exactly.'

Alice seemed quite happy. 'Well then,' she announced, 'we had best make a plan, hadn't we?'

'Wake up! Wake up!'

Sam was being shaken from a deep sleep. He came to slowly, his ankle throbbing and his mind confused. He could see light through leaves, and then everything flooded back fast. De Ville had found him! He woke fully with a start and sat up. He threw off the rug and jumped to his feet, ready to escape, when he realised that the person who had been shaking him was not Tiger De Ville. Cowering as far away from him as the strange, shadowy, leafy space they were in would allow was a young boy. He stared at Sam, open-mouthed.

'Who are you?' Sam asked, rubbing his eyes.

'Who are *you*?' cried the boy, curious rather than annoyed. 'And what are you doing *here*?'

'Well,' said Sam, feeling as though he might be in one of his dreams, 'it's a long story, but my name is Sam and I need to speak to the Duchess of Albion.'

'She's my aunt,' said the boy eagerly. 'But how did you get in here? Nobody's supposed to know about this, it's my secret den!'

'It was dark,' Sam replied. 'I was being chased and I fell in.'

'How thrilling!'

'Well not really, but if you can help me reach the Duchess—'

'You've eaten my chocolate!'

'I'm sorry. I was starving. I'll get you some more.'

'Oh, that's all right. I've got loads. Who was chasing you?'

Sam was still feeling slightly groggy from his heavy sleep, and did not know quite where to start. 'Someone who I think wants to . . . er, hurt the Queen.'

'WHAT? She won't like that. Is that what you want to tell my aunt?'

'Partly. You might find this hard to believe, but I think I know where Princess Alice is.'

'Do you? That's spiffing news. Do you really?' Sam felt that the boy did not fully appreciate the gravity of the situation. '*And* a message about hurting Grandmother. What fun.'

'Is Queen Victoria your gran, then?'

'Yes. I'm Prince Edward. But even I daredn't call her Gran. She'd have me thrown in the Tower! Can you walk? You keep rubbing your ankle.'

'Yes, I think so. It's a bit sore from when I fell in here.'

'Well, I'll get Nurse to have a look at it. I say this is terribly exciting. Let's go and speak with Mrs Goose –

she's the lady who's in charge downstairs at the house. To be totally frank, I think it's best if *I* speak to her. She's a frightful dragon, and she won't let you into the house looking like that, but I can usually get round her. Are you ready?'

'Yes,' replied Sam, surprised and relieved at this fortuitous turn of events.

'Jolly good. Come on, then, Sam – can I call you Sam?'

Sam smiled. 'Of course.' He felt slightly self-conscious addressing a prince. 'What shall I call you?'

'Oh, people call me all sorts of things, some of them dreadfully rude. My tutor calls me Duffer, but that's because I'm so clever. If you'll be my friend, *you* can call me Duffer. This is the smashingest holiday I've ever had here. It's usually boring as funerals.'

The young Prince scrambled out of his den on all fours, up a slope between two of the cluster of bushes beneath which he had created his secret hideaway. As Sam wriggled up it after him, he realised it was this slope that had saved him during last night's chase. He had caught his foot here and tumbled in. It was just visible in daylight. De Ville would only have found it at night if he had known it was there. Sam crawled out, blinking in the morning light. What he saw confirmed what he had suspected last night, that he had stumbled into the grounds of Osborne House. The gardens were immaculate. Beautifully shaped bushes and hedges. Impeccable lawns. A fountain. All perfectly maintained in matchless order. Sam shuddered as he took in where he was. Prince Edward, however, was deliciously unaware of the scale and significance of Sam's concerns. He was quite simply enjoying the best adventure of his life. He was jumping up and down with glee, and as Sam staggered away from the den, the Prince grabbed his hand.

'This way,' he cried, and dragged Sam in the direction of Osborne House, and the fearful Mrs Goose.

Back on the mainland, Billy and Potts had formed a plan of action. They crept from the woods, along the railway line, down the tunnel and back into the station. They were armed with a club each, chunky sticks they had found among the trees by the fork in the line. They hid, as Titch had done, under the train. There was no one to be seen. Nothing to be heard. They shuffled along quietly under the train until they reached a point where they could see through the arch into the interior. Still nothing. It seemed safe enough for them to venture out. They were heaving themselves up on to the platform, when they heard voices. They shot back down again, out of sight.

The two guards they had seen last night came running through the arch on to the platform. The first man was shaking his head, saying, 'No. No. No. I won't do it.'

The man behind was shouting. 'It's an order! Take it!' He was holding out a revolver. 'Take it.'

The first guard still refused. 'I won't do it.'

'The Professor wants them out of the way.'

'They haven't *done* anything!'

'They're evidence. They must be got rid of.'

'They're just kids! I can't shoot innocent children.'

Billy and Potts froze. They could hardly believe what they were hearing.

The head guard thrust the revolver out again. 'They must be eliminated. All three of them.'

Billy and Potts grabbed each other.

'Free of 'em!' whispered Potts. 'That's why we ain't seen Titch.'

'You're right, Potty, Titch has been captured.'

Again the junior guard protested, but he was weakening. 'It's not right, chief. You know it's not right.'

'Right doesn't come into it. It's necessary. Take the gun!' Billy and Potts were willing the man not to. 'If *you* don't shoot them,' said the head guard, 'I *will*. But I'll kill you first.'

To Billy and Potts's alarm, the junior guard took the revolver. He looked defeated, but he took it. 'Give me a couple of minutes,' he said miserably. 'I'll do it.'

'Do it now. Do it fast. The longer you leave it the harder it will be.' The head guard turned on his heels and went back through the arch. Billy and Potts watched in horror as the junior guard took a large key from a chain on his belt and made his way reluctantly back into the central complex.

''E's gonna shoot 'em, Billy.'

'What can we do?'

Potts was shaking with fury. He wanted to act, but didn't know how. Billy also felt helpless with rage and fear. They both knew that if they went to the aid of the three captives now, they would probably be shot as well.

'I 'ave to go, Billy!' Potts whispered furiously. 'If I don't do sumfing, I'll never forgive myself.'

'I know, Potty, I know. It just seems pointless.'

'It's Edie.'

'And Titch.'

'We can't just stand by, can we?'

'No,' said Billy. 'We can't. Come on.'

The two lads scrambled up on to the platform. They stood looking at each other, gripping their clubs, frightened, determined. Knowing this might be the last thing they ever did, they lacked the nerve to charge into the caves.

'Potts.'

'Yeah?'

'You're my best mate ever.'

'Fanks, Billy. You're mine.'

'Shall we?'

'We 'ave to, Billy boy. For Edie.'

'For Sam and Titch.'

'And Mr 'Olmes.'

'Good luck, then.'

'You too. Come on.'

They ran from the platform, heading for the prison cell. They had just run through the arch, when they heard the first shot. It stopped them in their tracks and echoed round the caves. They stood pinned to the spot, thick with guilt for being too late. Before they could move, they heard two more shots. They were devastated by the thought of their friends

Titch and Edie being killed so ruthlessly, to say nothing of little Princess Alice. The deafening sound reverberated through the interior of the caves. They could hear the echo, dying its way along the tunnel. Potts held his head in his hands. Billy dropped his club and went to him. He put his arms round his best friend, and the two of them just stood there, aching, defeated, lost.

When Watson finally came to, he was in the darkest dark he had ever known. An impenetrable dark, immeasurable. Even when his eyes had grown accustomed to the blackness, he could still see nothing. He could not see his hand in front of his face, he thought with bitter irony, because his hands were roped behind his back. His ankles were also tied. He had no idea of the shape of his prison, or the size, or even the location of it. He wondered how Sam had fared – if he had got away from De Ville. He prayed that Billy and Potts had met up with Titch and rescued Edie. He thought desperately of Holmes. How things might have been different had the Great Detective still been alive. Poor Watson. He had never felt so powerless.

* * *

At Osborne House, Prince Edward led Sam to the kitchen entrance and left him outside while he ran in to find Mrs Goose. One of the gardeners, taking his wheelbarrow out to work, stopped and stared at Sam, open-mouthed. He felt like a scarecrow. A maid stuck her head round the door to take a peep at him and ran back inside giggling. Sam began to wonder if it was going to be quite so easy as he had imagined to get his message to the Duchess.

He was still hoping that Prince Edward would bring the Duchess out with him, when the fearful Mrs Goose herself appeared with the young Prince, whose tail was very much between his legs – he obviously hadn't managed to win her over this time! She examined Sam with an unforgiving eye, as though he was an exhibit in a museum. He decided he would keep his mouth shut and await the dragon's verdict. Having circled him once, Mrs Goose gave Prince Edward a withering look and shook her head.

'I don't know,' she said. 'I don't know what you're thinking of, Master Edward.' She looked Sam directly in the eye. 'You stay here. If you move, I shall have them set the dogs on you.' She turned and strode away. 'Come with me, Master Edward.'

As he trotted after her, the young Prince turned to

Sam and shrugged. Mrs Goose took him by the collar and guided him firmly into the house. Sam was left standing.

Billy had his arms around Potts, who was numb with grief, when Titch and Edie appeared, running for their lives.

'Potts! Billy! Quick!' whispered Edie urgently.

The two lads were too astonished to move. They thought they were looking at a ghost. Ghosts!

'Edie! Wot?!'

'Come on, Potts. Move.'

'Titch!' cried Billy.

'Come on!' Titch grabbed him and started shoving him towards the platform. Edie took Potts by the hand and dragged him after her. Behind them came the guard. In his hand was a smoking gun. Over his shoulder was Alice.

'Go on!' he whispered vehemently. 'Quick!'

They ran into the deserted station. They sped past the train, along the platform, down on to the line, and did not stop for breath until they emerged from the tunnel into the trees. There was no one following them, but even when they reached the outside world, they kept moving, heading for safety.

As they ran, Billy and Potts worked out that Alice, Edie and Titch had been saved by the guard, who was now leading them through the forest. He had fired three shots to fool his boss. Princess Alice was now running happily alongside Edie, as fast as her little legs would carry her. By the time they reached the cliff edge, they were all breathless, but happy. The relief that they had been rescued, the added pleasure of being together and the sheer thrill of being alive produced a kind of wonder. They stood looking out over the sea, hand in hand, gulping in the heady air of freedom.

Alice was the first to speak. 'Look!'

'What is it, Alice?'

'The royal ferry.'

'Wow!'

'What day is it?' Alice asked.

'Friday,' the guard replied.

'The thirteenth. My uncles and aunts will be on it. And Papa going to Osborne for Christmas. The children were all going yesterday.'

'Flippin' 'eck!'

'Wow!'

Titch was quiet. The ferry looked safe, but she couldn't get Edie's vision of crowns rolling down hills and trains coming off rails out of her mind. 'I hope they're going to be all right,' she said under her breath.

'So do I,' said Edie ominously.

Stamping his feet against the cold, Sam began to wonder if there was any point at all in waiting for the return of the ghastly Mrs Goose or Prince Edward. Members of the household staff continued to regard him with distrust. By the time Sam's fingers and toes were blue, the young Prince emerged from the kitchen door, followed not by Mrs Goose, but by a tall thin man with curvature of the spine, whom Edward introduced unwillingly as Mr Spooner. Prince Edward wriggled, and made apologetic faces at Sam behind Spooner's back.

'So, young man,' Spooner addressed Sam with oily familiarity, 'you are the Prince's new friend, are you? How nice to meet you. And your name is . . .'

'It's Sam!' interrupted Prince Edward, annoyed. 'I told you.'

'So you did. So you did. I do apologise,' Spooner crawled, rubbing his hands apologetically. 'And you have a message, I believe, for the Duchess?'

Reluctantly, Sam nodded. He had never taken such an instant dislike to anyone. One look at Spooner and he was convinced the man was one of Moriarty's agents.

'May I perhaps know what the message is?' Spooner enquired.

'I'm sorry,' Sam responded. 'I don't really know who you are, and I need to speak directly to the Duchess. It's private.'

Spooner was offended. 'There's no need to be like that about it. I am merely trying to help. Had it not been for my intervention, Mrs Goose would have turned you away without any hearing at all. Am I not right, Prince Edward?' Edward was obliged to agree. 'Perhaps I should not have bothered to come to your rescue at all,' Spooner burbled on, sulking.

Sam didn't know what to say. 'I didn't mean to be rude, sir. It's just that it's private.'

'Oh very well, very well. I am quite trustworthy, young man,' he concluded tartly. 'Never mind, come with me.' He moved off towards the kitchen door, gesturing impatiently for the two boys to follow. 'Let's get you cleaned up. I am sure the young Prince will know where to find the Duchess. My name is Spooner, by the way, humble assistant to Maestro Leinster.'

Sam was obliged to follow Spooner through the kitchens, where people stopped peeling and chopping to gape at him. He was relieved when they got upstairs, except that Spooner made him carry his shoes to avoid soiling the very fine light-green carpets. When they reached the main hall, Spooner looked at Sam as though he was something the cat had brought in, and said, '*We* should get cleaned up.' He indicated a guest bathroom off the hall, and suggested to Prince Edward that he should find his aunt, while Sam made himself presentable. As the young Prince trudged off unwillingly to seek the Duchess, Spooner manoeuvred Sam into the bathroom.

Sam saw himself in the mirror and was horrified. He washed his face and hands frantically. He felt extremely uncomfortable in the cramped room, his every move scrutinised by the grotesque Spooner, who added insult to injury by questioning him. 'How did you get into the grounds? Were you alone?' The questions pummelled Sam. Then Spooner tried to be nice! 'Poor boy, you look as though you have had a miserable time. Anything I can do to help, please . . . just ask.'

Sam was embarrassed and didn't know what to say. 'There's only one person I would really like to talk to,' he mumbled.

'And who is that, if I may be so bold?'

'Someone I can't talk to because he's dead,' Sam

muttered, wishing he could get out of this interrogation, to say nothing of the poky bathroom!

'I am sorry to hear your friend . . . is dead,' commiserated Spooner. 'Were you very close?' he said, holding out a towel for Sam, who squirmed.

He snatched the towel, and countered angrily, 'He was a detective. A very great one, actually.'

'Really? As great as the famed Sherlock Holmes?'

This absolutely confirmed Sam's suspicions about Spooner. Who else would have made such a guess, but an agent of Professor Moriarty's?

'It *was* Mr Holmes actually,' he said boldly, and added, with a touch of resentment aimed at Spooner, '*He* would *help*! *He* would know what to do.'

Spooner drew back and sighed. 'I despair of you, Wiggins. If you have a question for Mr Holmes, ask him!'

'I told you,' said Sam, incredulously, 'he's dead. And how do you know my name is Wiggins? Who *are* you?'

'Who am I?' Spooner leaned close to Sam and whispered, 'Wiggins, your powers of observation are woefully underdeveloped. If you wish to ask Mr Holmes a question, please do so. I shall be delighted to answer.'

'Mr Holmes is dead!'

'I have yet to be convinced of that, Wiggins.' Sam recoiled. Spooner's voice sounded different. Sam examined him intensely, and his jaw dropped. 'Really, Sam.' Spooner smiled. 'You ought to know me by now.'

'Mr Holmes!'

'Ssshhh. We don't want anyone else to know, do we?'

'You're dead, Mr Holmes,' said Sam blankly.

'Reports of my death have been greatly exaggerated, Sam.'

'Mr Holmes!' Sam whispered, awestruck.

'Indeed, Sam. It is I. Dry your face. Quickly.'

Not knowing quite whether to laugh or cry, Sam did as he was told. Holmes handed him a comb.

'You need to redo that ponytail of yours. It looks a frightful mess.'

'Of course, Mr Holmes. I don't believe this.'

'Believe it! We have work to do.'

'It's wonderful to see you. We thought you'd drowned.'

'I took advantage of the accident to disappear.'

'It took me ages to work out what your note meant.'

'You have my half-hunter, then. Splendid. My note was vague, Sam, I admit. I was unsure of Moriarty's plans until I got to Osborne.'

Sam could still hardly believe his eyes. 'Thank heavens you're here, sir.'

'Thank heavens *you* are here, Sam. And by the way,' Holmes added with a wicked smile, 'what the Devil took you so long to find me?'

12

FRIDAY THE THIRTEENTH

The reception for the royal ferry at Ryde Station was the most majestic that had ever been seen on the Isle of Wight. The bunting featured the flags of the visiting German principalities, a red carpet snaked grandly from the quay, and over all, the Union Jack flew proudly. The band of the Royal Marines entertained a large crowd with 'Men of Harlech' and 'Rule Britannia'. A white winter sun set the seal on proceedings.

The Duke of Albion shepherded the Queen's relatives down the gangplank. The locals had never before seen the Saxe-Coburgs, the Hohenzollerns and the Princes of Schleswig-Holstein, who were sporting their finest regalia – the men in plumed helmets, flowing capes and swords, their wives, hatted, bejewelled, in ornate dresses. As they left the ferry, the crowd clapped and

cheered. Before they transferred to the Queen's train, however, the royals had to watch the Marines in a display of marching and countermarching, and inspect the guard. Their arrival was an occasion, and the islanders were intent on making the most of it.

Some of the crowd were simply waiting to take the first available public ferry back to the mainland, and saw the razzmatazz as a bonus. But there was one man who wanted the spectacle to be over as quickly as possible because he was in a hurry to be away. Tiger De Ville was hovering near the back, doing his best not to be seen – not easy for a man of his stature. As the royal party were conveyed along the pier by the Mayor of Ryde, who was looking so pleased with himself he was in danger of exploding, De Ville edged nearer to the waiting ferry. Within hours, he thought, these overdressed boobies would all be dead. Within hours he would be with Professor Moriarty in the caves. Then they would be away to London, where Moriarty would be assuming the reins of power. De Ville found it hard not to gloat, but he was a professional to his toes. He kept his head down, remained as inconspicuous as he could, and waited with seeming patience to board the ferry.

* * *

The Duchess of Albion was beside herself with relief and anticipation, having been informed that it was at least known where Princess Alice was being kept prisoner. Sam, having delivered the good news, had been provided with some decent clothes, and was bringing Holmes up to date.

'De Ville was here last night, Mr Holmes.'

'Are you certain, Sam? Tiger De Ville?'

'Yes, sir. I'd know him anywhere.'

'De Ville. Here. I wonder why.'

'It's Dr Watson I'm really worried about, though, sir. He was being taken to a cache. What's a cache?'

'A cache? An arms or explosives store. Where *was* this cache, do you think?'

'I don't know, but I last saw the Doctor down by the railway tunnel.'

'The tunnel?' Holmes leaned forward and put his chin in his hands. 'Mmmmn. When I wrote the words *Look to the Queen there*, I feared an attempt on Her Majesty's life. I believe I have foiled Moriarty's evil plans, but a cache . . .' Jumping sharply to his feet, Holmes explained to Sam that he had been keeping a particularly close eye on two of the Irish labourers who had installed a lift in the house. Holmes paced round the room, recalling an evening when he had watched them leave Osborne. 'They *could* have been going towards . . . the tunnel,' Holmes mused. 'The tunnel. Mmmm.' He pondered Sam's evidence, and wondered if there was yet more to Moriarty's villainous schemes than he had previously considered. 'The tunnel, Sam. A cache. Watson. I wonder . . .'

'Not long, now, Alice,' said Edie.

Alice was jumping up and down with glee at the thought of seeing her mother and little sister Eleanor again. She was so excited that Edie was worried she would slip into the sea.

'Sure, Alice, be careful. Come away from the edge.'

Alice, Edie, Potts, Billy and Titch were standing with the kind guard, their saviour, queuing with the large crowd of people waiting to cross to the Isle of Wight. The first ferry had just come in from the island. The anchor was dropped, the prow and stern ropes tethered. The gangplank clunked into position on the quayside. When those currently disembarking were all gone, the barrier would be lifted and people would be allowed on board. Everyone pressed forward, keen to get underway.

Titch suddenly grabbed Potts. 'Potts! Edie! Look!' As the arrivals surged off the boat, the figure of Tiger De

Ville stood head and shoulders above most of the passengers. Although he had his head down in an attempt to be inconspicuous, nothing could disguise his hair, the black V, the mark of the tiger. People leaving the boat were being directed along the quay, separated by nothing more than a rope from those waiting to board. They realised that De Ville would pass within inches of them.

''E's lookin' flippin' cagey,' Potts remarked flippantly.

'Keep your head down, Potts,' Titch snapped. 'Down! All of you!'

Edie pulled Alice close and they ducked.

'What's De Ville been up to on the Isle of Wight?' Billy asked.

'Moriarty had the telescope in his office trained on the island,' Titch whispered.

'Of course. On some railway tunnel. It's on your map, Titch.'

'I only had a quick look, but I'm sure that's what it was.'

'Keep down,' said Billy urgently. 'He's getting near. He mustn't see us.'

They stopped talking and clung to each other, huddling up as close as they could to the people in front of them for cover. They each had their reasons to be wary of De Ville. He was the first person Alice had seen when they removed her blindfold after the kidnap, and she was scared stiff of him. Edie had not forgotten the moment when De Ville had swept her off the ladder in the station and thrown her on to the train. Potts had seen him do it. Titch knew that De Ville was reputed to be the second most dangerous man alive. Billy was the only one who had never seen him before, so as the other four did their best to remain hidden, keeping their backs to De Ville, Billy attempted to conceal them, at the same time keeping a wary eye on De Ville's progress. The line of people moving in the other direction progressed at a reasonable speed, but as De Ville approached, it slowed. As he came nearer to them, their hearts almost stopped beating.

'He's about five yards away. Stay down,' hissed Billy.

De Ville's queue nudged slowly forward. When he was dead level with them, it stopped completely. He could have reached out with one of his huge arms and scooped Edie up again. Or Alice. At one moment De Ville looked directly at Billy, the savage eyes glaring through him. Billy stopped breathing. He did his best to smile. De Ville turned away in contempt, drew on his cigar, and the queue started inching forward again. He was gone.

When he was out of hearing, Billy whispered, 'We're all right. He's passed.'

'Phew.'

'Wow! Scar-*y*.'

'Are you all right, Alice?' Edie enquired, taking her hand.

'No. I don't like this. It's much nicer on the royal ferry. You don't have all this stupid queuing.'

Edie was surprised by Alice's answer. 'Ah, well, now you know what it's like for the rest of us.'

'Yes. Horrible. Has that nasty man really gone?'

'Sure.'

'He always smells of cigars. Pooh. I shall see that Papa is particularly hard on him.'

''Ere. Look. They're all off the ferry,' Potts observed. 'We shall be movin' in a minute. Fantastic. Never been on a ferry before! Wot a trip!'

'Potts! Don't get larky.'

'Just tryin' to cheer us up!'

'We'd best get the tickets ready,' said Billy. They turned to the guard who had saved their lives. To their astonishment, he wasn't there. 'Hey! Where's he gone? He had the tickets.'

In alarm, they looked about for their saviour, but he was nowhere to be seen.

'What a pity,' remarked Alice.

'Shame 'e's gone.'

'Sure. He was always nice.'

'Perhaps he'll come back,' said Billy hopefully.

'That would be good. He would have got an especially nice reward,' Alice commented in that direct way of hers, as though she was talking about a piece of cake rather than the man to whom they owed their lives.

'Wot are we goin' to do about the tickets, tho'?' Potts asked. ''E 'ad 'em!'

'They're in your hat,' Alice pointed out.

'Wot?'

'Sure, Alice is right,' Edie remarked. 'They're in your hatband.'

Potts removed his bowler.

'Actually you could do with a new hat,' Alice went on. 'That one is in a shocking state. There is a much better one in the dressing-up box at Osborne. You can have that.'

'This 'at belonged to my Uncle 'Ector, Alice. Don't you dare speak ill of it. But look, you lot!' From the band of Hector's battered old bowler, Potts took their tickets. 'They're all 'ere!' Potts flicked through them. 'You lucky people! 'E must have popped 'em in there

219

when we was 'idin' from old Tiger. I wonder why 'e's done a bunk?'

Titch pointed out that the guard, too, was hiding from De Ville.

'Of course,' said Billy. 'He wouldn't want to be seen by De Ville any more than us!'

'Yeah. 'Is life's at risk now as much as ours, I suppose.' Potts stood on tiptoe and peered about. 'I can't see 'im nowhere. Can you?'

None of them could see him.

'I wish he was still with us,' said Alice. 'He carried me for miles.'

They were all upset that he had gone, and felt more vulnerable without him.

'No mopin',' said Potts. 'Per'aps 'e'll come back when it's safe. Look, the queue's movin'. We can go on board – at last! We shall soon be by a nice big fire in a fancy room in Osborne 'Ouse, drinkin' 'ot milk and chattin' wiv 'Er Maj. Wot's your gran like, Alice?'

Alice was somewhat alarmed by the thought of Potts meeting Queen Victoria. 'Potts,' she said thoughtfully, 'Grandmother is very nice, but rather . . . well, *very* strict. Worse than Papa.'

'Wow!' Billy was not sure he liked the sound of Queen Victoria.

Unlike Billy, Potts was not alert to the dangers Princess Alice was doing her best to convey. 'Can she knit?' he asked. 'My gran knits like mad!'

Alice's brow puckered. 'I think perhaps not,' she replied in her gravest tones. 'And if you will take my advice . . .'

'Yeah?'

'You will not ask her questions.'

''Ow we supposed to chat then?' Potts enquired. 'If I can't ask 'er—?'

'It's just that people like *you*,' Alice interrupted firmly, 'people not in the family, are not supposed to ask a royal person questions.'

''Oo made that one up? You can't live like that, Alice.'

'We do,' Alice replied with absolute conviction.

'You mean I can't ask 'er if she fancies a cuppa? Or if she'd like a dance? Or where the lav is?'

Alice was horrified. 'It's a rule, Potts.'

'Well, it's barkin', innit? Come on. On to the gangplank, boys and girls. A life on the ocean wave. You lucky people! Wot's up, Titch?'

'I'm looking forward to seeing Sam, that's all.'

'Course. We all are.'

'I hope he's all right.'

'Course 'e's all right.'

'I'm worried by Edie, too.'

'Wot?'

'She saw some stuff about a train . . .'

Billy gave Potts a nudge with his elbow. 'Potts! The ticket-collector.'

'Woops. Sorry, guv. Five juniors, my good man.' He counted the tickets. 'One two free four, and moi makes five. 'Ang on to this spare adult for us, will you, in case our friend turns up? Fank you. All on board!'

The ticket-collector was concerned by the five scruffy children straining to get on deck. But their tickets were in order, so he let them pass, although he could not resist issuing a warning.

'No messing about, now, you lot.'

'Worry not, my good sir,' replied Potts. 'They are wiv me.' He offered Edie his arm and led them on board. 'Cheer up, Titch. Tell you wot . . .' – Potts was on a roll – 'even now, Sam and the Doc will be savourin' the comforts of the royal 'ouse'old. Anuvver sherry, good Sir Doctor? And you, Your Maj – would'st thou anuvver cuppa like – laced wiv gin, of course? That is, if Your 'Ighness doth not mind me askin' you a question in the first place like.'

'Potts!'

'I'm serious. I'll bet you Sam and Sir Doc are 'avin a ball. One flippin' great, royal bloomin' ball!'

Potts would have lost his bet, twice over. Dr Watson was still tied up, cold and hungry, in the explosives cache in the tunnel. Sam and Holmes – still disguised as Mr Spooner – were keen to go and look for him, and Prince Edward was keen to take part in this great adventure. When pressed by the Duchess of Albion, he announced that he was going hunting with his chums. Mr Spooner calmed the Duchess's anxiety and promised to take great care of the eager young Prince.

In order to find Watson, the three of them retraced Sam's steps from the night before. They set off through the grounds of Osborne House to Prince Edward's den. When they reached it, Holmes scouted round and found traces of ash. He examined it in the minutest detail, sniffing it, rubbing it between thumb and forefinger, scrutinising the residue and testing the speed with which the ash fluttered to the ground.

'When he was looking for me,' said Sam, 'I heard him light that.'

'No doubt you smelled it, too, Sam. The Monte Cristo Number Three is a Cuban cigar, noted for its pungent aroma,' Holmes observed as Sam led them to the place where he and De Ville had crossed the wall. They helped Prince Edward over. It was then a question of working their way back to the tunnel, to where Sam had last seen Dr Watson. As Holmes wanted to get there as fast as possible, Sam did his best to retrace his steps, whilst Holmes looked for any indication that Watson might have been brought in the other direction. He ranged widely, searching for evidence, but always returned to the main route that Sam had taken. Sam was fascinated by Holmes's skill in tracking. There was little in the way of footsteps to observe, because the cold ground was too hard, but there were broken twigs, indentations in gravel, broken tufts of grass, recently fallen branches that had been knocked off in the chase, all of which revealed to Holmes a hidden story. He could have found his way without Sam. They crossed the road, heading towards the railway embankment.

'Still no indication that Watson was brought this way,' Holmes declared. 'On, Sam! Quickly!'

Prince Edward was less talkative than usual, intrigued by the change in Mr Spooner. He had to run to keep pace, for Holmes's speed tested even Sam. Sam had observed before that when Holmes was in pursuit of something, or some*one*, all his senses were heightened. His focus was fierce. He was fanatical. He seemed almost to glow.

'Mr Spooner?' said Prince Edward tentatively, cowed by the intensity of Holmes's concentration. There was no reply, and a lengthy pause, as Holmes, on his knees, examined a bush. He came away from it with a strand of wool. Ignoring the Prince's question, he turned to Sam.

'De Ville was wearing a tweed suit. Am I right? Chestnut brown, flecked with cream?'

'Yes, sir,' Sam replied, taking care not to name Holmes in front of their young companion.

'A creature of habit, our De Ville,' Holmes remarked, setting off again at breakneck speed. 'H. Huntsman of Savile Row was always his tailor of choice. Watson would not have been so attired. This way, I think.'

'Mr Spooner?' Prince Edward was trotting along by Holmes's side, determined to ask his question.

'Yes, young man?'

'You seem very different.'

'Do I?'

'Yes. Much nicer than you were. Not so stooped and . . .'

'And?'

'I hope you won't think me rude . . .'

Momentarily, Holmes reverted to his impersonation of Spooner, bending down and rounding on the young Prince, without for a second slackening his speed. 'Try me.'

Prince Edward jumped. Literally. 'No-no, it doesn't matter,' he cried. He had been going to say, 'stooped . . . and *creepy*', but he lost his nerve. 'What I really want to know is, if your job usually involves hunting like this.'

'What do *you* think?' Holmes said evasively, bending down low to look closely at a disturbed divot of grass.

'Well, I don't really know. But what I was thinking was . . . if this is what being the assistant to a painter is like, I'd rather like to be one! Wouldn't you, Sam?'

'I'd love it, Prince Edward.'

They reached the railway embankment. Holmes paced to and fro along the top, looking down the sharp slope to the rails. 'Ah ha! This, I believe, is where De Ville slid down the bank on his return. I am confident at least that Watson, wherever he is, was not brought up here. Shall we perhaps take the less precipitous route down?' As they walked down the gentler part of the slope to the railway line, Holmes took Prince Edward by the hand. 'The most difficult part of being a painter's assistant, young man, is being brave and sensible. Can you be brave *and* sensible at the same time?'

'Brave as you like, because I don't think. That's what mother says. But sensible . . .'

Holmes held Edward by both hands and knelt to speak to him. 'Prince Edward. I want you to do something for me. Something of very great importance. Something that might be quite dangerous. Are you prepared to help me?'

'How dangerous?'

'Well, if you are brave *and* sensible . . . not very.'

'Jolly good! Fire away!'

'I want you to take this large white handkerchief –' Holmes took it from his pocket and shook it open, '– and walk about a hundred yards.' Holmes angled the young prince so that he was looking up the line towards Ryde, away from the tunnel. 'I want you to wait there for the train.'

'With all our relatives on?'

'Exactly so. When you see the train coming, I want you to try and stop it.'

'Stop it? But they're coming for Christmas, and—'

'I know. But it is *very important to try and stop it,*' Holmes said emphatically. 'By waving this handkerchief. Do you think you can manage that?'

'I can try.'

'Good. That is very brave. Promise me you will also be very sensible.'

'Promise. My tutor *will* be surprised that you think I'm sensible.'

'You will only be really sensible if you do nothing to endanger your life. Do you understand me?'

'Not really.' Prince Edward could not work out how he might lose his life performing such a simple task as waving a hanky to stop a train.

'Well . . . if the train driver does not see you, or does not seem prepared to stop the train, you must make absolutely sure that you get out of the way in time.'

'I'm extremely *clever*—'

'This is very serious, Edward. Try and stop the train, but under no circumstances put your life at risk.'

'Yes. I see. My life will be at risk, will it?'

'Only if you are not sensible. So . . . be sensible.'

'What I lack in sensible, I will try and make up for with clever. All right? Shall I go *now*?'

'The train is still at Ryde.' Holmes glanced quickly at his half-hunter. 'It should be leaving in the next few minutes. Sam, would you take Prince Edward to a suitable point in the line. And tie that handkerchief to a stick for him. Prince Edward . . . if you fail to stop the train . . .'

'Yes?'

'I want you to run as fast as you can . . . *away* from this tunnel behind us.'

'Why?'

'Because if you *follow* the train, and my fears turn out to be justified, you will not live to tell the tale.'

'Golly gosh.' The Prince was beginning to realise just how momentous the situation was. 'And that wouldn't be very sensible, would it?'

'No. Off you go with Sam.'

Sam set off. 'Come on, Duffer.'

'Careful, or I'll have you sent to the Tower!' Edward ran after Sam, chattering nervously. 'Golly gosh, Sam, I hope I manage to stop the train. I hope we can have some more holidays like this. I know it's frightfully dangerous, but it is just completely the most brilliant hol' ever. In fact this beats life back home . . .'

Holmes was neither listening nor watching. As he waited for Sam to return, he walked at a snail's pace along the railway line, leaning forward at right angles, examining the ground in great detail. He slowly approached the dark, intimidating tunnel mouth.

The Duke of Albion was not a great fan of display marching. His view was that it was impressive the first time you saw it, but after that, it quickly became boring. He ushered the royal guests to their seats in a specially erected marquee at the side of the parade ground, and prayed that the Royal Marines would not get too carried away. The day was cold, and he longed for the marching to be over so that he could lead the royal party to the warmth of Osborne House. There was a stirring roll on the drums. The band struck up. The Duke suppressed a yawn and watched politely as the marching began.

The ferry was making easy headway towards Ryde Pier, on a calm sea, with a gentle breeze. Potts made them all stand at the prow of the boat, relishing the sea air.

'This knocks spots off London town, this do! The roar o' the surf. The crash o' the waves.'

Titch smiled. 'There's not a wave in sight, Potts!'

'Poetic licence. No bloomin' fog. No 'orrible smells.'

'I'm feeling a bit queasy,' said Alice, putting her hand to her mouth.

Titch was used to boats and the sea. She put a

reassuring hand on Alice's back. 'Just breathe deep, Alice, and think of your mum and Eleanor.'

'Dead right, Titch. Breathe deep, the lot of you. Clear yer lungs out! 'Ey, Billy. P'raps we should open our first 'otel down 'ere! You know, take the workers out o' their filthy factories to experience proper maritime air, wot?'

'That's not a bad idea, Potty. We could—'

'Edie! Edie, are *you* feelin' a bit woozy 'n' all?' Edie did not respond to Potts's question. She was deathly white and still.

'What is it, Edie?' Billy asked.

'I fink she's away, Billy. 'Ey, Edie. Talk to me. Tell me. I'm listenin'.'

Edie stood trance-like. 'Sure. It's the train. I can see the train again.'

'Train? Wot's this about a train, Titch?'

Before Titch could reply, Alice went to Edie and took her hand. 'When she had one of her turns, Potts, she saw a tunnel and a train coming off the rails. And crowns, rolling down a hill.'

'Wot?'

'She saw Eleanor, too, my baby sister. But the *really* bad turn was the train.'

Titch was busy thinking. 'Alice.'

'Yes, Titch?'

'When your family leaves the pier, how do they get to Osborne House?'

'I told you, Grandmother has a private railway. It's a most beautiful engine, and it goes nearly all the way to the house. They will be on it very soon, although Papa told me they were going to have to watch loads of boring marching and stuff first.'

'Tell me, Alice,' Titch pursued, 'is there a tunnel on the line?'

'Yes,' replied Alice.

Titch turned to Billy. 'I've got a terrible feeling we may be too late.'

'Late?' cried Potts. 'Wot you on about? Sam and Sir Doc are "looking to" ol' Queen Vic. We've rescued Alice. Conquerin' 'eroes. That's wot we are! 'Ow can we be late?'

'I know, Potts, but I saw a tunnel through Moriarty's telescope, and Edie's always right, isn't she?'

'Never fails.'

'Well, what if the train with Alice's family comes off the rails?' Titch asked.

'Wot?'

'If it's *made* to come off the rails.'

'Wow! You mean if it's attacked?' cried Billy.

'Ay. Crowns rolling down a hill. That's what Edie saw.'

'Blimey, Titch, I never thought o' that. You could be on to sumfing.' He put his arms round Edie to warm her. 'I'd better get 'er inside. She's dead cold.'

'Can you move her?'

'I'll carry 'er. Give us an 'and, Alice.' Potts gathered Edie gently in his arms and, guided by Alice, carried her towards the public cabin.

'What can we do, Titch?'

'It depends, Billy. If the royal train ain't left for Osborne by the time we get there, we might be able to stop it.'

'And if it *has* left?'

'Just hope I'm wrong about the tunnel.'

Titch and Billy reflected on the dreadful possibility of an attack on the train. The sea breeze seemed chill on their faces.

'Edie's always right,' Billy observed coolly. 'It may not be what you think, but she's always right.'

'Ay.'

'I don't like this, Titch.'

'Nor me, Billy. It don't look good at all. Go and fetch Alice, will you?'

'What for?'

'Cos when the ferry gets to Ryde, we're going to have

233

to act real fast. And the only way to get through might be to use Alice.'

'Good thinking, Titch.'

Billy ran off, and Titch turned her eyes to the distant pier. She fancied she could hear band music drifting in snatches over the water, which was a good sign: as long as the band was playing, the train would not depart. She wondered if she was right about the threat to the train, and if Sam – wherever he was – was also aware of the possible danger. She wished he was with her. Everything was better when they were together. Titch suddenly felt responsible for the others, responsible for saving lives. She was also very apprehensive about what they might find when they landed on the Isle of Wight.

13

WIRED

The Duke of Albion was greatly relieved when the music finally ended and the soldiers were still, their breath clearly visible in the cold air. He addressed his neighbours in impeccable German: 'Meine freunde . . . My friends . . . the moment has come for us to leave. We have to pay our respects to the Commander of the Regiment and then we may travel on to Osborne.' He got the impression he was not the only one who was looking forward to a warm fireside. The visiting dignitaries rose and made their way from their stand at the side of the parade-ground to inspect the guard – the last of their public duties before boarding the train. The Duke stole a look at his watch and congratulated himself that his arrangements were all going smoothly, to the minute.

* * *

By the time Sam rejoined Holmes, the Great Detective was on his knees. Sam stood over him.

'This is where the Doctor was hit, sir.'

'Is Prince Edward all right?'

'Bit nervous. Very excited.'

'Good. He will be unable to stop the train, of course, but it will keep him occupied, out of our way and, above all, safe.' Holmes moved nearer the tunnel mouth, walking on the rails to avoid disturbing any evidence, and indicating to Sam that he should do the same. 'There are clear signs of Watson's presence back there. As you say, that is where he was hit. What is less evident is what happened to him afterwards. This large gravel does not readily yield clues. Did De Ville name his companion, by any chance?'

'No, sir.'

'Was there sufficient light for you to observe Watson's assailant?'

'He was big. He had an axe handle.'

'Just as I feared – Reilly, one of Moriarty's men.' Holmes dropped to his knees and looked closely at the gravel. While he was thus engaged, Sam noticed something inside the tunnel. He nipped past Holmes and walked into the darkness.

'Look, sir.' Holmes raised his eyes. 'The axe handle

he used to fell Dr Watson. Here. At the base of the tunnel wall.'

'Very good. Well done.' Holmes dropped to his knees, looking carefully at the ground to one side of the rail, and crawled slowly towards Sam. 'Oil from a flashlamp, and a shard of broken glass,' he observed to himself. 'Signs of a struggle.' When he reached Sam, he stood. 'Poor Watson was dragged – certainly as far as this point. From here, where Reilly jettisoned the axe shaft, I suspect he was carried. I believe Watson is in the tunnel.'

'Do you think the cache is *in* the tunnel, as well, then?'

Holmes spoke slowly and deliberately. 'I do.' His voice was laden with meaning.

'Oh no!'

'Exactly, Sam. They aim to blow up the train. And with it, of course . . .'

Sam was suddenly aware just how important Watson was to him. 'We have to get the Doctor out before the train comes.'

Holmes again glanced at his half-hunter. 'The train must be on the point of departure, Sam. We have not a moment to lose. Come with me. Drag your hand along the tunnel wall. You take that side.'

Holmes set off into the darkness, trailing his arm along the right-hand side of the tunnel. Sam followed, taking the left. 'We must discover if our dear friend Watson is being held in this foul place.'

'It's very dark, sir.'

'Your eyes will settle, Sam, but it is, I must admit, *exceedingly* dark. Fool that I am, I have come ill prepared, but I have a few matches with me. I must use them sparingly. Forward.'

As the ferry approached the harbour, Billy, Titch and Alice caught a brief glimpse of the royal train, racing-green and gold, just as Alice had described it, gleaming and steaming in the white midday sun. Potts was in the cabin caring for Edie, who was still in a mild state of trance. As the boat came to rest at the dockside, the others were straining to be first off the ferry.

Prompted by Titch, they had convinced the captain of the ferry that Alice was indeed a princess – granddaughter to Queen Victoria. It had taken all Billy's charm but they had finally persuaded the captain that there was a potential emergency, which they might be able to prevent if they could reach the royal train before it left Ryde Station. Consequently, the first mate had been summoned to assist them, and as soon as the gangplank touched the quay, he led them to dry ground, pointing them in the direction of the station. If they ran fast enough, they might just be able to stop the train leaving. Thanking him, they raced off.

Titch was out in front, followed by Billy, who was a bit on the chubby side for sprinting, and Alice, who was running faster than she had ever run before. They left the pier and tore on to the footbridge that would take them to the station. When they reached the barrier at the head of the platform, the train was still there. They were within yards of Alice's father, but the inspector would not let them pass. They pleaded with him, but he would not allow them on to the platform. They told him who Alice was, but of course he didn't believe them. Alice started shouting to her father – she couldn't see him, but she knew he was there. She yelled at Mr Perkins, the station-master, who she could see, but it was futile. Her voice was drowned by the whistle of the engine and the grind of the wheels, as the train began to leave the station.

At Osborne House there was an air of tangible excitement as the great moment for Queen Victoria to use her lift for the first time drew nearer. Prince Edward had done his job well, and the Queen, if not exactly excited at the prospect of inaugurating this new 'gadget' as she insisted on calling it, was secretly looking forward to using it. She was feeling almost light-headed, having learned that her favourite granddaughter had at last been located. She was confident Alice would soon be rescued and surrounded by all those close to her. Tomorrow was Prince Albert Day. There would be fireworks. Prince Albert had adored fireworks, and the display commissioned in his honour was spectacular. As she sat by her bedroom fire, awaiting her daughter, the Duchess of Albion, Queen Victoria looked at the countless, ornately framed photographs of her family, which she herself had coloured, and smiled contentedly.

The station-master's attention was distracted, away from the departing train, to the trio of rowdy young children shouting at the ticket barrier. Mr Perkins did not like noise. He particularly did not like noise when the royal train was in his station. He stalked over to the barrier and was about to speak firmly to the offending youngsters when he stopped dead in his tracks.

'Princess Alice!' he exclaimed, shocked to see the Princess looking so filthy and bedraggled.

'Mr Perkins!' cried Alice. 'We're trying to stop the train.'

'Too late now, I'm afraid. But why are you here? And in such a state? I expected to see you yesterday when all the other children came through.'

'It's a long story, Mr Perkins, but we must stop the train travelling to Osborne altogether.'

Mr Perkins was confused. 'Why on earth should we want to do that, Princess Alice?'

'We think it might be in danger, don't we?' She pointed to Billy and Titch, who were nodding madly in agreement. 'This is Billy and this is Titch, and they are my friends and they rescued me because I've been kidnapped and held prisoner in a cave and you must listen to us because our friend Edie – who will be here very soon with Potts who's looking after her – had a nasty sort of a dream sort of vision thing about trains coming off rails and crowns tumbling down a hill and Potts says whenever Edie sees things like that it always happens so we've got to stop the train in case there's a terrible accident.'

Mr Perkins was a slow thinker whose life was ruled by timetables. Alice's rush of words was altogether too much for him. He didn't understand it. He didn't like it. He needed time. 'I tell you what, Princess Alice, and you two,' he said, pointing a wary finger at Billy and Titch, 'why don't we all go to my office and see if we can't come to something of an understanding there, eh?'

Princess Alice was about to start bossing Mr Perkins, but Billy intervened. 'I think that's a jolly good idea, sir. But would you mind if we went quickly because if we're right about the train, sir, there really isn't a whole lot of time.'

Mr Perkins was taken with Billy's courteous manner. He led the children along the platform to his office. 'Here we are. We'll soon have this sorted out, Miss Alice. In you go.' And in they went.

Sam and Holmes walked into the deepening darkness, testing the tunnel walls. Sam stopped suddenly and asked Holmes to wait for a moment. He dropped to the ground and laid his ear to one of the rails.

'The train is on the way, sir.'

'Very good, Sam. We must move faster. If there is to be an explosion, I would prefer to avoid it.'

'Me too, Mr Holmes,' Sam replied, groping forward as fast as he dared. 'How long have we got?'

'It is not far from Ryde to Osborne, Sam. I calculate eight to ten minutes at the most. Depending, of course, on the speed of the train.'

The gravel floor made their footing unsure. Cobwebs trailed over their faces. The pitch-dark was intimidating. Something flew at Sam and whizzed past his ear. He heard it coming, but couldn't see it. He yelped with shock.

'A bat, Sam. Never fear. They will not hit you. It is believed they navigate by sound. Quickly, onwards.'

As they felt their way deeper into the tunnel, Holmes talked. 'I wonder if that was a barbestelle bat. I would much like to see one. They are rare, but the lepidoptera of this region are peculiarly suited to them.' Sam sensed that Holmes was talking to relieve the tension. Suddenly a swarm of bats flew at them, squeaking and screaming, and disappeared up the tunnel. 'They might even be roosting in this tunnel. I wonder if they have been disturbed in some way.' The tunnel was so long that they could see no light at the far end. Sam looked back, and was alarmed to discover they had also lost sight of the light from which they had come. The precious minutes ticked by. Although their footsteps sounded loudly, Sam fancied he could hear the approaching train.

'Mr Holmes!'

'What is it, Sam?'

'I have come to a break in the brickwork.'

'Very good, Sam. I am going to light a match.'

Holmes felt his way towards Sam, who could hear the rattle of the matches in the box, the grating noise of the match on the glass paper on the side of the box, and the relief of light as the flame sputtered to life.

'Ah ha!' said Holmes keenly. 'As I expected.'

Set back in a recess in the tunnel wall was a small door. Sam ran to it. Holmes's match went out and the porous dark returned. Sam felt for the handle. The door was locked. He hammered on it.

'Ssssshhhh. Quiet now, Sam. Let us listen.'

In the deathly silence, as the echo of Holmes's voice died away, they could hear noises from behind the door, scuffling sounds, muffled cries. Holmes lit another match.

Sam looked around, and then, pointing at the floor, he yelled, 'Look, Mr Holmes. A cable. Half buried in the gravel.'

'Villains!' Holmes exclaimed angrily.

'What is it, Mr Holmes?'

'This cable runs underneath the door, Sam. It also runs the other way, towards the tunnel exit. Where, I have no doubt, Moriarty's men will be waiting with some form of detonator. This confirms our deepest fears. It is the cache. It is wired to explode as the train comes through. And I am afraid that poor Watson is locked inside. Heartless villains!'

The match went out, and in the dark, Sam could hear Holmes kicking violently at the door.

'Mr Holmes!'

'Yes?' Holmes grunted with the effort of barging at the door with his shoulder.

'I brought the axe handle. Would that be any use?'

'It might indeed, Sam. Good lad! Let me have it.'

Sam felt for Holmes's outstretched hand and gave him the axe shaft. He could hear Holmes's fingers exploring the door, searching for a thinner area of wood, a panel perhaps, where he might break through.

'Good. Good. That ought to do,' Holmes muttered to himself. He then placed his mouth to the keyhole and spoke clearly. 'If you are there, my dear Watson, kindly move away from the door.' After a few moments, Sam heard a loud crash and a splintering noise. 'Excellent!' cried Holmes. Sam could hear him kicking at the broken wood, which now began to shatter easily. In no time, Holmes created a hole, through which he held another lighted match and peered.

'Is the Doctor there, sir?'

'He is indeed, Sam. Very much the worse for wear. Have no fear, Watson!' he called. 'Sam will have you out of this accursed hole in a trice. Sam, I am going to leave you. You should be able to get through this door now. Get Watson out of here as fast as you possibly can, *and* out of the tunnel. Continue in the same direction in which we were walking – away from Ryde – it will give you a few more precious seconds in which to reach safety.' Sam was already scrambling through the hole in the door. Fumblingly, Holmes handed him the matchbox. 'Here. There is only one match left. You have more need of it than I. I am going to follow this cable, and see if I can prevent the explosion altogether. If only I was not in this wretched disguise, I would have my penknife with me, and we could put Watson out of danger instantly. Goodbye, Sam. Give the Doctor my regards.'

As Sam tended Watson, trussed up in the dark, he could hear Holmes moving off hurriedly along the tunnel.

Reilly sat in the small copse overlooking the tunnel, humiliated and nervous. O'Hare had cowed him into a brooding silence. The plunger that would detonate the arms cache, obliterating the train, its passengers and Dr Watson, sat between them. They looked down at the tranquil scene below. The grass was green, a few sheep grazed idly, the railway line meandered reassuringly towards Osborne.

'O'Hare?'

O'Hare breathed in, suppressing his anger. 'Yes, Reilly?'

'Do you think the kid will come back for the Doctor?'

'There's been no sign of him,' O'Hare replied, trying to shut Reilly up. He was successful for some minutes. Then . . .

'O'Hare?'

'Keep your mouth shut, Reilly. The lift is wired. It'll blow up when the Queen reaches the ground floor. The tunnel is wired. The train will come. You will call the signal. I will press the plunger.' He eyed his companion wearily. 'All right?'

'Yes.' But Reilly remained anxious. 'How does the plunger work?'

O'Hare was near the end of his tether. 'I pull the T-bar right out of the casing, all right? Then, in order to blow the cache, I press it back down again.'

'I see,' Reilly said slowly, rubbing his brow, still perplexed.

'There will be a large explosion, Reilly. In the carnage and the chaos, we shall leave. A boat is waiting. All right?'

Reilly nodded sullenly. Several moments passed. He scratched his head. 'O'Hare.'

O'Hare glared at him, awaiting the fast-approaching moment of destruction with relish. He pictured, not the rural idyll that lay below them, but the volcanic carnage of the explosion – the earth erupting upwards, mingling with bits of iron, steel, and the bodies of the nobility that he so hated.

'I think about things, O'Hare. And I get agitated.'

'Reilly. The lift will be going off real soon. Listen out for it.' He looked at his watch. 'The train has just left Ryde. Lucky for us they are such clock-watchers. Any minute, you can take your place, ready to give me the signal. Till then shut up. All right?'

Reilly was silent again, but he was still agitated, troubled by the thought that the explosion they were about to trigger would change the world as they knew it for ever.

14

THREE – TWO – ONE ...

Sam was so relieved to have found Watson, he flung his arms around him. He then put all his effort into removing the gag, which had been tied savagely tight. When it finally came away, the poor Doctor was barely able to speak.

'Sam. Sam, dear boy,' he gasped. Quite apart from the horrors of the freezing black night, when he had heard Holmes's voice, and seen Spooner's ghostly face by the light of a match, he thought he was losing his mind.

'Quick, Doctor! We have to hurry.' Sam wrestled with the ropes at Watson's wrists.

'Sam. Dear Sam,' was all Watson could utter through his parched, bruised lips. 'How good to see you. That man who was here reminded me of Holmes.'

'It *was* Mr Holmes,' Sam shouted.

Watson was in too much of a daze to cope with this information, but when his hands were free, Sam urged him to work fast, and untie his heavily bound feet, while he endeavoured to increase the size of the getaway hole in the door. It was nightmarish for both of them, working in the dark. Sam explained, between violent attacks on the door with the axe shaft, that Holmes was alive and in disguise as part of his plan to foil Moriarty. He strove to convince Watson of the absolute need to get out of the cache. When the Doctor was able to move, Sam used up the last of his matches. Taking care that no stray sparks should go near the dynamite, he showed Watson the hole in the door. Sam then scrambled through.

'Come on, sir! Give me your hand.' Watson struggled to get through. Sam was yelling, 'Come on, Doctor! Mr Holmes is afraid that this dynamite cache will be blown as the train comes through the tunnel! And the train,' he screamed, 'IS ON ITS WAY.'

Watson was stunned and physically stiff, but he at last understood the reason for Sam's desperation, and managed to squeeze through the hole. Sam grasped the Doctor's hand, wrenched him to his feet and dragged him, stumbling, up the line towards the tunnel mouth.

* * *

Mr Perkins was not used to having three frenzied children in his office. The station-master found it very hard indeed to believe their story of royal sabotage. What he could not quite dismiss was the presence of Princess Alice. He was very proud of his association with the royal family, and although the two children with Alice looked most unlikely companions, he was extremely impressed with the Princess. Billy and Titch were amazed by her dramatic gifts. She begged, she pleaded, she flung herself at Mr Perkins's knees. She positively battered him with her story, and she did not give up until Mr Perkins agreed to help.

Mr Perkins duly summoned Giles, the driver of the station gig, and ordered him to prepare his horse instantly in order to pursue the train. The gig was brought up and the four of them jumped on board. Alice sat beside Giles. Titch and Billy squashed into the back seat, on either side of Mr Perkins. Off they set after the train – they could still see smoke rising from its funnel in the distance.

'Faster, Giles! Faster!' cried Alice, leaping up and down.

'Careful, Alice,' said Billy. 'Hang on to her, Titch.'

Titch leaned forward and took Alice's arm. 'Sit down, Alice.'

Alice sat, but did not stop bullying the driver. 'Faster, Giles!' she insisted.

'I can't *go* no faster than this Miss Alice,' Giles replied. 'Old horse be doing his best!'

'Well, it's not good enough!' Alice shouted regally.

Giles whipped the poor horse, who was quite unaccustomed to such demands for speed, and the gig clattered off along the road faster than ever before.

'We are going the wrong way,' Alice pointed out, tapping the driver on his shoulder.

'Don't worry, Miss Alice,' Giles replied, trying to remain calm, 'the road do bend round, and then us do run alongside the track till us do reach the tunnel. Then the road do veer off towards Osborne.'

At mention of the tunnel, Billy and Titch exchanged glances. 'It's the tunnel we need to get to, Mr Perkins, before the train,' said Billy.

'Why?'

'We think the danger is in the tunnel.'

'Shall we make it?' asked Titch.

'Well, going at this sort of speed,' called Mr Perkins, holding on to his top hat, 'I think we might.'

'Faster,' cried Alice. 'Faster!'

* * *

On board the train, the Duke of Albion made sure that all the dignitaries had rugs to help them shake off the cold of the parade ground. For those who wanted it, there was a warming glass of brandy. The train was cosy and chugged along merrily. They were all anticipating the comforts of Osborne, until there was a rather surprising shriek of brakes. The train skidded to a halt. In his many journeys to Osborne, the Duke had never known this to happen. Bags lurched off overhead racks, brandy slurped out of glasses, suitcases slithered from under seats. Alarmed, the Duke lowered the window in order to discover the cause of their delay.

Everyone was equally concerned. 'What is the problem?'

Leaning out of the window, the Duke was relieved to discover that it was nothing serious. Pulling on the leather strap to close the window, he turned to the anxious faces within, smiled and said, 'Sheep.'

'What?! What is "sheep"?'

'I'm sorry, but there are sheep on the line – baaa – schafe – sheep.'

'Ah! Schafe! How do you say? Sheeps?'

'Sheep. I apologise, but it is not serious and we shall be moving again very shortly.'

Good humour soon reasserted itself, glasses were

replenished and rugs retucked while the offending sheep were removed from the line.

'Not long,' the Duke called. 'Very soon we shall be on our way to Osborne. And I should warn anyone afraid of the dark – just before we arrive at Osborne, we shall come to a tunnel where, for a brief period, everything will go black.'

Prince Edward waited on the railway bank for the train to come. He jumped up and down to keep warm. He could see smoke from the engine, and ran into the middle of the line to see why it was not getting any closer. He was rather fed up that it didn't seem to be moving. Shoving his hands deep in his pockets, he stomped back to the stick with the hanky on that Sam had rigged up for him. As he strolled up the bank, kicking idly at the grass, he was surprised to see one of the men who had worked on the lift at Osborne coming towards him.

'Hallo!' he called happily, waving. 'What are you doing here?'

'What in the devil's name are *you* doing here?' countered Reilly, breaking into a run.

The Prince sensed from Reilly's aggressive response that it would not be an altogether brilliant idea to tell him the truth. 'Oh. I often come down here for a bit of fun,' he said backing away, 'and the train will be arriving soon, so I thought I'd come and wave at all my uncles and aunties . . .'

'Give me that stick.'

'I'd rather not actually, if you don't mind, Mr . . . I'm sorry I don't know your name,' said the young Prince, keeping a healthy distance between himself and Reilly.

'You don't need to.' Reilly lunged at the stick.

The Prince whipped it out of his way. He was now quite certain that whatever this man was doing, it would be wise to avoid him. Reilly advanced on him. The Prince turned and broke into a run. After sprinting as fast as he could for about half a minute, he stopped and looked back. The man was holding a gun, cursing and fuming, kicking the ground angrily.

'I knew something would go wrong,' he was shouting. 'I knew it.' Suddenly, with a howl of frustration he hurled the revolver into the trees. The Prince could not begin to understand why he had thrown his weapon away, or why he had not followed him, but his instinct told him to keep running, that it would be sensible to put as much distance as possible between himself and the big angry man with the red hair.

As his legs pounded away, his mind was working fast. He remembered that Mr Spooner had advised him to get away from the tunnel if he failed to stop the train. He was already running towards Ryde, and he calculated that if he continued to run in that direction, he would make himself safer *and* meet the train earlier. He considered this to be a very sensible course of action, and he was beginning to enjoy this unfamiliar feeling of being sensible.

When Sam and Watson tottered out of the tunnel, blinking in the sun, their eyes were immediately drawn to a cable which Holmes had unearthed, lying on the ground. It snaked up to the top of the slope where, by a copse, they could see two figures grappling. Sam recognised Mr Spooner as one of them.

'That's Mr Holmes, Doctor,' Sam yelled, 'with the humpy back.'

The poor Doctor was still reeling from lack of food and drink, and the daylight was such a shock to him after his night in the cache that his eyes actually hurt. It took him a moment to piece things together. 'Holmes?' he asked, peering at the two fighting men. When he realised what Sam meant, he jumped high off the ground, yelling, 'Holmes! Holmes!'

Holmes was an expert in martial arts, but he had met his match on this occasion. O'Hare lacked skill, but he was brutally strong, and he was wielding the branch of a tree.

'Do you have your revolver, Doctor?' Sam enquired.

'I am afraid not, Sam. It was taken from me. But quick. Let us assist poor Holmes.'

This, Sam realised, was why he so adored Watson – he was a man of unquestioning, undying loyalty. With no thought for his own wretched condition or safety, he staggered off up the slope to assist his friend, Holmes. Sam easily overtook him.

The sight of Sam and Watson running up the slope caught O'Hare's eye, and while he was thus distracted, Holmes got in a sharp kick to the ribs that winded him. Enraged, he swung his branch wildly and caught Holmes a nasty glancing blow. Holmes went down, gripping his head.

'Fear not, Holmes!' cried Watson. 'Help is at hand.'

Sam reached O'Hare. Dodging the flailing branch, he grabbed the Irishman by the leg. Holmes dragged himself to his feet, and struggled to disarm him. By the time Watson joined them, Holmes and Sam were gaining the upper hand. Weak from his miserable night, Watson was precious little help, but it was he who saw the train approaching.

'Look, Holmes! The train!' he cried.

Holmes turned. Sam looked. Spurred on by the prospect of failure, O'Hare shrugged them off with a mighty yell and ran towards the plunger concealed in the copse.

With the train underway again, the Duke was comfortably settled in his seat. His mind filled with memories of his daughter, Princess Alice – as a tiny baby, taking her first steps in the Long Gallery at the palace, the feel of her glorious silky hair, playing with the Queen's doll's house – his last image of her before she had been so cruelly plucked from their home. That was less than two weeks ago, but it seemed like a lifetime.

The Prince of Saxe-Coburg, sitting facing the Duke, touched him on the knee and asked him if he would like to see Princess Alice. The Prince's question caught the Duke off guard, preoccupied as he was with thoughts of Alice. He was unsure how to answer. 'I am afraid,' he said, 'that I have not seen Alice for some days.'

'Ya,' replied the Prince, 'I am knowing this, but what I ask is, would you like *now* to see her? Yes?'

Still confused, the Duke said, 'I would like more than anything in the world to see Alice now.'

'Then would you out of the window please look?'

The Duke had a strange feeling that something was being lost in the translation. How could he possibly see Alice through the train window? However, out of politeness, he looked. To his astonishment, there she was!

She was standing next to the driver of a pony and trap, which also contained two scruffy children and Mr Perkins, the station-master. Alice's beautiful white dress was filthy, her golden hair was greasy and lank, and she badly needed scrubbing. But it was undeniably Alice. She was leaping up and down, held by the smaller of the two urchins, and she was yelling in a most un-princess-like manner. The Duke let the window down, allowing a gust of cold air and smoke into the carriage, and leaned out to wave. Alice was shouting still – as were the other children – but there was too much noise from the engine, and the thunder of the wheels, for the Duke to hear what she was saying. He was overcome with relief to know that she was alive and free, and clearly unharmed, but this glimpse of his daughter was fleeting. As the train drew slowly away from its sheep stop, the gig had pulled up level, but as the engine picked up speed, the gig could not compete. So no sooner had the Duke seen Alice, than she was taken from him, as the gig lost ground against the accelerating train.

The Duke did not allow the frustrations or seeming madness of the moment to worry him. He had seen Alice. They would soon be united. The train was nearing Osborne, so was the gig. Mr Perkins was the soul of reliability. What, thought the Duke, could possibly go wrong? He closed the window and resumed his seat. The Prince and his wife were about to enquire what was going on, when suddenly, the Duke jumped up again, rushed to the window and reopened it.

'What on this earth is happening?' cried the Prince, confused.

The Duke was leaning out of the window again, waving and calling loudly, 'What is it? What is it?!'

The Prince of Saxe-Coburg could see that the Duke was addressing a young boy brandishing a stick with a white hanky on. He was flailing the stick frantically, and yelling inaudibly. Like the fleeting vision of Alice, this unusual image shot swiftly by the carriage window. The Duke turned and addressed the Prince gravely.

'I don't know what is going on,' he said, 'but I think I must try and stop the train.'

'How? You are having no means of access to the engine.'

'Perhaps there is a blockage further up the line,' mused the Duke. 'Maybe the tunnel has caved in . . .'

'Unless you are using the roof!'

'The roof. Of course. I must try.' Again the Duke released the window strap and a further blast of freezing air, mingled with smoke and soot, burst into the carriage.

'Is this being totally necessary, my dear sir?'

'Why else would they be trying so desperately to capture our attention?'

'Indeed, ya. Why else?'

The Duke, with his body facing the carriage, struggled out of the window. The Prince wanted to help, but could not see how. He could see the Duke's legs, thrashing wildly for some fixed point of contact. He grabbed a flailing foot, held it firmly to the side of the window and supported it from below.

The Prince just heard the Duke's cry of 'Thank you!' The last thing he saw was the Duke's legs disappearing upwards.

'Papa! Papa!' screamed Alice, stunned by the sight of her father climbing on to the roof of the train. The gig

– having lost the chase – was trotting along the road by the side of the railway line at a steady pace, but Titch was still holding on to Alice, who was quite beside herself, leaping up and down, shouting and crying. She was inconsolable; indeed, they were all alarmed by the sight of the Duke slithering along the train roof, crawling slowly towards the engine, battered by freezing winds, smoke and steam. At precisely the same moment, everyone in the gig realised he was in great danger. They could see the tunnel.

'Noooo!' cried Alice. 'Papa!'

'Stone me!' said Titch. 'He's going to be—'

'Wow!' yelled Billy, grabbing Titch's arm. 'I hope he isn't—'

The driver stopped the gig. They all stared in horror. The train sped towards the tunnel.

'Oh dear,' said Mr Perkins, under his breath. 'Oh dear.'

The Duchess of Albion collected Queen Victoria from Her Majesty's bedroom suite. They walked arm in arm along the landing to the new lift. It had been designed with great discretion so that it looked to all appearances like a large cupboard.

The Queen glanced over her shoulder. 'Just look at

the Grand Staircase, my dear – so perfectly proportioned. I shall use it for going *down*stairs. How does one make an entrance from a lift?'

A waiting servant opened the lift doors to reveal a criss-cross grille which barred access to the lift itself, although through it the Duchess was pleased to see that it had been superbly appointed in red and gold, with a fine Persian carpet and an ornate mirror. There was even an upright chair for the Queen to use if she so desired. The grille was drawn back. The Queen and her daughter entered, somewhat tentatively – it was unfamiliar to them and they were nervous of it. The Queen nodded to the servant, who joined them, and was on the point of closing the outer door when Princess Eleanor ran up.

'Mummy.'

'Yes, dearest,' replied the Duchess. 'I thought you were downstairs with nanny.'

'May I come with you?'

'Mama,' the Duchess asked, 'would you mind if Eleanor was to join us?'

The Queen did not in the least object, and Eleanor tiptoed into the lift. 'Before we descend,' the Queen enquired, 'are we absolutely sure that the official photographer is ready? I do not wish to waste my time repeating this journey for the sake of the camera, always assuming we get down at all!'

'Yes, Mama. I had my maid check before I came to fetch you. Everyone is there. Many of the staff, and all the children – except Eleanor of course.'

Eleanor snuggled close to her mother.

'Mind the doors,' said the Duchess. 'It is time, Mama. Shall we go?'

The Queen smiled and nodded. The servant closed the lift door, then pulled the grille across. The Duchess indicated that he might press the button marked G for Ground Floor. With a slight judder, the lift began slowly to descend.

Strict instructions had been given to the manufacturers that it should not alarm the Queen by its speed. To Her Majesty, it seemed to be taking a lifetime, inching down interminably slowly.

'It would be quicker for even me to walk,' she remarked tartly.

'But the real benefits, Mama, will be on the way *up* stairs,' said the Duchess sweetly.

'That,' replied the Queen, 'I cannot deny.'

'And should you ever wish to visit the viewing room on the sixth floor . . .' The Duchess smiled. 'How are you, Eleanor, my dear?'

'Rather bored,' Eleanor commented shyly. 'It's a bit disappointing. I keep waiting for something to happen.'

'The speed can be adjusted,' said the footman. 'We shall soon be there now.'

Gradually, the lift neared its destination.

O'Hare had not expected to be interrupted, so he had not prepared the plunger. His first task therefore, having temporarily beaten off his attackers, was to draw the T-bar out, ready for the imminent arrival of the train. With Holmes and Sam bearing down hard on him, he stopped, picked up another shorter branch, and assaulted Holmes violently – if he could get rid of the adult, the kid would be no problem. The Doctor was still too feeble – and too far away – to be of any concern.

Sam again grabbed one of O'Hare's legs, and hung on tight. Holmes kept just outside O'Hare's range, as the enraged Irishman thrashed out at him with his branch. O'Hare couldn't get near enough to Holmes, because Sam's hold on his leg restricted him, so the Irishman whacked the boy hard on the neck and shoulders. Sam yelped, and almost lost grip. Holmes used this moment to try and get closer, but O'Hare was fast, and as Holmes closed on him, O'Hare delivered another blow to the side of Holmes's head – a fierce upwards blow – and Holmes, already weakened by the first colossal strike, went down again. O'Hare kicked Sam off and made a dash for the plunger, a few yards away. Holmes was groggy, and Watson had only just caught up with them.

Looking back over his shoulder, Sam could see that the train was on the point of entering the tunnel. O'Hare was standing over the plunger, and with ghoulish glee he drew the T-bar out from its base. Sam was unsure what to do. And he knew he only had seconds.

'Wiggins!' called Holmes. 'Stop him pushing down the plunger. Understand? The plunger!'

'Alice!' Prince Edward ran up to the gig yelling joyously. 'Alice!!'

'Duffer!' she replied, delighted to see her favourite cousin bounding towards them. 'Eddie, this is Billy and this is Titch and – look!' Alice pointed at the train.

Before the young Prince was able to welcome Alice back from the horrors of her kidnap, they all stood together, watching the train. The Duke was still crawling along the carriage roof towards the engine.

They could dimly hear his cries of 'Stop! Stop the train!', but the engine driver and fireman, intent on making up time lost to the sheep, were piling on coal, and unable to hear.

'UNCLE!' yelled Prince Edward.

'PapAAAAA!' screamed Alice. They all held their breath as the engine entered the tunnel. They were afraid they were going to see the Duke scraped off the top of the train, but he lay as flat as was humanly possible and, miraculously, disappeared into the tunnel in one piece.

They breathed a huge collective sigh of relief.

'Hallo, everybody! I'm Alice's cousin – Edward.' The Prince grinned infectiously. 'Welcome back, Alice! This is the most brilliant hol' ever. You're going to have oodles of fun!'

In his headquarters, Professor Moriarty's telescope was directed at the tunnel. He watched the train disappear, and as it sped towards the cache, he smiled, a thin evil smile. He spoke quietly to the man with him without removing his eye from the lens. 'Well, De Ville . . .'

'Yes, Professor?'

'We are on the brink of success.'

De Ville rarely heard the Professor sound pleased. In

response, he drew deeply on his cigar, and regarded the Professor with a look of discreet content. The gold on his front teeth glinted.

O'Hare stood poised with the plunger raised. In the distance, Reilly's cry signalled that the train had entered the tunnel. O'Hare was holding Sam at bay and counting gleefully – he only had to hold out for ten seconds before the train reached the cache.

'Ten – nine – eight . . .'

Sam feinted and dodged and got a bit nearer.

'Seven – six – five . . .'

Watson helped Holmes to his feet and together they approached. 'Do not do it!' they cried. 'Have pity!'

'Four . . .' O'Hare began laughing maniacally, 'Ha ha . . .'

Sam was desperate. He leaped in close but was obliged to jump away again to avoid the flailing branch.

'Three . . . ha!'

Sam did not see how he could get close enough to O'Hare to prevent him pressing down the plunger, but as he jumped back, he tripped on the cable which Holmes had uncovered. His fingers scrabbled at the cold earth and he managed to release enough cable to hold.

'TWO!' cried O'Hare in an ecstasy of glee and fury. 'Ha HAAA!' He leaned down hard on the plunger with one hand, using the stick to keep Sam, Holmes and Watson at bay with the other.

'OOOOooone!'

Sam tugged hard on the cable. It snagged under the freezing ground where it had been buried, and for a moment Sam feared he was too late, but it suddenly snapped free, and Sam was able to yank the plunger from under O'Hare as he shouted 'Conta-a-act!' O'Hare brought his full weight to bear on the T-bar as the plunger was whisked from beneath him. His cry was cut short, and he collapsed idiotically amidst a flurry of furious curses. He jumped to his feet – still holding the T-bar – screaming, 'I'll kill those royal swine!' – and set the plunger upright again, determined to detonate the explosives cache.

Sam, thinking he had prevented O'Hare blowing up the cache, let go of the cable and latched on to O'Hare's leg again. Sam could not see, but Holmes and Watson witnessed helplessly as O'Hare steadied himself with crazed determination against Sam's attempts to pull him down. Leaning forward on the plunger, he rammed it viciously back into its case, igniting the dynamite in the cache.

They all knew he had been successful because the earth started to tremble. It grew into a vast subterranean rumble, like an earthquake. Everyone felt it – Sam, Holmes, Watson and O'Hare himself. They stared in disbelief as the ground shifted beneath them. Reilly, who was cowering at the edge of the forest, felt it. Everyone in the gig felt it. And so did the occupants of the juddering lift in far-off Osborne House, who thought, for a moment, that something had gone wrong with the machinery. The footman offered to support the Queen, who grabbed the handrail and held on to it firmly. Princess Eleanor grasped her mother's dress. The Queen turned to the Duchess in alarm. The Duchess returned her look of concern. The four of them stood frozen with fear, as the lift, to the sound of distant thunder, finally came to rest on the ground floor.

15

SKY HIGH

There was an enormous muffled roar. The ground over the tunnel began to change shape as the crust of the earth seemed to crack, lines appearing in the grass. There was a pause, as if nothing more was going to occur. Then the ground above the tunnel from where the explosion came, dropped for a second, before a violent volcanic eruption spewed pieces of grass and soil high into the air, accompanied by an ear-splitting boom. It echoed and re-echoed as out of the bowels of the earth flames spouted. What had been the tunnel appeared an inferno, belching forth huge gobbets of soil, brick and metal. The ground heaved and fumed and spat. Even O'Hare was surprised by the scale of it, laughing madly as smoke billowed from the vast roaring trench that opened up before them. As he stood watching his masterpiece with an expression of

infantile wonder on his face, Holmes came up behind him and felled him with a huge blow from the discarded branch. Holmes was angry at the chaos, and he vented his fury on the perpetrator.

Below their feet, the earth began to settle, but from above fell debris of all kinds, hissing out of the blackened sky like filthy red-hot rain. Slowly, the hillside re-formed. What had been the tunnel bubbled and burped. From the epicentre of the explosion spurted blue and yellow jets of fire, with an attendant smell – a nauseating combination of sulphur and cordite, oil, soot and gas.

Nothing had stopped the train – not Prince Edward, not Princess Alice, not the Duke – but the noise of the monstrous blast behind them reached even the ears of the engine driver. People sat in their carriages paralysed with shock as the train screeched to a halt. The Duke vaulted from the carriage roof, and watched in amazement as divots of soil and lumps of brick and metal rained down around him. He covered his head with his hands, looked back at the carnage and wondered how on earth they had possibly survived. He calculated that the rear of the train had cleared the tunnel just as the explosion occurred. They had avoided death by seconds.

As the smoke drifted away, it revealed a disordered mountain. Twisting upwards out of the mangled heap of soil, brick and metal were the railway lines, sticking up like straws out of a glass. Bizarrely, as the land resumed something of its normal shape, he could see a long indentation – the shape of what had been the tunnel – running, like a glacier of seething mud, through what had been the hillside.

The sound of the explosion died away. The only noise to break the stillness was the bubble and hiss of the tunnel remains – echoed strangely by the puffing of the stationary train, which, like the earth, seemed almost to breathe. A wounded sheep tottered drunkenly about, dazed and bleeding. Gradually, people returned to their senses.

Reilly's worst fears had been confirmed. It had gone wrong. He could not make out much now through the drifting smoke, but he had seen the engine emerge from the far end of the tunnel before O'Hare pressed the plunger. He had no idea what had delayed O'Hare, but he had no wish to go to the aid of the man who had put him down, and whose foolish overconfidence had, in his view, led to the failure of the tunnel bomb. Reilly had worked himself to a standstill getting all the dynamite there, and his efforts had been wasted.

Furious, Reilly stood by the edge of the trees and considered his options. He regretted having thrown Watson's revolver away, and began to search for it. With the gun, he would make for the south of the island and take the getaway boat for himself. Damn O'Hare.

Reilly staggered through the trees looking for the weapon, cursing himself for not having hung on to it, wondering why he had heard only one explosion. Perhaps the dynamite O'Hare had wired to the lift had exploded at the same time as the cache, which was why Reilly had not heard it. Perhaps it had not gone off at all. Reilly reached the area where he thought the gun had landed and crawled about, examining the ground closely. He was searching like this when a voice surprised him.

'Is this what you are looking for?'

He looked up, startled, and there to his amazement were two boys. He recognised Prince Edward, but who the chubby kid holding the gun was, he had no idea. It didn't matter: the boy was holding Watson's gun, and aiming it straight at him.

'Give that to me,' he said, rising and advancing threateningly towards the kid.

'I don't think so,' said Billy backing away, clinging to the heavy gun and keeping it aimed at Reilly.

Reilly stopped. 'You wouldn't use that thing, boy.'

'Not unless you forced me to.'

'Don't be daft. You're a kid.'

Prince Edward didn't trust Reilly. 'Watch him, Billy! He'll try and get it off you!' he cried, leaping up and down in a frenzy. 'Billy!'

The Prince was right. Reilly lunged at Billy, who eluded him, warning him again, 'I *will* shoot, mister.'

'You won't shoot, Billy,' said Reilly calmly. 'You don't know how to use a gun properly. You're too young.'

'You're wrong,' Billy replied sagely. 'I have used this gun before. The man it belongs to showed me.'

'Ha!' Reilly sneered. 'You won't be seeing him again, fatso!'

'Why not?' asked Billy, confused and hurt.

'He went up sky high with the arms cache.'

'What?'

'Interfering swine!' cried Reilly, lunging at the gun again. 'I could see bits of him coming down out of the sky!' he taunted.

Billy turned white.

'Watch him, Billy!' cried Prince Edward. 'He's too close.' The Prince was excited but scared. Trying to be sensible, he recognised that the stakes were getting dangerously high.

'If you've killed Dr Watson,' Billy stammered, 'it would be all right for me to kill you. And with *his* gun.' Holding the gun firmly in both hands, he shook it boldly at Reilly. 'It would be justice!'

Reilly laughed openly at Billy's attempts at manliness. As he manoeuvred his way subtly closer to the gun, Reilly pointed at Prince Edward. 'Something you don't know is that your grandmother – and anyone else near that stupid lift at Osborne House – has also been blown to bits.'

'What do you mean?' Edward enquired earnestly.

Reilly no longer threatened; he stood still for a second, affecting sympathy. 'The lift was wired, like the tunnel.' Edward gulped. 'Aah. Poor little Prince. Lost his dear old gran, eh?'

Reilly was gaining the upper hand. He had bewildered both boys. The Prince was coming to terms with the possible murder of his grandmother, and Billy was stunned by the news of Watson's death. His head reeling, his concentration on the gun wavered. Reilly pounced. Instinctively, Billy fired. The gun went off with a huge flash. The sound echoed through the trees. The kickback flung Billy on to his back, where he lay, dazed, expecting Reilly to jump on him, grab the revolver and shoot him. But nothing happened. Cautiously Billy raised himself on to one elbow to see what Reilly was doing.

The Prince helped Billy to his feet, and the pair of them gaped at Reilly's prostrate form.

'You got him, Billy. You got him! You fired the gun!'

'I did. Wow! I really did. Have I killed him?'

They peered closely. 'He's moving.'

Reilly lay there, blood oozing from his ankle. Billy circled him, keeping his distance.

Reilly opened his eyes and glared at Billy. 'You swine,' he breathed, his brow furrowed with pain. 'You fat swine. I'll kill you. Fatso.' He began struggling towards Billy, but the wound was too much for him. He gave up, yelled with fury and beat the ground with his fists.

'Prince Edward,' said Billy, 'I'll stay here and take care of this bloke, if you go and get help. All right?'

'Oh, yes. Oh definitely yes. I'll go and get help,' said the Prince. But he didn't move. He couldn't tear his eyes from the whining, bleeding figure of Reilly.

'Off you go then,' said Billy.

'What?'

'Off you go.'

'Oh yes. Sorry. Bye then.' He set off through the trees, looking back frequently to see if Billy was safe. He ran in the direction of Osborne House, worrying about his grandmother.

Billy kept the gun trained on Reilly. He knelt down, several yards away, and spoke coldly. 'By the way, mister, if you call me fat again, I'll shoot your *other* ankle. Do you hear? I'm not fat, I've got big bones. Understand?'

Reilly groaned.

'Understand?' said Billy firmly.

Reilly nodded.

'Good.'

Billy smiled.

Using the cable from the plunger, Holmes lashed O'Hare's wrists behind his back. O'Hare lay cursing fitfully. Watson looked on as Holmes put his foot to the knot and pulled it tight.

'You are very lucky to be alive, my dear Watson. I cannot tell you how glad I am to see you in one piece.'

Watson was still dazed by his fearful night in the cache, and the scale of the explosion which he had so narrowly avoided. 'I can't believe I'm seeing you at all, Holmes.' He shook his head in amazement.

Sam was concerned. 'Are you all right, Doctor?'

Watson put his hand on Sam's head. 'Well, thanks to you, Sam – and to Holmes of course – I'm still here, but I confess I am a trifle shaken.'

Holmes was in a hurry to get on. 'Sam, I want you to run to Osborne House and bring the security guards back here as fast as you can.'

'Now, sir?'

'Immediately. For this villain.' He indicated O'Hare, lashed and semiconscious. 'Watson and I have business to attend to.'

'Business, Holmes?'

'We must get to the mainland as fast as we can. Moriarty and De Ville will assume their vile plot has been successful, and we may just catch them. On your way, Sam.'

'Right, Mr Holmes, I'll be off. Goodbye, Doctor.'

'Goodbye, Sam. And thank you again for saving my life. Go on, do as Holmes asks. I'll see you later.'

Somewhat reluctantly, Sam began making his way towards Osborne.

Holmes turned to Watson. 'Well, Watson, are you up to it?'

'I am not harmed, Holmes, but I *am* suffering from shock. I am also somewhat dirty, and desperate for something to eat and drink.'

'We cannot let the way we look prevent us from acting, Watson. Look at me! A fright in this idiotic disguise! We shall brush you down as we go. We shall get food and drink at the pier-head. I had the foresight to leave an overnight bag, containing my own clothes and some nourishment of a sort, with the station-master. Time is not on our side. We must take the first available ferry to the mainland. First I shall speak to the Duke – who I see below on what remains of terra firma – and we shall leave instantly.' So saying, he strode down through the rubble in the direction of the stationary train.

As Watson dusted himself down, he watched Holmes speaking to the Duke of Albion. The Great Detective then poked his head into a couple of the carriages, seemingly to reassure people that they were now safe. He bounded back to Watson as though he had not a care in the world.

'All right, Watson?' Before the Doctor had time to reply, Holmes was on his way. 'Time to leave,' he cried. 'The game is afoot!'

As Sam neared Osborne House, he saw Prince Edward in front of him.

'Eddie!' he called. 'Eddie!'

Like Sam, the Prince was running as hard as he could, and didn't hear.

'DUFFER!' yelled Sam.

The Prince looked back and saw Sam haring towards him.

'Hi! Sam! Where are you going?'

'I have to find the security guards.'

'Mr Wickham? He's a chum of mine. I'm looking for him, too.'

'Are you all right, Eddie?'

'Yes, but what about that bang, eh?'

'What about it?!! Show me where we have to go.'

As they ran, they exchanged stories.

Skirting the fallout from the explosion, Holmes and Watson saw the station gig. In it, Mr Perkins sat unmoving, stunned. He and the driver were contemplating the damaged hillside and the extended crater below them. The poor horse was still quivering with shock. Giles was giving him lumps of sugar to soothe his shattered nerves.

'This is most fortunate, Watson,' cried Holmes, advancing towards the station-master. 'Mr Perkins! What, pray, are you doing here? This is well out of your way!'

'Who are you, sir?' replied Mr Perkins, coming very slowly to life.

'I met you at the station with the Queen but a few days ago, Mr Perkins. I left a valise with you for safe-keeping. My name is Spooner! Do you not recall?'

'No, Mr Spooner, I regret to say, in my present state, I do not recall.'

Holmes persevered. 'Never mind, Mr Perkins, I would be most grateful if you and your driver could escort myself and this good gentleman –' he nodded at Watson, who was still some way off, '– back to your station. We must take the ferry to the mainland on a matter of national urgency.'

'I'm afraid that will not be possible, sir. I am responsible for those two young persons down there.' He looked in the direction of two children negotiating their way round the end of the tunnel remains.

'Ah!' cried Holmes. 'I recognise the lad in shorts.' Addressing Mr Perkins, he added, 'The young lady is, of course, Princess Alice?'

'It is indeed,' said Mr Perkins.

'I hoped as much.' Holmes smiled at Watson, who had finally caught up with him. He pointed at the carefree figure of a young girl in a torn, dirty white dress, jumping over the smoking ruins of the tunnel, helped by Titch.

'Titch,' said Watson under his breath. '*And* Princess Alice. How wonderful.'

'They are looking for the Princess's father,' Mr Perkins continued, 'who was in . . . I should say . . . *on* the train.'

'This is very good news indeed,' said Holmes. Looking again at Titch and Princess Alice, he remarked, 'Well done, the Irregulars. Mr Perkins. I have just spoken to Princess Alice's father. He is alive and well, and she will encounter him in a few minutes, with everybody else on the train. They all survived safely. If your mind is at rest on that matter, may I ask you now to convey myself and Dr Watson to Ryde with all possible speed?'

Mr Perkins remained unmoved by Holmes's request.

'Mr Perkins,' said Holmes, a touch of steel entering his voice, 'if we make haste, it is remotely possible that we shall apprehend the evil man behind Alice's kidnap, this fearful explosion, and indeed, an entirely separate assassination attempt on the life of the Queen, which I am happy to say I foiled personally! I would not like to hold you in any way responsible for our failure to capture the criminal mastermind of our age.'

The force of Holmes's demand was not lost on Mr Perkins. Turning to the driver, who was equally stunned by Holmes's outburst, he asked, 'What do you think, Giles?'

The driver tore his astonished eyes away from Holmes, looked up at Mr Perkins and said, 'I do think it be time to go home anyway, Mr Perkins. Us can accommodate these two gentlemen, don't you think?'

'Excellent!' cried Holmes. 'Thank you, Giles. Jump up, Watson!'

Unaware that they had been spotted by Holmes and Watson, Titch and Princess Alice worked their way carefully round the base of the collapsed tunnel. Lower down the hillside, the ground was unaffected by the blast and they ran quickly round, and over, scattered debris, towards the stationary train which was puffing gently in the distance. Hopping on to, and over, a mound of brickwork, Alice commented, 'I hope Papa is all right. If he was hit by stuff like this, he will have a frightful headache.'

'Ay,' Titch agreed wryly, amused by Alice's directness. 'He'll be fine.'

They ran, jumped and dodged their way to the train. As they approached, up the hill, their progress was hampered by broken sleepers and stones. They could not see any passengers, and realised that they had all gathered on the other side of the train. Edging their way across the rails, they were about to emerge into full view when Alice suddenly became nervous, aware of the mess she was in.

'Titch,' she said. 'I'm a bit scared. Papa might be cross with me.'

'Cross?'

'For having disappeared.'

'You didn't disappear, Alice, you were kidnapped.'

'I know. But I look such a fright.'

Alice had displayed real excitement, seeing her father on top of the train, and Titch was surprised that she was now overcome with nerves at the prospect of coming face to face with him.

'Don't fret, Alice,' said Titch reassuringly. 'You stay here.' Leaving the Princess concealed behind the train, Titch made her way slowly towards the huddle of stranded passengers. They were preoccupied, discussing their recent near disaster. They did not see her.

'Excuse me,' said Titch.

One of the dignitaries looked over his shoulder with such chilling disdain that Titch froze.

'What do you think you're doing, boy?'

'I'm looking for the Duke of Albion, please,' Titch stammered.

The nobleman turned round fully and looked down his nose at Titch. 'I am he.'

'Well,' Titch spluttered, 'I've got your daughter for you, sir.'

'Don't waste my time,' answered the Duke dismissively.

'Princess Alice is here, sir,' Titch protested.

'I recognise you,' the Duke declared suddenly. 'You were with Alice and Mr Perkins in the station gig.' He advanced towards Titch aggressively. 'Where *is* Alice?' he demanded, and added, in a threatening tone, 'What have you done with her?'

Titch began to understand something of Alice's nervousness about her father. He was intimidating. Haughty. Cold.

Titch had been frightened of her own father but it surprised her to realise that fathers from a noble background could also be so intimidating. She squared up to the Duke. 'Listen, Mr Duke of Albion,' she said, with all the courage she could muster, 'me and my mates have been through one hell of a lot to rescue your flipping daughter. And at times she were as snooty as you. She asked me to come and get you cos she's scared of you. Scared of her own father. Think about that. If you can't behave decent after all she's been through – and her – *longing* to see you – you don't deserve to have a daughter, you don't.' The Duke's jaw dropped, but before he could reply, Titch stalked off.

When Titch came round the end of the train, she found the young Princess with her head in her hands.

'Eee, Alice, buck up, lass. Don't let him get you down.'

'That's what I was afraid of, Titch,' Alice sobbed. 'He can be like that.'

'You come with me.' Titch took firm hold of Alice's arm and pulled her round the corner of the carriage. The Duke had followed Titch and they almost bumped into him.

He stood, frozen, staring at the distraught ragamuffin child in disbelief. 'Alice?' he asked. 'Is that you?' Alice nodded. 'Come here,' said the Duke hesitantly. Alice did as she was told, unwillingly, with her chin down. 'Let me look at you.'

Alice fell towards her father and put her arms around him, sobbing loudly.

'Now, Alice,' said the Duke, 'there's no need for that. You're home now.' Alice clung to him. The Duke looked back at Titch through narrowed eyes. Titch stood her ground, waiting for an apology that did not come.

'As for you, young man . . .' said the Duke, 'in just a few moments, we shall be getting back on board.' He pointed at the train. 'Would you care to join us?'

'Of course she will,' cried Alice. 'She *saved* me! She and Edie and Potts and Billy, but her more than anyone. She *found* me! She travelled underneath a train. She brought Beaky . . .' Alice ran to Titch and took her hand. 'It was her more than anyone!'

'Her?' said the Duke, looking at Titch. 'What *are* you talking about, Alice?'

Alice suddenly realised what she had been saying. She turned to Titch penitently. 'Sorry, Titch,' she mumbled. 'Sorry. It just came out.'

'Don't fret, Alice. Let's just get on the train, shall we?'

'Yes.' Alice was ashamed. 'I want to see Mama,' she said sullenly.

'All in good time,' replied the Duke. 'Your mother is at Osborne.' He lifted Alice on to the carriage steps. When she and Titch had been suitably placed, he helped people back to their seats with his customary politeness. The Duke then came and sat next to his daughter. Titch watched.

'I am greatly relieved to have you back, my dear,' he said. 'When we've got you cleaned up, you must tell me what you've been up to.'

Alice sat, staring at the floor, on the verge of more tears. Titch was not surprised. She herself was shocked by the Duke's coldness. If he had any deep emotions at being reunited with his daughter, they were so firmly under his control that they were invisible.

In the meantime, fallen debris had been removed from the track, and word was given to the driver that the train might proceed to Osborne.

16

THE EMPRESS OF INDIA

'Mr Wickham! I demand an explanation!' The Queen was at her most intimidating – not openly angry, but coldly furious. The lift had unnerved her. The tunnel blast had frightened her. In the many years of her reign, there had been more than one attempt to assassinate her, and this explosion felt like another.

The man to whom the Queen was speaking was the head of her personal security force at Osborne. The tunnel bomb had taken him entirely by surprise. Unused to threats of any kind, the scale of this attack was way beyond his wildest expectations. Reeling from shock, Mr Wickham had been ordered to Her Majesty's sitting-room, a large first-floor room with a bow window overlooking the grounds and the Solent, in which the Queen conducted the royal business of state when in residence. One was only summoned there for the gravest of reasons. Mr Wickham was nervous.

As he drew breath to offer excuses for the failure of his small team, the door burst open and Prince Edward stormed in with Sam. They were followed hotly by Mrs Goose, who was doing her best to prevent them entering the room. Nerves were on edge. The Queen, Mr Wickham and the entourage jumped out of their skins. Prince Edward was young and eager but he realised that he and Sam had entered the lion's den. He skidded to a halt in front of his grandmother and stood panting, staring at the Queen.

'Sorry, Grandmama! Sorry sorry.'

'Edward.' The Queen fixed him with her most ferocious glare.

'Yes, Grandmama.'

'What do you mean by breaking into my sitting-room unannounced?'

'Sorry, but Sam and I – that's Sam, by the way, over there – weren't really looking for you. You just happen to be in here. Sorry. We wanted Mr Wickham because we've captured the men responsible for the big bang. Did you hear it?'

The Queen was momentarily silenced. 'I should imagine it was heard in London, Edward!'

'Yes, it was pretty whopping, wasn't it? Well, Mr

Spooner and Sam have tied up one of the villains. The other – one of the workmen with the red hair? – our friend Billy shot him in the foot, and he won't be going far, I can tell you. Ha! So we were looking for Wickers to go and arrest them, and . . . throw them in the Tower!'

The Queen looked across her desk in disbelief. 'Edward, you know how strongly I disapprove of telling fibs.'

'Yes, Grandmama, I do, but this is not a fib. Honest. Cross fingers, hope to die and all that stuff. Tell her, Sam.' The Prince went to Sam who was hovering just inside the room. Sam's clothes were in shreds, he was scratched and muddy, and oily soot from the tunnel blackened him from head to foot. He looked like a sweep's boy who had just emerged from the chimney. The Prince led him from beneath the eagle eye of Mrs Goose into the royal presence. Sam was so overawed by being in front of the Queen that he lost his tongue. Prince Edward nudged him. Sam made a funny sort of self-conscious bow. As he leaned forward, he noticed that his shoes were filthy. He remembered being made to carry his shoes by Mr Spooner. He raised his foot to see if he had made a mark on the carpet. He had. He started undoing his laces, then realised that everyone in the room was waiting for him to speak.

'Sorry, your Maj— er, Your Queenship. Yes. What Duffer says is quite true.'

'Duffer?' said the Queen, in shock.

'The Eddie, I mean the Prince. Prince Edward.' People were hypnotised by the pantomime Sam was performing, removing his shoes in front of the Queen. 'The two men have been apprehended, Your High— Victoria . . . ship.' Sam was wrestling to get his left shoe off. 'One of them was arrested by Mr Ho— er, Spooner, just like Duff— Eddie, the Prince said.'

'Mr Spooner?' The Queen and her entourage were beginning to wonder if the two boys had completely lost their wits.

'Yes, Your Majestic,' said Sam, hopping up and down as he finally managed to pull his second shoe off, 'Mr Spooner is in fact Mr Sherlock Holmes in disguise, you see. Sorry. I should have made that clear.' Sam was now standing holding his dirty shoes, feeling more confident. 'Sorry about the mess, and the shoes and the barging in and that, but it's really important that these men get arrested quickly like, cos Mr Holmes and Dr Watson have gone to Ryde – they have to get the ferry because they want to capture the men behind it all, Professor Moriarty and his sidekick, who—'

'Sam,' whispered Prince Edward, taking Sam's elbow.

'Yes?'

'You can stop now.'

'Oh.' Sam became self-conscious again. He bowed, and backed away from the Queen, encouraged to do so by the Prince. 'Beg pardon, Your Highship. But what Duffer – the Edward – says is absolutely true.'

The Queen could not quite believe that she had witnessed this extraordinary display, and was gathering herself to speak, when Mr Wickham courageously took the floor.

'Ma'am.' He bowed discreetly to the Queen. 'I think you should leave this one with me for the moment, if I might be so bold. The good news is that there are apparently no fatalities, no injuries, and—'

'By the way, I forgot,' Sam piped up. All eyes turned to him. Was there to be more from this ill-dressed, ill-mannered urchin? 'We've rescued Princess Alice.' The silence was so intense that Sam felt he was expected to continue. 'She's probably a bit grubby – like me, I'm afraid – but she's all right.' The shocked silence continued. So did Sam. 'Sorry. Should have mentioned that earlier. Well, I did actually, to the Duchess of Arsenal, but I wasn't exactly sure then that we had in fact rescued Alice. We were on her trail, like . . .'

Prince Edward came to Sam's support. 'It's true, Grandmama. I've seen her.'

Mr Wickham was about to lead Sam from the room, when the Queen found her voice.

'Bring the boy here, Mr Wickham.' The head of security hesitated. 'Bring him here.' Mr Wickham guided Sam to the centre of the room.

'Take his shoes.' Mr Wickham took Sam's battered shoes and handed them to Mrs Goose. He bowed and backed away, leaving Sam isolated again, in front of Queen Victoria.

'Your name is Sam,' said the Queen – a statement, not a question.

'Yes, Your Honour. Sam Wiggins, Your Honour.'

'When you address me, Sam Wiggins, you say Ma'am. And you say it just like that, in such a way that it rhymes with Sam. Do you understand?'

'Yes.'

'Yes what?'

'Yes, Ma'am.'

'Good.' The Queen fixed her eye intently on Sam. 'Sam. Is Prince Edward telling me the truth? Are *you* telling me the truth?'

'Yes. Ma'am.'

'The whole truth?'

'And nothing but the truth. So help me. Ma'am.'

'You have rescued Princess Alice, and caught the men responsible for the explosion?' – a question that sounded like a statement.

'Yes, Ma'am.'

The Queen turned her attention to Prince Edward. 'Before you go with Mr Wickham, Edward – is your nickname really Duffer?'

'Yes, Grandmama, I am rather afraid it is.'

'A prince of the realm called Duffer. What is the country coming to? Edward. Do you know where both these villains are?'

'Yes, Grandmama.'

'Take Mr Wickham to them. Sam. Stay where you are. I wish to question you. Mrs Goose.'

'Ma'am?'

'Find Princess Alice and bring her to me immediately.'

'Ma'am.'

Mr Wickham, Prince Edward and Mrs Goose bowed and left the room. The remaining staff – an equerry, two ladies-in-waiting and a footman – were intrigued by the Queen's behaviour. They could not imagine what she could possibly have to say to the filthy urchin standing before her, shoeless, whose feet, they noted, were almost as dirty as his shoes. The Queen rose, walked round her desk and sat in an upright chair, close to Sam. Sam was getting worried.

'Sam,' said the Queen severely, 'I want you to understand that these circumstances are most unusual.'

'I do, Ma'am. Not half.'

'Be quiet for a moment. We have just suffered a rather unpleasant attack upon our person and our property, so the normal protocols are not being properly observed. Do you follow?'

'Proticol?'

'Rules.'

'I see, Ma'am.'

'Good. I sense that you know rather more about this affair than I do. Indeed one suspects that you know a good deal more about it than Mr Wickham, which is not at all as it should be. Am I right?' – definitely a question. A rather frightening one.

'That rather depends on how much you know, Ma'am.'

'Indeed. I think you should take it that I know nothing. So . . . can you inform me?'

'That rather depends, too, Ma'am.'

'On what, may I ask?'

'On how long you've got, Ma'am. There's a lot to tell.'

The Queen did not answer. She looked at him beadily for some time. Sam was afraid he had gone too far. Her eyes still on Sam, she addressed the footman.

'Bring me that stool.' In silence the footman brought the stool.

'Here,' said the Queen, imperiously. The footman duly placed the stool by Her Majesty.

'Sam.'

'Yes, Ma'am?'

'Sit down.'

The entourage could not believe what was happening.

Sam felt self-conscious again. 'I'm dirty, Ma'am. Very dirty.'

'It is a stool. It can be cleaned. What you have to say is, I believe, of great importance to us, and to our country. We wish to hear it. Sit down.'

Unwillingly, Sam did as he was told. He fancied the Queen was going to send him to the Tower – according to Duffer, that was the fate of most court offenders.

'Now, Sam,' said Her Majesty, sitting up very straight and placing her hands together in her lap, 'tell me everything.'

* * *

'Hell and damnation. Blast! Blast! Blast!' Sherlock Holmes stood in Professor Moriarty's deserted office, looking out over the River Solent towards the Isle of Wight. 'This whole extraordinary subterranean complex has been cleaned out, Watson. There is not a trace of him. As always, he has vanished. What a mind the man has. What breathtaking skills. If only he were to use his perverted brain for the good of mankind, what might he not achieve?'

'As you have observed many times, my dear Holmes. Of more than one criminal, in fact.'

'Indeed, Watson, but Moriarty is truly exceptional. At least,' he sighed, 'between us, we have managed to foil his wicked plans. It was easy for me to cut the wires which would have caused the Queen's lift to blow up, and the Irregulars . . . ? Well, the Irregulars have excelled themselves on this occasion.'

Watson did not respond. He had always disagreed with Holmes about using children to help solve crimes, and they had had so many close shaves he was beginning to wonder if their luck might soon run out. He felt guilty that he had involved them in this case. It had led them all into dark and dangerous waters.

'You know, Holmes, I haven't really got over your death, yet. Let alone your resurrection!'

'My dear Watson. What would I do without you?' This was the nearest Holmes came to expressing his deep fondness for the doctor. 'Enough of this. We must away to London, and quickly.'

'Unless you have particular need of me, Holmes, I think I should go back to Osborne. The Irregulars are all there, and I feel . . . well . . . responsible for them.'

Holmes appeared to ignore the Doctor's concerns. 'Come, Watson, let us return to civilisation as fast as we can, and shake off the atmosphere of this evil place.' He strode out of Moriarty's office and along the empty corridor, past the cell where Edie, Alice and Titch had been imprisoned. Watson trailed behind him, looking with amazement at the intricate network of passages and rooms that Moriarty had created. Through the archway on to the platform he followed Holmes, and gaped in wonder at the deserted underground station.

'Astonishing, Holmes.'

'It is, Watson. These caves were hollowed out nearly one hundred years ago to help us defend our country from Napoleon. Moriarty has used them cunningly against us. Ironic, isn't it?'

'Moriarty being the Napoleon of Crime, you mean?'

'I do, Watson. Come along.' Holmes strode along the platform, jumped on to the rails and stalked off along the tunnel towards the woods. Watson had to run to catch up with him. 'Watson, we shall not catch Moriarty, but it would be splendid if we could trace De Ville. He was here, quite recently.'

'How do you know that, Holmes?'

'The aroma from his cigars. It was particularly potent in what had evidently been Moriarty's office. You may return to Osborne if you wish, Watson, but I can assure you those children are more than capable of looking after themselves.'

'I'm fond of them, Holmes.'

'Sentimental piffle, Watson. It will be the death of you. If Potts and his boss, the dubious Mr Dyke, were to give me odds, I would lay a bet that the Irregulars are having the time of their lives!'

Holmes was right. The Irregulars were in seventh heaven. Sam and the Queen had got on famously, and when Prince Edward returned with the news that O'Hare and Reilly had been arrested, Alice was with him. He persuaded Her Majesty to invite Sam and his friends to stay on to see the fireworks, as a thank-you for everything they had done. The Irregulars had consequently been installed in the Swiss Cottage in the grounds of Osborne House, as all the bedrooms in the main house were taken by the Queen's royal guests.

On Prince Albert Day, they were grandly dressed. After the memorial service in the local church, they were taken to see the enormous Christmas tree in the Durbar Room. After a feast of a lunch they went back to their palatial lodgings to await the fireworks. The Swiss Cottage was a large chalet that Prince Albert had built in the grounds of Osborne as an educational centre for the royal children. To the Irregulars, who lived rough lives on the streets of London, it was little short of paradise. Potts and Edie were chatting in the sitting-room.

'Stone me, Edie! This is the life! I thought this place might be a bit neat, but this is the bee's flippin' knees! 'Ave you seen the kitchen downstairs?'

'Sure. You could cook up a storm in there, couldn't you?'

'I could live 'ere for ever. Totally independent, like. Got your own vegetable garden outside.'

'It's not bad, is it? Nice clean clothes, too. And crisp clean sheets on the bed! I can't wait to sleep in them again tonight. Hot water whenever you want it. Warm towels! That's my favourite, Potty – warm towels. Who thought that one up?'

'I bet it were ol' Beau Nash, Edie. 'E pampered

'imself rotten, 'e did. Picture the scene. Steppin' from 'is perfumed bath one ice-cold mornin', Beau Nash – famous dandy – addresses 'is valet thus. "Whilst indulgin' in my bath, my man, I come up with the notion that when I steps out the tub, instead of 'andin' me this strip of freezin' cotton, wot you gives me is a towel wot you 'ave 'eld in front of the fire for five minutes." Thus was the warm towel invented. Old Beau become rather partial to it, and invents the warm towel *rail*. 'E's so proud of it 'e tells the King. And 'Is Royal H knighted 'im for it. Wot d'yer reckon?'

'You're off the wall, Potty,' said Edie, laughing.

'I do me best. I tell you sumfing tho', Edie. In them there clothes wot they given yer, you look more flippin' gorgeous than I ever seen yer! You look bloomin' edible.'

'Ah, get on with you.'

'No! You do! Your 'air is shinin' sumfing smashin'. An' you got beautiful 'air to start wiv. And them silk green ribbons! I ain't never seen the like.'

'Sure. You don't look so bad yourself.'

'D'yer like it?' Potts asked, taking a peek at his new suit in the mirror.

'I do, Potty. I love it.'

'It's a bit on the big side, but it's dead posh.'

'It is that.'

'At least it ain't got no 'oles in, like me old whistle!'

'Whistle?'

'Whistle and flute – suit!'

Edie laughed. 'Wot d'yer reckon Sam'll say?'

'Hey, Potty. What about Titch?'

'Sure. He'll be thrilled.'

At this moment, Billy tore into the room. 'Listen, you two—'

'Look at *you*!' cried Potts, interrupting. 'I shall never call you "turnip" again! Edie, look at Billy, will yer?'

'Shuttup, Potts, Sam's got a problem.'

'Wot? You mean 'is new pants?'

'Don't get larky, Potts.'

'Hexcuse me, Yer Maj, but these 'ere knickerbockers – they doth not fit the contours of my—'

'POTTY!'

'There's no need to shout, turnip.'

'Quit larking, will you? This is serious.'

'Wot?!'

'Sam's been thinking . . .'

'Get on,' said Edie smiling.

''E orter take a flippin' 'oliday from finkin'.'

'He can't. You know what he's like. He wants to contact Mr Holmes and the Doc.'

'Wot abaht?'

'Major Sebastian Tiger De Ville . . .'

'That's Lestrade's problem now.'

'. . . and he wants to get a cable to Mr Holmes.'

'Mr 'Olmes'll be back in London,' Potts stated.

'We thought he might come back here,' said Billy. 'Him and the old Doc.'

'Sure. Mr Holmes will be heading for London like Potty says, won't he?'

'Billy, if Sam wants to get a cable to Mr 'Olmes, 'e should 'ave a word wiv 'is mate, the Prince. Wot's the point of 'avin' contacts in 'igh places, if you don't use 'em.'

'Sam doesn't like to.'

'Where is 'e?'

'Sam? Upstairs.'

'Leave this wiv me, Billy. By the way, wot's 'appenin' abaht supper?'

'That butler chap who runs this place said they were going to bring something down about six this evening.'

'Sure, I can't believe this!'

'You deserve it, Edie, after wot you been through,' quipped Potts from the door. 'So does Titch. 'As Sam actually *seen* Titch yet, Billy?'

'No. He's busy thinking.'

'Course.'

'But guess what else the butler told me.'

'Wot?'

'He said that the Queen was thinking of coming down to see us all before supper.'

'Wot!?!'

'To express her thanks in person, he said. What about that, eh?'

'Old Queen Vic. My gran would 'ave an 'eart attack if she knew!'

'So would Mrs Hudson! She'd go nuts – us meeting the Queen.'

'Sure, this is Alice's doing.'

'You know what Duffer told me.'

'Wot, Billy?'

'That Queen Victoria is also the Empress of India.'

'You're 'avin' me on, Billy.'

'Honest. So we get to meet a Queen and an Empress at the same time!'

'Cor blimey! Wot a trip! Been on a train. Seen the sea. Been on a ferry! I'll just go an' sort this cable out fer Sam, all right, you two?'

'Sure. See ya, Potty!'

'Cheers, Potts.'

'Tara, turnip.'

17

FIREWORKS

Mrs Hudson was sitting by the stove in the kitchen at 22lb Baker Street, when Sherlock Holmes walked in, dressed in his deerstalker hat and Aberdeen cape.

'Mr Holmes!' screamed Mrs Hudson. 'You're dead!' And she fainted.

Holmes was unusually understanding. He fetched the smelling salts, and explained everything to Mrs Hudson in great detail. When she came to, she was beside herself, laughing and crying, and fussing over Holmes – 'Well, did you ever? You must come and see my room, Mr Holmes, sir. The decorator's done a lovely job while you've been dead!'

'With pleasure, Mrs Hudson. As soon as you are quite yourself,' said Holmes sweetly.

'Perhaps Dr Watson would like to see it, too.'

'Watson has returned to the Isle of Wight, Mrs Hudson.'

'How nice.'

'Nice? It is nonsensical. He went back to take care of the Irregulars. I pointed out that they are more than capable of looking after themselves. In the meantime—'

Holmes was interrupted by a loud knock on the front door.

'I will go, Mrs Hudson. You stay here in the warm.'

Mrs Hudson sank back into her chair, quite overcome by the notion that death had improved the Great Detective – she had never known him so thoughtful. Moments later, Holmes was back in the kitchen. He held a telegram in his hand.

'What is it, sir?'

'It's a cable from Wiggins, Mrs Hudson. From the Isle of Wight.'

'What does it say?'

'Just five words – *De Ville. St John's Crypt.*'

'What does that mean?'

'Wiggins is quite remarkable, Mrs Hudson. Quite remarkable!'

'But what does it mean, sir?'

'Wiggins informed me that the Constable of the Tower served alongside the Duke of Albion.'

'Yes?'

'The Constable is Princess Alice's godfather.'

'I know that.'

'Sam believes the Constable was instrumental in her kidnap – under threat of blackmail from De Ville, of course. De Ville is now in hiding, Mrs Hudson. If Sam is right, the Constable is being forced to assist him.'

'I still don't follow, Mr Holmes.'

'St John's Crypt – in the Tower – contains a secret chamber where the Crown Jewels were once stored. Sam's telegram suggests that is where De Ville is to be found. I must leave without delay.'

'Do you not wish to see my room first, Mr Holmes?'

'Much as I would love to see the new decorations, Mrs Hudson, my immediate presence is required at the Tower.' He grabbed his deerstalker, and as he donned his Aberdeen cape, he teased his housekeeper. 'I have no need to go to your room, my dear Mrs Hudson, to enjoy the decorations! The delicately patterned wallpaper is very much to my liking; rose madder – the new colour of the paintwork – is one I adore; and the decorative paper strip, featuring a repeated pattern of dog roses, could have been chosen by myself.'

Poor Mrs Hudson felt faint again. 'I don't know how you do it, Mr Holmes. I think you're still dead.'

'Mrs Hudson, there is nothing fantastic in my knowledge. The decorator left his equipment in the hall, along with remnants of wallpaper and a tin of rose madder paint. Over which I tripped. Careless oaf!'

And with that, caped and hatted, he swept from the room.

Prince Edward tore through the gardens of Osborne House with Princess Alice hard on his heels. Swiss Cottage was quite a long way from the house.

'Come on, Alice. We've got to be first to tell them!'

'Coming, Duffer!' cried Alice, panting.

When the two royal children broke into the chalet, the Irregulars had just eaten. Full to bursting, they were sitting round talking about the extraordinary events that had brought them to Osborne House. When they heard the door, for a moment they thought it might be the Queen. Before they could heave themselves out of their comfy chairs, Edward and Alice rushed into the room.

'Hallo, you lot!' cried Edward.

'Hallo!' Alice ran across and jumped on to the sofa between Edie and Titch.

'Hallo, Alice, pet,' said Edie, putting her arm round the shining Princess. 'Shove up, Titch, make a bit of room. What's all this about, Alice?'

'Can I tell them? Please!'

'Oh, all right,' said Edward. 'But only because you were kidnapped and nearly got shot and stuff.'

'Thanks, Duffer.' Alice beamed.

'What is it, Alice?' asked Billy.

Alice slid forward to the edge of the sofa, where she sat, her legs dangling. 'There's a gentleman just arrived at the house who says he knows you, and would like to see you.'

'Wot's his moniker, Alice?'

'Moniker?'

'Really, Potty!' Edie slapped Potts playfully on the wrist. 'Moniker is London slang, Alice. It means *name*.'

'His name . . . is Dr Watson.'

'Watson?' shouted Sam, leaping to his feet. 'Where is he?'

'The old Doc!' yelled Potts. 'Yippee!'

'Dr W!' cried Titch.

'Wow!' said Billy.

Alice was amazed by the way the Irregulars lit up with glee at her announcement. She sat open-mouthed as they bounded about, jumping in the air and clapping their hands. Edie and Potts did a little jig.

'Where is he?' Sam repeated.

'He'll be here any minute, I should think,' said Edward.

As the Prince spoke, a footman led Watson into the room. As one, the Irregulars streamed across the room and swooped on him. Watson was overcome by the wildness of their greeting, and with his own pleasure at seeing the Irregulars again. They jostled him, they hugged him, they held him, they competed with each other for his attention, they almost knocked him over with the force of their feelings.

Alice could not help but remember her own meeting with her father. He had been lovely to her since, and told her repeatedly how glad he was that she was well, and that he had been worried sick and that they had searched high and low for her. But Alice's father, in private, at his most emotional, came nowhere near the tornado of spontaneous affection that had greeted the arrival of Dr Watson.

When things had calmed down, Watson slumped into the sofa. He was still looking a bit the worse for wear. He had brushed his coat, and acquired a new hat, but he was fatigued, and still suffering from delayed shock. 'I am delighted to see you all again,' he grinned. 'And in one piece.'

'You, too!' they shouted.

'Sure, it's grand to see you.'

'You nearly got blown ter bits, Doc!'

'If it hadn't been for Sam . . .' mused the Doctor.

'And Mr Holmes,' added Sam.

'Indeed, indeed,' said Watson, 'it was a very close thing. Far *too* close for my liking. But let me look at you all, dressed up to the nines! My oh my! You all look . . .' Watson hesitated.

'What's the matter?' asked Edie.

'Well,' said Watson, 'I was so knocked out – almost knocked *over* – by your welcome . . . I've only just realised that Titch isn't here.'

The Irregulars were suddenly very quiet.

Edie nudged Sam. 'Sure, Sam. You tell him.'

Sam stood sheepishly in front of the Doctor. 'Well, sir. We've got a bit of a surprise for you.'

'What? Is Titch all right? Has something happened?'

'Titch is fine. And, by the way, sir, Titch is *here*.'

Watson looked about, confused. 'What? Where?'

'Right here, sir.' Sam held out his hand. A very pretty girl, elegantly dressed in a pale blue gown, with white socks and neat blue pumps, took it. Sam led her in front of Dr Watson, and she curtsied to him. Watson was speechless. He had long had suspicions about Titch, but he had not expected her to transform

into such a beauty.

'It's me, Doctor. Titch.' Titch's voice was unmistakeable – the Lancashire accent, the deep, slightly rasping, boyish sound.

'Heavens above . . .' exclaimed Watson. 'Is this . . . Titch? Well, Titch, you look . . . you don't look at all Titch-like. You look positively . . . well . . . angelic!'

Titch was about to answer, when a footman appeared in the doorway. 'Ladies and gentlemen . . .' he announced, 'Her Majesty the Queen.'

Before they could gather themselves, the Queen had entered the room. Watson leaped to his feet and encouraged the Irregulars to do likewise. They bowed and curtsied. The Queen smiled.

'Well,' she remarked warmly, 'you all look much better. A lot cleaner and a great deal smarter.' She turned to the footman. 'Seat, please.'

The footman helped the Queen to sit down. She nodded curtly in acknowledgement, looking at each of the Irregulars in turn.

'I've heard a lot about you all. From Sam.'

Edie was trembling, Billy's mouth was dry, Titch's palms were sweating. Even Potts was cowed into silence, now that he had actually come face to face with his sovereign – the Empress of India! Sam was less fussed, having had a long conversation with her earlier.

'Sam, come here,' ordered the Queen. 'Tell me who everyone is.'

Sam went and stood by her. He ran his finger round the inside of his collar to free it a little – he had never worn a stiff collar with a tie before. He felt rather odd in his unfamiliar clothes.

He cleared his throat. 'I presume you know Dr Watson, Ma'am.'

'I do indeed. I have already spoken to him. What I neglected to say when we met so briefly, Doctor, is that I am a great admirer of your writing. I have read, I think, all of your books to date!'

'Thank you, Ma'am.' Watson bowed stiffly, still feeling the after-effects of his night in the arms cache.

After a slight pause, Sam said, 'Well, Ma'am, this is Edie. She's—'

'She's my best friend, Grandmama,' cried Alice. 'She's Irish so she's not always easy to understand, but she's really nice. And she can tell the future, too.'

'Really, Alice?'

'Well sort of, and anyway you'll like her a lot.'

'I am sure I will. Hallo, Edie.'

Edie curtsied. She wanted to reply but didn't quite know how to address the Queen. Sam came to her rescue.

'When you speak to Her Majesty, you call her Ma'am.'

'As in Sam,' said the Queen.

'Thank you . . . Ma'am.'

'Thank *you*, Edie, for looking after Alice. Her behaviour has improved greatly since she came back to us, and I think I know why.'

'Sure, she's a darling. We're all very fond of her. Ma'am.'

There was an embarrassed pause before Sam stepped in again.

'And this, Ma'am –' Sam indicated Titch, '– this is Pat. We call her Titch.' Glowing with pride, Sam was about to explain how brave Titch had been, when Alice jumped down from the sofa and ran to the Queen. 'It's Titch that really found us, me and Edie, Grandmama, by travelling underneath the train we were in, and exploring the caves where we were imprisoned, and then sending her pet pigeon Beaky home with a message! She used to look like a boy, but we persuaded her to put a dress on tonight. Doesn't she look pretty?'

'She does indeed, Alice. How wonderful to meet you, Titch, and to have this chance to thank you personally for all that you did. I shall be eternally grateful. We all shall.'

'My pleasure, Ma'am,' said Titch. Very quietly.

'This is Billy, Ma'am,' Sam went on. 'He works for Sherlock Holmes and the Doctor. Helped with the rescue.'

'Hallo, Billy. I am aware of your bravery.'

'Hallo, Your Maj, sorry, Your Ma'am. Oh dear, I'm a bit nervous. I mean Ma'am, Ma'am.' Billy bowed deeply.

The Queen was touched. 'Thank you, Billy. Might I ask how you came to be in possession of a gun, Billy?' the Queen asked with some concern.

'Duffer – I mean Prince Edward – found it and gave it to me. It belongs to Dr Watson.'

'I am speechless. Well done both of you. I am most impressed.' The Queen turned back to Sam, indicating that he should continue his introductions.

The only one left was Potts. Sam had left Potts till last intentionally. He was very nervous, as they all were, about how Potts would react when he met Queen Victoria. Sam was hopeful that Potts would behave – he had been unusually quiet in chapel and over lunch, and he was looking more respectable than Sam had ever seen him. Sam crossed his fingers behind his back and prayed.

'And this, Ma'am, is Potts. He was with Billy when they got the prisoners out of the caves.'

The Queen smiled benignly at Potts, and thanked him.

'It's a great 'onour to meet you, Ma'am,' said Potts. Sam breathed a sigh of relief.

'Do you have a Christian name, Potts?'

'I do, Ma'am. It's Eli, but I don't like it. So my mates call me Potts. They sometimes call me Potty. Cos I am a bit. But I'd be grateful, if you would stick to Potts. Or Potty. Up to you, Ma'am. Just not Eli.'

'Of course,' said Her Majesty, without a flicker.

Sam felt that they were nearing thin ice. Sensing that Potts was on the verge of asking the Queen questions, he tried to steer the subject round to Prince Edward, but Potts was gaining in confidence, and when he came and stood directly under the Queen's nose, they all got rather twitchy. The Queen herself was not remotely troubled by Potts's behaviour. She looked him directly in the eye and demanded simply, 'Well, Potts?'

'It's like this, Ma'am . . .' said Potts. 'Oh dear. This is where it gets tricky.'

'Tricky?'

'Alice told me that I can't ask you questions. But I can't really find out wot I wanner know unless I do. And I don't wanner be sent to the Tower nor nuffing, but, to be 'onest, I'm a bit curious.' There was a brief pause, and then Potts remembered to add 'Ma'am.'

'Well, Potts, in society, it is considered impolite to ask the royal family questions. That is all.'

'Then how do we have a chat, Yer Maj?' The Queen stiffened. 'I mean I'm real interested in you and wot it's like being Queen 'n' that, but if I can't ask you questions, then I'll never know nuffing abaht you, will I?'

Alice and the Irregulars were getting deeply worried. They felt Potts was about to ruin everything. Dr Watson was finding it hard to suppress a smile, and Prince Edward thought it was huge fun watching his grandmother cope with this cockney sparrow.

The Queen put on her most formidable look. 'Well, Potts. You don't like to be called Eli, and members of the royal family do not like to be asked questions by impertinent upstarts who do not understand the rules.'

The onlookers were unsure just how much anger the Queen was suppressing, but Potts soldiered on, unabashed. 'Ma'am, wot I wanner know is not impolite nor nuffing. I'm just interested in whether or not you can knit, like my gran.'

Everyone tensed. The Queen took a moment before answering.

'Well, young man, you may know that one *can* knit.

Although one must confess that one has not knitted for some years.'

'Fank you, one. I mean Ma'am. I had a feelin' you were a knitter. My gran is the most amazin' knitter. She can knit everyfing from woolly jumpers to 'ot-water bottle covers. The only fing wot she's no good at is socks. She can't turn the 'eel proper. I know it's not easy to turn the 'eel, but she just knits tubes, and sews the ends up. That can be a bit uncomfy like. Can you turn the 'eel, Ma'am? Woops, sorry, that were a question, weren't it? Ow! There's anuvver. Off with his head! No intention of offendin'. I'll shut up now. Beggin' yer P, Mrs Ma'am. Sorry.'

The silence in the room was palpable. Even Prince Edward was scared. No longer slouching, he was sitting bolt upright, expecting the worst. His grandmother could be very frightening, and he had never seen anyone speak to her as Potts had just done. Watson's smile had frozen on his face. Sam wished he was in another room, another country! Billy and Titch were gaping. Edie was particularly concerned for her beloved Potts. Alice went to take her grandmother's hand and was about to speak, when the Queen got up. Very slowly she approached Potts. Potts began to tremble. He knew he had gone too far.

'Potts . . .' said the Queen, as she moved round him, scrutinising him through her pince-nez.

'Yes, Ma'am?'

Edie put her hands over her mouth, stifling a cry – she was convinced Potts was about to be banished.

'Have you ever considered a career in the music hall?'

Potts took a moment to take this question in. 'No, Ma'am. I ain't.'

'Well,' said the Queen, 'you should. You are a very entertaining little boy.'

'Fank you, Ma'am,' said Potts nervously. 'I do me best.'

'I can see you do,' said the Queen, completing her examination of Potts and returning to her seat.

'What one would like you to know, Potts . . .' Potts was now rigid with fear, and the room was still tense, fearing the Queen was about to give Potts a severe ticking-off. 'What one would like you to know, is that one *can* knit, but that one prefers embroidery.'

'Does one?' said Potts, sighing with relief. 'Fank you. Ma'am. Fank you for sharin' that personal detail wiv me, your 'umble subject. And for not sendin' me to the Tower. I *mean* well, Ma'am.'

'I can see that, Potts. Your good intentions are written all over you.'

'My gran likes embroidery, too, Ma'am. She done a cushion for your Silver Jubilee which were the talk of our street. Wot sort of fings do you embroider, like?'

'One rather likes flowers, Potts. Roses.'

'Amazin'! Wot a coincidence. So does my gran. You two orter get togevver one afternoon. She makes a Victoria sponge cake to die for 'n' all. You'd love it. Sorry I'm goin' on a bit. But it's not every day you meet a queen.'

'Nor is it every day, Potts, that I have the opportunity to thank a group of the most extraordinary children I have ever met.' She rose. 'You may give me your hand now, Alice. We are going. No, Edward, you cannot stay and play with Sam. We have duties to perform. Firework duties.' Turning to the Irregulars, she said, 'If there is anything you require, please do not hesitate to ask one of the staff.' The Queen and Alice glided gracefully to the door. Prince Edward joined them. The Irregulars all bowed, led by Dr Watson. Before leaving, the Queen addressed them again. 'I have been considering what I can do for you in the nature of a reward—'

'Yippee!' cried Potts, jumping in the air. 'Reward time!'

'Potts!' said the Queen sternly – *so* sternly that Potts

stopped jumping and apologised.

'By way of thanks, what one would like each of you to do,' the Queen continued, 'is to write a letter in which you lay out what might be done to help you personally.'

'Wow!' said Billy, overcome.

'You are the bee's knees, Yer Maj,' cried Potts.

'Potts! One more interruption and you will be boiled in oil!' said the Queen.

'Beg pardon, Ma'am.'

A close observer might have seen the Queen wink secretively at Potts, before she resumed, 'You will give your letters to Dr Watson, and he will convey them to us. We look forward very much indeed to seeing you at the fireworks display. Warm coats will be provided. Until later, then. Goodbye.' She led Edward and Alice regally from the room. The Irregulars stood speechless.

After several minutes, Billy just said, 'Wow!'

'Wot a flippin' queen, eh?'

'Sure. You were lucky not to get sent to a penal colony, Potty.'

'Tell you wot tho', in the end we 'ad quite a nice chat, Her Maj and me. Didn't we?'

'*You* enjoyed it, Potty,' commented Sam.

'I fink you're bein' a bit ungenerous there, Sam. I

fink *she* enjoyed it 'n' all! Flippin' loved it.'

'Potts.'

'Yes, Dr Watson?'

'I think I'd better have a word with you about this fireworks display.'

'Wot kind of a word?'

'A "How to behave at a Royal Fireworks Display" kind of a word, Potts.'

'Yeah. You're right, Doc. I'll 'ave to watch my tongue.'

'You will, Potts. For one very good reason . . .'

'Wot?'

Watson turned to Sam, Titch, Edie and Billy – and grinned. 'We don't want our Potts being boiled in oil! Do we?'

DR WATSON'S DIARY

AN UNPUBLISHED FRAGMENT

DR WATSON

Professor Moriarty, as Holmes predicted, evaded capture and has disappeared without trace, so the story is not yet over. Despite the sense of triumph that we experienced in rescuing Princess Alice, Edie and Titch, and the sense of justice we felt in the arrest of Reilly and O'Hare, there is the ever present fear that Moriarty will strike again in his evil quest for power. The shadow cast by this case is long.

Thanks to Sam's cable to Holmes, Major Sebastian Tiger De Ville was arrested at the Tower. As Sam suspected, he was concealed in St John's Crypt. De Ville had blackmailed the Constable into terrified compliance. The Constable is not to be prosecuted, but he has been given a dishonourable discharge in spite of his many years' loyal service, because of his role in the kidnap of the Princess. De Ville's fate will be a great deal harsher!

Mr J. Wilson Booth Senior, of the Anglo-American Trans-Atlantic Cable Company, visited 22lb again, to apologise personally to me for his lack of faith in the Great Detective. Holmes happened to be there. He was desolate that he had failed to prevent the sinking of the *Arcadia*. He had already been aware of Moriarty's designs on the Queen, and explained to Booth that he took advantage of the disaster to 'disappear'. Booth was pleased to inform Holmes that three members of the crew of the *Arcadia* had been apprehended. Holmes had observed them, escaping by rowing-boat prior to the explosion. When arrested, they confessed to being Moriarty's agents. Booth recognised that with such huge forces working against him, there was little more that Holmes could have done – he had prevented one disaster when he detached the limpet bomb from the side of the ship.

Mr Booth's story ended well. He was devastated by the loss of life when the *Arcadia* sank, but insurance covered the ship, and most importantly, the cable-laying had been completed in time for the President of America to ring the Prime Minister of Great Britain – the first transatlantic telephone conversation!

Our 'holiday' at Osborne concluded very happily. The Queen insisted on a display of normality, in spite of the horrendous events of the preceding days. After the fireworks, we stayed on for a few days, during which several rather extraordinary friendships were cemented. When we returned home, they were, I think, as sad to see us go as we were to leave. Before our departure, I was able to give the Queen the letters she had requested from the Irregulars. Her Majesty was so impressed with the unselfish nature of their requests that she returned them to me for my perusal and safe-keeping. Here they are:

BILLY CHIZZELL

Dear Queen Victoria,

Thank you very much for asking us to write to you. I didn't do anything like as much to help in the rescue as Titch, and what I would like for a reward is actually for her (and Sam) because she really deserves it. Titch and Sam share a basement room somewhere in Marylebone – they won't tell us where exactly, they keep it secret. I do know that it's in an unoccupied house, and I don't think it's very nice, but if they weren't there they would be living on the streets and that would be even worse. I have a proper home and I hate the thought of them all cold and bleak. I would love to find them somewhere nicer, but I haven't got enough money. Do you think, for my reward, you could give Dr Watson enough to help Titch and Sam find somewhere nice to live? That would make me very happy.

It was such a privilege to meet you, and to see the Duchess of Albion again. I looked after her when she came to Baker Street and we first heard that Princess Alice had been kidnapped. The Duchess was very unhappy then. It was nice to see her smiling. With Alice!

Thank you for having us. It was very kind of you, specially as you already had so many guests staying.

Best wishes and thanks,

William Chizzell

TITCH

Dear Ma'am,

I asked Dr Watson if it was right to call you Ma'am in this letter and he told me how to spell it. Sorry about my writing but Sam's only just taught me and I'm not very good yet. I'm better at capitals.

As long as I have my friend, Sam, I don't really need much. And if I do, Dr Watson always helps out. So for my reward I would like you please to do something to help Billy. He is learning about hotels and wants to have his own one day (with Potts). I am sure you know all there is to know about hotels and could help him. The sort of thing he would be brilliant at is being that butler chap who looks after us here in the Swiss Cottage. Billy's really thoughtful and kind. He's especially good when people are in a state and need helping. Ask Alice's mum. Perhaps you could send him to butler school. I hope it's all right to ask for this. You have already been very kind to us, but thank you in advance.

Patricia 'Titch' Simpson

EDIE MCARDLE

Dearest Queen,

Sure, I can't thank you enough for all your kindness. What I would like most of all in the world is to help Potts and my pa to set up their own business. It's a sort of dream they have. They want to provide decent, bottled drinking water for people. Potts comes from a part of Soho where they had terrible cholera and there was a clever doctor man who worked out that it was in their drinking water. I know Potts's family were struck by the cholera, ages before he was born, and he's always talking to my pa about 'drinking water you can trust'. It's not a bad idea, is it? If they could but get started I know it would take off, because they are both so hard-working. And if they had their own company, me and Ma and my sisters would all be better off, too. Thanks so much for asking us to write to you. And for the lovely holiday.

As my pa always says, may the road rise up to meet you, and may the sun shine warm upon your back. Thanks a million.

Edie McArdle

POTTS

Your Majesty,

You'll ave to forgive my spellin. Doctor W give up on me! Fanks for evryfing – the nice new outfit, (lovely weskote!), the brilliant grub and the regal ospitality. And for not sendin me to the Tower when I got a bit carried away the first time we met. I meant wot I said abaht my gran tho – you and er wud get on famous. I'll get er to send you a slab of that sponge cake wot I menchioned!

As for this reward fing, which is andsome of you – you don't *ave* to do it – can you please elp my friend Edie? She's the most bootiful person wot I know, and the Doc and I are doin wot we can for er, but er minces are not in great nick, and I'm opin that you will know the top eye bloke in the country, wot might be able to elp er out. This would mean more to me than anyfing, so I ope you can fix it. She also needs a new gaff, but the minces is more important.

It was great meetin you. Fanks again. Your umble subject,

E. Potts eskwire

P.S. Fantastik fireworks! Specially that rocket wot they let me light!

SAM WIGGINS

Dear Queen Victoria,

I can hardly say what my feelings are about meeting all of you. You were so kind and thoughtful to us, and we are just ordinary kids off the street. You never made us feel awkward or inferior or anything. And I really hope I shall see Duffer again, although I understand that might not be possible, given our different stations in life. But thank you. It's changed the way I feel about having a queen.

I hope you don't mind, but I want to tell you about my dad. He was a soldier, and he lost his life fighting in Khartoum – I always say 'for King and Country', but of course, you were on the throne at the time. From now on I shall say 'for Queen and Country'! The best reward I could have would be to have my dad back, because I miss him a lot. But you can't do that, so I have two requests . . .

The man who has done most for us is Dr Watson. For me, he's sort of taken the place of my dad. He is a hard-working doctor and he's always thinking about other people. He is a really good man. As Queen, there must be all sorts of doctor jobs that you could give him. Could you make him a royal doctor? He'd look after your family better than anyone. It would warm my heart to have someone help *him*, who's forever helping other people.

Also, would it be out of the question to give Beaky, Titch's pet pigeon, the Victoria Cross for exceptional bravery? It took him nearly three days to fly back with the message that saved Alice. He was shot, and lost loads of blood, but he never gave up.

With big thanks. I know you'll do your best for me.

Samuel Wiggins

I find these letters most affecting, and I find it hard to express the full extent of my admiration and fondness for these remarkable children. I am as proud of them as if I were their father.

h HODDER *Look out for more Baker Street Mysteries*

THE DRAGON TATTOO

By Tim Pigott-Smith

Sherlock Holmes has disappeared.

As page-boy Billy Chizzel searches London for his master, he is helped by the other Irregulars – Potts, Edie, Sam and Titch.

And so they are drawn into the dangerous world of the Dragon Clan of Shanghai . . .

THE ROSE OF AFRICA

By Tim Pigott-Smith

The Rose of Africa: a famous diamond.
Beautiful. Valuable. Stolen.

When Potts's Uncle Hector is blamed for
the theft, things don't quite add up. Can the
Irregulars unravel the case and prove Uncle
Hector innocent?